THE ROAD TO HELL

THE ROAD TO HELL

Gillian Galbraith

Polygon

First published in 2012 by Polygon,
an imprint of Birlinn Ltd
West Newington House
10 Newington Road
Edinburgh
EH9 1QS

www.polygonbooks.co.uk

ISBN 978 1 84697 225 6
eBook ISBN 978 0 85790 176 7

British Library Cataloguing-in-Publication Data
A catalogue record for this book is available from
the British Library.

Set in Italian Garamond BT at Birlinn Ltd

Printed and bound in Great Britain by the MPG Books Group

ACKNOWLEDGEMENTS

Maureen Allison
Colin Browning
Douglas Edington
Lesmoir Edington
Robert Galbraith
Daisy Galbraith
Diana Griffiths
Christine Johnson (Bethany Christian Trust)
Jinty Kerr
Alan Montgomery
Roger Orr
Aidan O'Neill
Dr David Sadler

DEDICATION

To Hamish, with all my love

I

The middle-aged woman in the poorly-fitting yellow anorak was twisting the ring on her finger, first one way and then the other, all the while trying to slide it over the enlarged, inflamed middle joint. She appeared not to notice the queue of people growing behind her. Now bowing her head and starting to lick her finger with her tongue in an attempt to ease it, she muttered to the assistant, 'Got any soap, dear?'

The embarrassed girl, dressed all in black, shook her head, then peered up from beneath her straw-coloured, floppy fringe, eyeing the line of increasingly restive customers with concern. Looking at them, she shifted her weight from one foot to the other, rocking nervously from side to side. After a further minute had passed without any progress, she asked, pleadingly, 'Maybe we could get on with things, while you're getting the ring off? Have you got the paperwork with you? Your passport, your driving licence?'

'Eh?' the woman snapped irritably, concentration broken on her all-engrossing task. A bubble of spit glistened on her lower lip.

'Your passport? Your driving licence?' the assistant repeated, tapping her finger on a yellowing, typed notice that was pinned to the wall detailing what was required of sellers. 'Like what it says here.'

'I've no passport, I've no need of one. And I don't drive either.'

'A household bill, maybe . . . electric, gas, something like that? That would do instead. Everybody has them.'

'Not this body, dear. I've not got any of them with me. But it's gold all right, if that's what's worrying you. It's my wedding band.' Then, giving herself a rest from the strenuous removal attempt and sounding wheezy and out of breath, she added, 'It had bloody better be anyway. Archie gave it me. You can bite it or whatever you do, check it with your teeth like the gypsies. But you'll need to wait until I've got it off my finger.' She removed her chewing gum and smiled winningly at the girl as if to charm her into submission.

'I'm sorry but we can't take it,' the assistant replied, shaking her head, 'not without the proper documentation.'

'Bingo!' said the woman, beaming even more broadly, holding the ring triumphantly between the still sticky thumb and forefinger of her right hand, and thrusting it at the assistant.

The girl shook her head again, mulishly, and as she did so, the lank curtain of her hair swung from side to side across her eyes. 'No documents, no sale. That's the rule in all Money Maker stores.'

The middle-aged woman, now chewing her gum again, appeared unabashed by her refusal and continued polishing the ring on the sleeve of her yellow anorak. In fact, seeing the girl's implacable expression and determined to get her way, she decided it would be wise to change tack. If charm was not to going to win the day then coercion would have to be used.

'Listen, dear,' she said, moving forwards and brandishing the ring in the girl's face, 'you've a big sign outside saying "All gold wanted – good prices paid". Is my gold not good enough for you, then?' Both of her fists were now parked on her well-padded hips and her feet were set wide apart, like a boxer readying himself for a fight. After wrestling with the ring for the last five minutes she had no intention of giving up now. Immoveable, she looked round at the queue of people behind her, suppressing a smirk as she recognised them for what they were, her unwilling allies. Few could resist the silent pressure that they were unwittingly exerting, certainly not this stick-thin teenager. A puff of wind and she would drift skywards.

'I'd like the money today, dear, and this is gold. Right? Got that? Your sign outside says nothing about paperwork. Gold is gold, OK?'

The girl pressed a button on her counter to summon assistance but no ringing sound came from it. She tried again, pressing harder but only eliciting a faint clicking noise for her pains.

'Shit!' she murmured to herself, looking down at the button and hitting it crossly one final time. In doing so she hurt her knuckles, and started rubbing them against her shoulder.

'Your alarm button not working then? Now, my gold?' the woman said quietly, between chews. 'There are lots of people waiting, dear. They'll be getting awfully impatient, you know, some of them may just walk out . . .'

'Eric! Eric!' implored the flustered girl, waving to attract a male assistant's attention. 'I'm needing some help over here.'

At her words, the youth put down his orange duster and moved away from the bank of widescreen plasma TVs that he had been standing beside and watching. He, too, wore only black clothing. He was heavily built and walked with the muscle-bound, wide-legged gait of a professional

3

bruiser. All the TV screens around him showed the same picture. A blonde woman in a leotard sat on an exercise bicycle, pedalling effortlessly while smiling inanely at the camera. Any accompanying sales spiel was lost as the sound was turned off.

'I'll attend to you, flower,' he said coming up to the woman and cupping her elbow with his meaty hand, attempting to waltz her slowly towards another empty counter.

'Get your mitts off me, son, or you'll hear my alarm button go off all right, just you wait and see. I'll shout the place down.' She disentangled herself from his grasp.

'OK, OK. But if you'll not move we'll have to get help – police help,' he said in a hushed tone, looking into her face, taking his mobile from his pocket and crooking an index finger above the keypad. Realising she had been outmanoeuvred, she turned her back on him and strutted out of the queue, keeping her chin held high in an attempt to preserve the shreds of her dignity. There were other places, after all, plenty of them less finicky with their paperwork than this one, less choosy when gold was on offer. Grasping the handle of one of the double glass doors, she toyed momentarily with the idea, the luxury, of threatening them with the trading standards people. But it would be an empty threat and only annoy them further, which would be pointless.

Three hours later, in the same Money Maker store, DS Alice Rice looked up at the CCTV camera pointing directly at her and took her place at the head of the queue. The reflection staring back at her in the lens was as distorted as that on the back of a spoon, splaying out her nose and making her eyes appear small and piglike. She looked more like fifty than forty, she thought, and her dark hair appeared to be framing an entirely unfamiliar face.

'I've come for the notebook laptop,' she said to the lank-haired girl.

'We've a few of them in here at the moment. We've got an Apple, a Sony and a Toshiba, too, I think. But you'll need to go to that counter, over there, if you're buying.' She pointed to the far end of the shop. Stacked by the counter were turntables, battered cardboard boxes overflowing with DVDs and an army of upright Dyson vacuum cleaners.

Crossing the floor and stepping over the open boxes, Alice Rice addressed another black-clothed clone. 'The notebook laptop, please. Donny was going to phone you about it earlier, he said. I've come to collect it.'

'You from SART, then?' the man asked. 'Donny told us you'd be here by eleven. Eleven on the dot.' He sounded annoyed. Glancing at his watch to emphasise that the time had long since passed, he bent down and removed a smallish box from below his counter. Still frowning, and consulting the watch again to further underline his point, he handed the package over to the plain-clothed policewoman.

She wondered why he was so bothered about the time. He was not exactly run off his feet, she was his only customer. What possible difference could that half hour have made to him? The jerk. All the same, she was relieved that he had known exactly what she was supposed to be collecting. No one in the SART office had told her the make of the notebook they were after.

Once it was safely stored in her carrier bag, she decided to waste a few more minutes having a look around the store. Time had to be killed this morning and here was as good a place as any to do it in. The shop was warm, and browsing its contents might distract her, repel the repetitive thoughts which were constantly trying to invade her brain. It might, briefly, obliterate her obsession with her two o'clock appointment, her forthcoming tribunal hearing. Her very own, and imminent, personal disciplinary case.

As she wandered about the shop, she was struck by its resemblance to a wholesale outlet, but it seemed a strange, sinister variant of the species. Goods were piled high on all the available floor space, the walls were hung with them and not an inch of unused shelving was visible. But despite the bright strip-lighting, crisp decoration and the superabundance of merchandise, the place reeked of poverty and desperation. The assistants drifting about reminded her of undertakers in their black clothes, circulating within a Chapel of Rest. They spoke to everyone in hushed tones and their customers replied in the same way, as if they were embarrassed to find themselves in such a place. The body-language of the patrons conveyed one message and one message alone, that they were 'just looking'. They were not here to buy, and certainly not to sell.

In the absence of any apparent trade, it seemed a miracle the business survived at all, she thought. But a notice on the wall boasted that branches of the chain were to open from the Forth to the Clyde. Money Maker appeared to be flourishing in the ailing towns of the Central Belt like some kind of fungus living off a dying tree. According to the advertisement, its spores were soon to take root in the cold, grey streets of Kirkcaldy and on a disused lot by the dog-racing track in Thornton.

'Are you after anything special?' an assistant, who had glided silently to her side, asked her in a sibilant undertone.

'Just looking, thanks,' she caught herself whispering in return. After he had moved away, she turned her attention to the rear of the shop. High up on a wall hung a selection of crossed fishing rods and nets, and stacked immediately below them were a row of golf bags, shiny clubs protruding from each of them. On shelving to one side was a display of power tools, some in mint condition, but others mud-spattered and worn, as if plucked, still buzzing, from their building sites only minutes earlier. Nothing tempted her.

A customer coming in through the swing doors set a couple of tiny handwritten tickets on a nearby alarm clock fluttering in the artificial breeze, like the wings of a frantic insect. Catching sight in the distance of a silver-plated saxophone displayed against the blue silk lining of its case, Alice wandered over towards it, attracted by the beauty of its sinuous shape. Gazing at it, she felt an overwhelming urge to possess it. Maybe Ian would like to draw it, or even learn to play it? Of course, other lips, strangers' lips, would have blown into it, dribbled into it, and that might well put him off. Besides, the price of ninety-five pounds seemed steep, and money might be tight if the worst happened this afternoon. He might think she had chosen it with herself in mind, despite it being ostensibly a present for him? He would be right, and he could, and would, see right through her. But, with its fine filigree engravings it was a wondrous object. The sort of thing that would be appreciated by anybody, surely?

While she was still mulling things over, trying to talk herself out of buying it, a man joined her, also intent upon inspecting the musical instruments section. He smelt strongly of stale curry, and in his left hand he held a stick, on which he leant heavily. Hobbling past her, he came to a halt before a stand on which seven electric guitars were propped up. Humming to himself, he began slyly inspecting the instruments and their price tickets. As he bent over to examine one, he lost his balance and toppled into a large pile of treadmills and dumbbells stationed at the base of the stand.

'Feck!' he shouted, lying spreadeagled on the floor. Instantly, a pair of assistants appeared from nowhere. Yanking him up, one of them hissed at him, 'Forget it, Paddy. You're not getting it back unless we get the cash.'

The other stood in front of the guitars, his arms crossed, deliberately blocking the man's view with his body.

'I just need it the one night, boys,' the man pleaded. 'I've a gig booked in Ratho. I could give you the money after it's over and I'm paid.'

Alice decided that she had seen enough. Ian would not thank her for the saxophone. Like the rest of the items in the place, it would carry with it its story of shattered dreams, hobbies abandoned, jobs lost, mortgage payments now in the red. Almost every article was a tangible reminder of human misery or folly, including the saxophone, and that thought would certainly put him off. Her, too, thinking about it dispassionately.

And, of course, a fair few of the things there told a different story, as the SART boys knew only too well: one of housebreaking and heroin. Camouflaged among the once-treasured possessions were a mass of stolen goods.

Having had her fill of the place she walked towards the door. Next to the entrance were a couple of locked cabinets, both filled with an assortment of highly-polished jewellery, calculators and mobile phones. For a second, sunlight glinted off a golden bangle, the reflection temporarily blinding her. Another reflection danced on the pavement below, a third flitted about on a leather jacket worn by a passer-by. The cabinets, she noticed, had been angled artfully by the management, arranged to attract those outside the shop into it, acting as lures to draw them in like fish into a trap.

'Sure there's nothing I can help you with?' It was the same lisping male assistant as before. He smiled at her, as if to persuade her to come back inside. Behind him she could see Paddy being frogmarched to the exit, his stick waving uselessly in the air like the leg of an upended insect.

'No thanks . . . I've just been looking,' she said.

On Leith Walk, Alice headed southwards, trying to look into each of the dusty, old-fashioned shop fronts as she dawdled past them. She knew that if she allowed her mind to drift, she would find herself rehearsing her evidence again, answering questions which might never be posed, justifying herself to herself like a mad woman. How the hell had she got herself into a situation like this?

Suppressing her inner dialogue, she stared into the shop windows. To her eyes, they seemed anachronistic, a collection of fossils from an older, slower world of commerce, an age untouched by computer technology and internet shopping. There was an old-fashioned barber's shop complete with striped pole, a tattoo parlour with its proprietor's name dripping in blood-red letters, and cheek by jowl with it, a secondhand bookshop. Leith's glory days were long since over. A few of its street names,

Baltic Street and Madeira Place, hinted at its romantic past as a maritime port. Recently, city money had been pumped in to redevelop, renovate and restore the place, but despite the millions spent on it, its couthy character had never quite been extinguished. It was like an old Scots lady, her tartans now replaced by stylish silk clothes, but who betrayed her origins every time she opened her mouth.

Next to the bookshop was an office, deserted, with a Polish name emblazoned above the door and fly-posters pasted across its cobwebbed windows. Its abandoned state was easily enough explained, she thought. Nowadays, there were precious few Poles left in the capital to use its services, the cold wind of recession having blown most of them back to Warsaw, Cracow, Gdansk or wherever.

Maybe, after the hearing, she too would find herself jobless, she mused. Conscious that she was sinking into the quagmire of doubt again, she wrenched her attention back and began staring through the glass of a shoe repairer and locksmith's door. Deliberately, she focused on the display of mortise locks and Yale keys inside as if they were of interest, exhibits worthy of study. Moving onwards she forced herself, once more, to put her appointment out of her mind, to stop herself dwelling on her imminent professional nemesis. But with the hour growing closer it was becoming impossible.

In a final attempt, she halted to look in the window of the One-Stop Aquarium Shop, her eye momentarily caught by an iridescent fish darting about its tank, its tiny body glinting like a jewel in the clear water. But as she was watching it, unconsciously she started to finger the folded-up piece of paper in her pocket, feeling the edges of the Misconduct Form between her thumb and fore-finger. It was dog-eared and discoloured from too much handling, and on it were recorded the two charges laid against her.

She knew the wording by heart. The first was for revealing 'in a manner that was not for police purposes' that Robert Longman was a sex offender. The second was for 'stating to a named Professional Standards Department Officer in the course of his inquiries that she had not been the source of such information when she did know this to be false and for thereby carelessly or wilfully creating a falsehood'. In short, charge number one was for disclosing unnecessarily that Longman was a paedophile, and number two was for lying about having disclosed that information.

At the hearing this afternoon, she must keep her nerve, she told herself. Tell the truth, the whole truth and nothing but the truth. And if they did not believe her, then . . . then, then? Then so be it. But they would, because it was the truth. So they bloody must.

But envisaging the tribunal, she could feel the panic rising within her. How many times had she seen juries acquit those she knew to be guilty? In one case a complete confession taken by her had been withheld from a jury for procedural reasons. But it had convinced her, and she could still see the accused punching the air as the verdict was delivered. In another case, the newly-liberated man had been unable to resist gloating, goading them all as he left the courtroom by giving them chapter and verse of the offence, providing new and revolting details that only the guilty person could know. But miscarriages of justice went both ways, and the innocent were sometimes locked up.

How had she got into this mess? The answer was simple. All thanks to that bastard, Stevenson. But for his inability to control himself, and tell the truth, she would not now be teetering on the edge of dismissal.

Just a few more hours to kill, helping the boys in Gayfield, and then on to Fettes HQ, where all the formality and gravitas of the law would be on display to impress or intimidate her. As if the very word 'hearing' in itself was not enough to make a cold shiver run down her spine.

A double-decker bus hooted its horn at a passing cyclist, the man's helmeted head low down on his handlebars, and the noise brought her back to the present in the nick of time. A second later, in her preoccupied state, and she would have collided with a post from which was suspended one of the many 'I Love Leith' banners that had been hoisted the length of the Walk. Well, I don't, she declared cantankerously, surveying its litter-strewn pavements and stepping out of the way of an abandoned armchair. Who does? They protest too much. The feel-good slogan trumpets the burgh's unloved and miserable status, like a valentine some sad person sends to himself.

—

SART – the Search and Recovery Team – were based at Gayfield Square Police Station. The squat, toad-like shape of the sixties building with its warty, grey-harled surface, gave fair notice to all and sundry of the nature of the accommodation to be found within. There were suites of drab, functional rooms without ornament of any kind, all painted in tired shades of magnolia. Posters on the walls warned of the dangers posed by adulterated heroin and the use of dirty needles. Telephone numbers to ring in case of domestic abuse, child abuse or substance abuse were on display, and everything had been translated into at least four languages, English alone long since having become insufficient for the city's needs.

The office to which she had been seconded for the day was tucked away at the end of a narrow corridor on the second floor, and was as unobtrusive and low-key as its occupants. In order to get into it, Alice had to push with her shoulder against the door, dislodging as she did so a recently-recovered stolen bicycle which had been propped up against it. Donny McDaid, a plain-clothes constable and one of the stalwarts of the operation, had his sturdy, denim-clad legs up on his desk. A tattooed arm rested on the top of his computer. With his left hand he was busy fidgeting with the rubber band that held his ponytail in place.

'Any luck with the notebook?' he inquired genially as she entered.

'Yes.'

'Good on you.'

'Aye. Well done,' Fergus Walsh, another team member, chipped in. His eyes were roving over a white board on which the names and telephone numbers of all the pawnbrokers in the capital had been scrawled in black magic-marker. With a sleeve of his cotton jersey he rubbed out one entry and inserted another in its place.

'It wasn't that difficult,' Alice said defensively, handing over the laptop to Donny.

'Not for a quick learner like you, eh?' Fergus retorted, winking at Donny and returning to his desk.

'Tea?' Alice asked, turning towards the white plastic kettle and stained cups on the metal filing cabinet. Peering inside the kettle, she noticed that the furred-up element appeared to have burnt itself out and melted the plastic. She fished a couple of old teabags out of it.

'You're still on trial, mind,' Fergus said, then, regretting his crass choice of words, added quickly, '. . . as a tea maker, I mean.'

'But you'll be making it, eh – because you're a woman,' Donny added, seeing his colleague's embarrassment and trying to repair the damage.

'I'll be making it because I haven't a clue what to do in this place.'

'Like I said,' Donny retorted, still stroking the back of his head, 'because you're a woman.'

Sipping from the chipped mug, Alice stared at the screen in front of her. On it was a seemingly endless list of names and transactions carried out at Cash 4 U branches the previous day. As she scrolled down it the words began to merge into each other until her eyes glazed over in boredom, lost in a sea of now meaningless typescript.

'How do you do it? How can you tell what's dodgy and what's not, simply from that?' she asked Donny.

'Well,' he replied, 'see that entry? Number 313?'

'Yes. The Blackberry. Sorry, Blackberry Bold 9.'

'Never mind the type for now. Look at the name opposite it. It says Catherine Simpson, right?'

'Yes.'

'Well, she's no business having a phone like that. Know why?'

'No.'

'Easy,' Fergus butted in. 'She's at an address in Craigmillar. Blackberries don't grow in Craigmillar, now do they? And she's Kevin Thomson's girlfriend. That's what he does, see? He takes the stuff from someone else's house over in the New Town or wherever, then he uses

14

his girlfriend, his mum, his cousin, someone he thinks we don't know about, to sell the stuff in the pawns for him.'

'So this isn't the first time he's used her, then? Doesn't he ever learn?'

'Nope,' said Donny smugly, 'none of them do. We get their photos from the CCTV, sometimes their prints or DNA from the stuff and still they come back for more. They're half-witted junkies, most of them.'

'See, in this op we're like ghosts. We don't exist. They see us,' Fergus explained, 'in the pawns with them. We're checking up, but they think we're selling something like they are. They think we're just another punter. And out on the streets we've been taken for all sorts. A couple of days ago it was as a *Big Issue* seller, seriously.'

'Speak for yourself,' Donny retorted, stirring another spoonful of white sugar into his tea, then adding, 'and that was the day you were wearing your best clothes, too.'

Glancing up at the clock on the wall, Alice said, 'I've got to go. Time for my trial.'

'Break a leg,' Donny said wanly, holding up his hands for her to see, the index and middle fingers crossed on both of them.

2

The sight of the Fettes HQ building made Alice feel queasy. Its spare design was silhouetted against the leaden sky, and its bulk cast her into the shade, temporarily blotting out the insipid winter sun. Passing through the glass double doors, she noticed on the right-hand wall a mass of brightly-coloured, child-friendly pictures each bearing its own caption. All of them depicted a simple, straightforward world in which policemen in their smart uniforms were doing good, busily apprehending law-breakers and making the world a safer, better place. If only life was so simple, she thought ruefully.

'You're here for the hearing?' the burly man on the reception desk asked her as she approached. She nodded, her mouth dry and all inclination to speak having vanished.

'Rice or Stevenson?'

'Rice,' she replied faintly, noticing a former colleague and giving him a wave. But he did not return it, passing quickly by as if any longer in her presence might contaminate him.

'You DS Rice, then?' the receptionist demanded with unconcealed curiosity, viewing her, she thought, with the sort of interest he might once have shown in a condemned man.

'Yes. How d'you know?'

'By the colour of your face, love. You're as pale as a sheet. You're the options-in, eh?' She nodded again, wishing the expression still remained a mystery to her. Until six months earlier it would have been meaningless, but no longer. 'Options-in' or 'options-out' described the two possible types of disciplinary hearings. The first, reserved for trying more serious offences, allowed the panel to return any of six possible verdicts: a warning, a fine, an increment fine, reduction in rank, a requirement to resign or dismissal. Only the first three verdicts could be returned in the 'options-out' hearing and no lawyers were involved in them. They were kept in the family, as purely internal police matters. Now, she thought with regret, she could answer an exam question on disciplinary hearings and the procedures associated with them. Give a lecture on the subject if the need arose.

As she entered the Force Conference Room she had no idea what to expect. She had never before been admitted to this holy of holies. Striding through the doorway, trying to look as confident as an innocent person would, she immediately recognised Alec Norton, the lawyer appointed by the Police Federation to represent her. He was a lanky, unsmiling man with an excessively reserved manner, and at their first meeting she had not taken to him. On that occasion he had made her more frightened, not less, with his incessant note-taking and his uncompromising legal jargon. He crooked a long white finger at her and, as if in a trance, she came and sat beside him at his small table.

Seated opposite them at another small table, on the other side of the central table, sat a couple of women. One, a peroxide blonde, was dressed snappily in a black suit and crisp white blouse, and she was busily sticking

Post-it notes onto various of the papers in the pile in front of her. Her bright red nail varnish glinted in the strip-lighting and she glanced up, briefly, on Alice's entry. Her companion, clad in sombre grey, was absorbed in making bold horizontal strokes with a luminous marker on the paper in front of her. She was highlighting key passages in the document, completing her last-minute preparations. Looking at the two lawyers, Alice decided that the one in the black suit must be her adversary, the Presenting Officer – the prosecutor, in ordinary parlance.

In front of the large, south-facing window was a long table at which the panel was seated. The Chairman, Chief Superintendent Jim McLay, sat in the centre, and his assessors, Superintendents Docker and Scrafe, were arranged on either side of him like bookends. Decades ago, McLay had played rugby for Scotland, but his prodigious muscle had long since turned to fat and a single seat no longer contained him adequately. By chance, his companions were both unusually small, looking like a couple of pet monkeys beside him. This odd trio were huddled together in conversation, with the two superintendents leaning inwards towards the big man as if to catch his every word, now being imparted in a low resonating rumble. The clerk, another lawyer, sat alone at a table to their left and he appeared alert, like a sprinter hunched on his blocks, ready for the proceedings to begin. His eyes were fixed on the Presenting Officer.

The first witness called by the prosecution was the Sex Offender Management Officer. The man could not disguise his nervousness, although he was well acquainted with legal proceedings and had competently given evidence in both the High Court of Justiciary and the Sheriff Court many times throughout his career. And those were intimidating settings, courtrooms decked in wooden panelling with a colourful Royal Coat of Arms above the bench, places where black-robed macers whispered to bewigged clerks and judges in red robes sat on high, surveying their domains. But in this stuffy little conference room he was unable to decide where to put his hands, alternately hiding them behind his back and then swinging them forwards where they hung loosely, chimplike, in front of his groin. His unease was because here, in the Lothian and Borders headquarters, he was giving evidence against his own colleagues and in front of very senior officers. The latter were the very sort of men who might hold his own career in their hands. They would be judging him too, scrutinising him and his performance.

In a strong Aberdeenshire accent, he provided the panel with details of Reginald Alexander Longman, trawling through his record of previous convictions and, finally, explaining the regime currently applicable to high-risk sex offenders such as him, released on licence. Longman, he told them, had been tagged, was subject to twice-weekly checkups and was required to remain resident at an address in Causewayside.

Listening to him, Alice heard nothing that she had not already known on the day that fateful telephone call had come in to the St Leonard Street Station. The call that had begun it all, the garbled ten-minute conversation reporting a sexual assault on a little boy in the Ratcliffe Terrace area. The checks she had immediately run on the intelligence database and the criminal history system had produced precisely the sort of information that she was now hearing from the lips of this nervous constable. A catalogue of horror stretching over two decades, and for which Longman was responsible.

As a result of that intelligence, she and DS Stevenson had gone to check up on him at his address in Grange Loan. Not a street in the well-known leafy suburb of the Grange, a sizeable reservoir of New Club members, but its twin in name alone, a run-down place in a far less salubrious part of the capital. The street was narrow and mean, punctuated with graffiti-daubed wheelie bins, and, crucially, led off into Ratcliffe Terrace. And the proximity of Longman's home to the scene of the offence seemed an unlikely coincidence. From a past encounter, Alice already knew what he looked like.

Finding the man's home deserted, they knocked on all the neighbouring doors, trying to find out if anyone had seen or heard anything useful, anything that would help them with the investigation. Most doorways had paint peeling and a broken or nameless doorbell. From many of the houses they got no reply, despite bright lights inside and the curtains twitching on their approach. Curiosity alone was not enough to prompt a response, not when there was rent owing, the TV unlicensed and sheriff officers to keep at bay.

The sound of a dog barking greeted them in the common stairwell of the next tenement along. The steps themselves smelt of stale cooking, vomit and burnt plastic. Climbing them, DS Stevenson held his nose, gagging as he reached the second-floor landing.

There, when speaking to the inhabitants of the only occupied flat on it, he had, inadvertently, prefixed Longman's name with the word 'paedo'. From the expression of horror on the faces of the middle-aged couple it was immediately clear that neither of them had realised that their next-door neighbour was, as the man put it, a 'fucking kiddy-fiddler'.

'We've got bairns who come here!' the woman had added crossly, looking outraged.

The word had soon spread. Later that very evening, reports of a rabble attacking Longman's home and breaking down his door had come into the St Leonard's switchboard. Nothing of the man had been seen since. Now underground and, to date, untraceable, he had assaulted another child, this time a little girl in the Niddrie area of the city, and a live warrant had been issued for his arrest.

———

After answering a number of questions from the panel, the witness was attempting to explain how vulnerable sex offenders such as Longman were while living in the community, describing in graphic detail a previous attack on the man when his identity had been discovered by a colleague at work. He had been attacked with a broken bottle, its jagged edge gouging a hole in his forehead the size of a two pence piece. On another occasion, and at another address, his home had been set alight and he had received second-degree burns to his arms and legs while escaping the blaze.

None of the windows in the conference room were open, and as the hours passed, the air temperature was becoming increasingly uncomfortable. Sweat was now apparent in beads on the constable's forehead and the clerk had removed his jacket, hanging it neatly on the back of his chair. Alice too, was feeling the heat.

'Any further questions, Miss Howard?' the Chief Superintendent asked.

The black-suited lawyer shook her head. 'None, Sir,' she replied, closing her notebook with a businesslike snap.

'Your witness, Mr Norton,' McLay said, addressing Alice's lawyer.

'No questions, Sir,' the man replied, scratching the side of his nose with his forefinger, then bobbing up and down on his seat as if in a courtroom.

The next witness, Alice knew, was vital to her cause, and she, along with everyone else in the room, hung onto to every word of his examination-in-chief.

'Aye,' the man from the neighbouring tenement said, 'I remember the police coming and asking us questions. They took my parking space.'

'Mr Meldrum, did either of the police officers speaking to you mention the fact that Mr Longman was a sex offender – in fact, refer to him as a "paedo"?' Miss Howard inquired, against a backdrop of complete silence.

'Aye.'

Alice held her breath. On the reply made to the next question by this plump, red-faced man, her whole career might hang. The Chief Super was leaning over his table, his eyes glued to the witness's face.

'Which of them mentioned that fact? Was it the male or the female police officer?'

'Em . . . I'm pretty sure it was the man. He done all the talking.'

Alice heaved a sigh of relief and caught Alan Norton's eye. He blinked owlishly at her, smiling slightly, and then returned to his assiduous note-taking.

The next witness was the previous witness's wife. She entered the conference room and looked round it fearfully, registering that all eyes in the place were fixed upon her. She was dressed in an overly tight cream suit. Under one arm she clutched a beige handbag. It was her Sunday best, but the heels she had chosen to go with the ensemble were higher than those she usually wore to church. She had calculated that she would not have to walk too far, so there would be no danger of keeling over in them, as she had once done en route to the Ladies in the bingo hall. On TV programmes, her only insight into trials, witnesses stood still to give their evidence. She answered the questions in a faint, smoke-scarred voice and had to be warned by the chairman to speak up on three separate occasions. Finally, the crucial question was posed to her.

'Did either of the police officers you spoke to mention the fact that Mr Longman was a sex offender, either of them call him a "paedo"?'

She nodded her head by way of a reply, and had to be advised once more by Chief Superintendent McLay that for the sake of the recording they needed an audible answer.

'Aha,' she confirmed, her voice almost too low to be made out.

'Which one mentioned it, Mrs Meldrum – was it the man or the woman?'

Once more, complete and intense silence reigned until, finally, it was broken by her stuttering reply. Miss Howard was staring at the woman like a hawk, all her attention and energy focused on her prey, willing her to give a particular answer. Her victory depended upon it.

'It w . . . was . . . the m . . . man.'

For a second, shock transformed the black-suited lawyer's expression, but she recovered quickly and, in an even tone, said, 'You say that it was the man. Are you absolutely sure about that, Mrs Meldrum? Could it, in fact, have been the woman?'

'Aye, it could've,' the witness said, her bag now held across her chest as if to protect herself. 'At first I thought

23

it was her. But later me and Davie spoke about it, and I realised it wasn't her, it was him. I'm dead sure of that now. Certain it was him. The first time she spoke, like, was to tell him to keep quiet. She said, "That's enough, Bill", or something like that.'

Unexpectedly, Alice felt a long arm extend across her back and pat her shoulder, and she turned to see her lawyer's beaming face.

'We should be fine now,' he whispered conspiratorially to her, and then he returned his gaze to his opposite number. She was deep in discussion with her sidekick, and the clerk, having left his own table, appeared to be drawing something to the attention of the panel.

Giving evidence herself, for once in her career, Alice almost enjoyed the experience. She answered the critical question confidently and without hesitation: 'I did not inform any of Mr Longman's neighbours in Grange Loan or elsewhere that he was a sex offender, or a paedophile.'

She felt a little more nervous about the follow-up question. In a solemn tone, and looking straight at her, Alan Norton asked, 'Did you hear your colleague, DS Stevenson, so inform the occupants of the second-floor flat next to Longman's house, Mr and Mrs Meldrum?'

She had answered that particular question in her head on countless earlier occasions, in the office in St Leonard's Street, in the supermarket, while driving her car and in every room in her flat. Usually, incandescent with anger at her predicament, she had almost shouted out the word, 'Yes!' But here, now, at this hearing, she found herself hesitating. Even if the bastard had lied throughout the investigation in the full knowledge that she would be dragged into the proceedings, it went against the grain to 'tell' on him, inform against him. But if she did not do so then her own career might still be brought to a premature end, despite her innocence. And he would have no such bloody scruples. He had dropped her into this mess, and had this coming. So, loudly and as if she felt no qualm, she responded, 'Yes.'

After a short interval during which Alice put her hands behind her head, leant back on her chair and tried to relax, the two female lawyers began conversing in hushed voices, both of them suddenly looking tired and rather grim. Eventually, the black-suited one stood up and turned to address the Chief Superintendent. Glancing down at a bit of paper she was holding in her hand, she said, 'In all the circumstances, Sir, including the evidence given by Mr and Mrs Meldrum and DS Rice's own testimony, the prosecution move that the hearing be discontinued and that DS Alice Rice be found Not Guilty on all the charges laid against her.'

—

With the collapse of the first hearing, the timetable for the second was brought forward. The proceedings against DS Stevenson were to begin straight away. Looking out through the open doorway of the interview room, Alice saw his unmistakable snub-nosed profile as he proceeded down the corridor on his way to the Force Conference Room. Trying to read that day's copy of *The Times*, she could still overhear the voices of the Meldrums as they discussed what they would have for their tea later. Mrs Meldrum wanted a pizza and Mr Meldrum said that he would prefer a proper fry-up with eggs, bacon, sausages, black pudding and beans. Unable to agree, their voices got higher and higher, until footsteps could be heard followed by a harsh admonishment. There was a momentary silence, then a muted, 'Fine. Right. Well, I'll cook my own tea then!' from Mr Meldrum.

The next sound that Alice heard was more footsteps, two sets this time, heading in the direction of the hearing. She peered out of her room and caught sight of the departing figure of Mr Meldrum, a minder leading him along as if he was a child.

Her mind drifted onto Reginald Longman, still on the loose, no doubt sheltered as usual by some smitten woman, ignorant of his predilections and with a child in tow. The infant would be the draw for him, something unimaginable to its mother, until the worst happened and the cycle began again.

It was so easy for him. He did not resemble the tabloid caricature of a paedophile, an inadequate with thick glasses and a woolly hat pulled down over a Neanderthal forehead. Looking into his eyes at their last interview, Alice had been horrified how attractive he had seemed to her, making her doubt for a second that they had apprehended the right man. But the contents of his computer had shattered any first impression that he had made. And the mask had slipped when he saw her as he was being escorted from court, his face contorting in fury, spitting at her like a snake.

Attempting to put the image of him out of her mind, she picked up her paper and started to read it again, homing in on an article about the plight of the Siberian tiger. Forty minutes later, hearing the sound of more footsteps, she peeped out again and came face to face with Mrs Meldrum as she was being shepherded away to give her evidence. She would be next, Alice thought, and she prayed inwardly that the Meldrums would not, for some reason or other, change their testimony.

This time when Alice entered the conference room she was directed to take a seat close to the door, facing the large table and opposite the panel. Annigoni's picture of Queen Elizabeth wearing the Garter robes looked down regally upon the proceedings, the Prussian blue of her cloak now a little faded by sunlight. Alice was aware that William Stevenson was looking at her. His colour was not good and he appeared anxious, an uncharacteristic pleading expression in his eyes.

Once more she gave her evidence efficiently, describing the call, her investigations following upon it, the drive with DS Stevenson and finally their inquiries in Grange Loan. The Presenting Officer in the Stevenson case, another lawyer, was an untidy, grey-haired woman with specks of dandruff on her shoulders. She had the confident swagger of a battle-scarred fiscal, an old-timer who could cope with whatever emerged in the evidence. Looking relaxed, she introduced the 'house to house episode' as she called it.

'DS Rice. Did you at any stage mention the fact that Reginald Longman was a sex offender, a paedophile in fact, to either Mr or Mrs Meldrum?'

'No, I did not,' Alice replied.

'Did you . . .' the woman asked, holding the lapels of her crumpled, navy suit as if it was a gown, 'hear DS Stevenson tell either of the Meldrums that Mr Longman was a sex offender, a paedophile?'

'I did.' Alice answered quickly, deliberately avoiding meeting her colleague's eye.

'What expression did he use?'

'Paedo.'

DS Stevenson shook his head from side to side in an exaggerated fashion, signalling to everyone present that she was not telling the truth and should not be believed.

Giving evidence in his own defence, he maintained, as he had throughout all the investigations, that he had not told the Meldrums that Longman was a paedophile but that his fellow sergeant, DS Rice, had done so. Foolishly, he felt the need to embellish the scene and was soon reporting other conversations with the couple, unaware that in the previous hearing they had said that the meeting on the landing had finished almost as soon as it had begun.

Once all the evidence had been taken, the panel listened to the Senior Officer's report. Alice, who had remained in the room, was surprised to hear in the course of it that Stevenson had already picked up two regulation warnings in his sixteen-year career. One, a breach of regulation five, was for a trivial neglect of duty, and the other, a breach of regulation six, for misconduct involving the sexual harassment of a female colleague. Everyone in the room knew that the verdict was a foregone conclusion, so the Chief Superintendent surprised nobody when he finally delivered it in his booming baritone. Solemnly, and now sweating copiously in the heat, he declared that William Stevenson was required to resign in relation to both counts. Then, mopping his brow with his damp handkerchief, he rose and strode out of the room, the assessors following behind him like puppy dogs, desperate to keep up with their master's gigantic strides.

———

The drive home did not take long despite the rush hour traffic or, if it did, Alice was not aware of it. The elation she now felt made everything seem bright and blessed, and she could find fault with nothing. With her hands resting loosely on the steering wheel and with the radio playing an old Beach Boys hit, she set off, feeling as if a great weight had been lifted from her shoulders. She had survived, been left with no stain on her character and the system had worked. No more accusations, no more questions, and life, normality, could be resumed at last.

Looking across Carrington Road onto the east elevation of Fettes College, the edifice as picturesque as a French chateau with its lofty central tower straining to touch the sky, she felt only pleasure. The immense building appeared as benign and well ordered as the world itself now seemed to be.

Turning right at the lights on East Fettes Avenue onto Ferry Road she joined the eastbound traffic, the car now warming up nicely. Stationary on Inverleith Row, her attention was caught by a party of Japanese tourists who had clustered together near the gates to the Botanic Garden. In the spitting rain, they were hurriedly unpacking their umbrellas from their backpacks and putting them up to protect themselves. One, who had turned his back on the treacherous wind, had his sugar-pink brolly blown inside out, causing a ripple of consternation amongst the entire group.

As she observed the scene, the faint, rhythmic whirring sound made by her windscreen wipers suddenly and unexpectedly reminded her of her childhood. Rainy days all those years ago meant, if she was lucky, a trip to Haddington with her mother, to the newsagents to buy one of those miraculous colouring books. A single stroke from the wet paintbrush and the grey flowers would become blue, orange and purple, and the grey grass, lime green.

Even a lick to the paintbrush was enough for the magic to start to work.

Turning into Broughton Place her luck held, a residents' parking space was free and not too far from the door of her own building.

Locking the car door, she looked up at the third floor and saw, to her delight, that the lights were on in her flat. Ian was home. In seconds, she would be able to chat to him about her day, tell him all about the hearing and the 'Not Guilty' verdict.

She ran up the cold common stair and let herself in. Immediately she could hear the sound of animated voices, chuckling, talking together, deep in conversation. One of them was Ian's, and she recognised the other too. It belonged to Celia Naismith and, she thought, there was almost no one on the planet she would like to see less. In fact, in the whole infinite space of the Universe. The woman, petite and feline with unnaturally large unblinking brown eyes, somehow managed to undermine her by simply breathing the same air, by being in the same room. To date, on every occasion on which they had met, Alice had gone away feeling like a clodhopper, ungainly and ill-educated. That was the extent of the woman's talent, and, as far as she was concerned, it was about as welcome as the deadly song of the Siren.

Taking a deep breath she entered the drawing room, and from their positions sprawled comfortably on the carpet, both Ian and Celia looked up at her.

'We'll ask Alice, shall we?' Celia said, excitedly.

'OK,' Ian replied, sitting up, helping himself to a crisp and smiling warmly at Alice.

'We've been discussing Rothko,' Celia said, resting her head on her elbow, 'and I think that he was more influenced by Avery, but Ian thinks Still's fingerprints are more evident. What do you think?'

'No idea, I'm afraid,' Alice answered evenly, slumping down in an armchair and sipping from a nearby glass of wine that she hoped fervently belonged to Ian. For this conversation, some alcohol would be essential.

'Maybe the TRAP people were more influential on him?' Celia remarked.

'You mean De Kooning, Pollock and so on?' Ian asked.

'Yeah. What I really like about Rothko is the sheer unintellectuality of his later work, you know, the fact that he had the courage to emphasise feeling and physicality – put thought to one side. Feel the paint.'

Celia stretched, raising both her arms above her head, evidently entirely at home and at ease in Alice's home, in Alice's presence. 'Who do you like?' she asked innocently, turning her wide brown eyes on her hostess.

Here we go, Alice thought, feeling nervous and already, somehow, put on the spot. She tried to summon into her mind images she was fond of, but other than one of Francis Bacon's screaming popes, nothing came, and she did not even like that picture really. She found it disturbing, almost too powerful with its lumps of amorphous flesh.

'I quite like . . .' she began slowly, 'Lucian Freud. Some of his horse pictures, like *Mare Eating Hay*, and the strange early ones with animals in them . . . and some of Cadell's portraits.'

'Just figurative stuff, then?' The slightly puzzled, condescending tone used to frame the question let Alice know that she had failed the test. Having scented blood, Celia added, as if in clarification, 'You probably like things like Vettriano's *Singing Butler* and so on?'

'Celia!' Ian Melville said in a warning tone, but he followed it up with a little laugh to soften the rebuke. He was well aware of her views of the Scottish artist and had begun to realise that she was playing with Alice in, possibly, a not entirely benign way. Rather like a cat with a mouse.

'Yes, I do like figurative stuff, but I also like some of Eardley's later works,' Alice said, some random inspiration having come at last, 'those wild ones, the stormy ones . . . the ones painted at Catterline.'

'Just figures or landscapes, then?'

'Yes, I do like landscapes too . . .'

Perhaps, Alice thought, she should just retire from the joust with her lance not yet broken. She had not wanted to enter this contest; it just seemed to have happened. As it always did with Celia.

'What do you think of Rothko's aquarelles?'

Now her lance had been well and truly bloody snapped! Alice took a deep breath. What the hell was an 'aquarelle'? Before she had time to assemble her thoughts, or attempt to bluster, Ian tried to throw her a lifeline.

'Enough shop talk, painter talk, for the moment, I think. Alice, how did you get on at work today?'

Looking into his eyes, it was obvious that he had forgotten all about the hearing. If he had remembered he would have chosen some other diversionary topic. He knew how she had been feeling about it, how scared she was, how private the whole matter was to her.

She told herself that his lapse did not matter, after all he was trying to help her. Anyway, nothing would have induced her to talk about this afternoon's purgatory in front of Celia, whatever the result had been. The very idea of Alice being subjected to any kind of disciplinary proceedings would have her salivating at the mouth, inciting her to pose a barrage of ill-intentioned questions, each one designed to embarrass or elicit some further unflattering disclosure.

'I spent this morning with the SART – the Search and Rescue Team at Gayfield Square,' she said brightly, 'and it was very interesting. Friendly men, a clever system – they've got really close relationships with all the pawnshops in the city.'

'Bloody hell!' Celia expostulated, putting a hand across her mouth as if she was about to be sick. 'You spent this morning in porn shops? Porn shops – how horrible!'

'Not porn shops, P.A.W.N. shops,' Alice said, spelling the word out quickly. 'Actually they're quite respectable now. The manager of one of them told me that they now see themselves as part of the Financial Services Industry. That may be going a bit far, but they've got customer charters and everything. They're pretty tightly regulated nowadays, I think.'

'Still, I'm not sure that's how I'd want to spend my day, or even a minute of it, sniffing around the detritus of other people's lives, in and out of pawn shops, mixing with irresponsible losers or thieving scum,' retorted Celia, trying to catch Ian's eye in search of agreement, a manufactured expression of pity on her face. 'Someone's got to do it, I suppose,' she added, looking around for the crisps.

'Alice enjoys it. Don't you, darling?' Ian said, holding out his hand for her to take. She took it, aware that he was trying to defend her in his loyal, uncomplicated way.

'Yes, I do enjoy it. Not the "sniffing", as you call it, Celia, or even the visits to the pawnshops, which was a first for me, incidentally, or the "mixing" with thieving scum and "irresponsible losers", whoever exactly they are. What I enjoy is very simple in its way. Corny, even. Putting things right, restoring order . . . helping people out.'

'Beware of kryptonite, then!' Celia replied, taking another sip of her wine and laughing into her drink.

Alice felt tired and unwilling to spar any more. It was like fighting with smoke. She got to her feet, taking with her Ian's empty glass.

'I'm going to get some food. What about either of you?' she said, walking out of the room.

'We've arranged to eat with two of our pals from the studio, haven't we, Ian?' Celia shouted back. And Alice noted the use of the proprietarily inclusive 'we'. The use of it twice.

—

In the kitchen she heard herself slamming shut unit doors and clanging pots on the cooker as if in an unsubtle bid to get Ian's attention. Picking out a couple of eggs from the fridge, she managed to crack both of them, without breaking the yolks, into the frying pan. How is it, she wondered, that when I feel so disturbed, so uneasy in that woman's presence, he cannot see it and continues to invite her home? Is he blind? No doubt she is short of friends, and no surprise there, but she is most decid-edly *not* a 'lame duck'. Too bloody glamorous for that description, more's the pity. And it's too bad if she does live in her studio. She does not deserve to be allowed in here, certainly not under the lame duck exception. If she is any kind of bird, it is a bird of prey or, even more apt, a vulture. Whatever she is, Alice wanted to shout, isn't it obvious that she only deigns to talk to me in order to make me seem like an uncultured Philistine? She views me as some kind of troglodyte, happy to plod about attending to my mundane, distasteful police tasks. Wallowing in the blood and filth of society's dirty laundry like some kind of perverted washerwoman. Sodding aquarelles!

She pulled out a dictionary from the bookshelf beside the cooker and found the definition: 'A drawing done in transparent watercolours'. Pretty esoteric stuff. Come to that, did Celia know what 'plethoric' meant or 'adipocere'? Of course not, because she had never read a post-mortem report nor found a decomposing body. Words learnt through life or, more accurately, death.

And, she thought, irritably, I should have told her, unashamedly and confidently, that I don't like Rothko. He's just another link in the chain of art history, nothing more. I don't like huge blurred blocks of colour, and they don't move me one iota either. They bore me, and had he died fat and happy they would have been viewed quite differently. Intellect is required in art as it is in virtually any other worthwhile human activity except, perhaps, making love. There is a qualitative difference between such simple, childlike daubs and, say, Monet's *La Pie* and a place for both. Under a fridge magnet for the first along with the rest of the children's artwork, and on a gallery wall for the second.

'Alice?' Ian ended her heated, silent argument with herself.

'Yes?' she said coolly, her resentment with Celia still burning, bleeding into her reaction to him.

'We're off to Blanco's. I didn't realise you'd get back so early tonight. We all arranged it at lunch. Do you want to come too?'

'No thanks,' she answered, spooning hot oil over the eggs, the very idea of spending the evening with Celia, plus others who might be every bit as toxic, making her shudder inwardly.

'Bye, then,' Celia said sweetly, peering round the door and then adding, as she wrinkled her nose, 'Egg and chips! Don't you get enough of that kind of stuff in your works canteen?'

After she had eaten, Alice sat in the dark on the drawing-room floor, leaning against the front of an armchair and stroking the dog's soft head. The solitude was blissful. Bach's *Goldberg Variations* were playing and she was familiar with the recording, anticipating each note on the piano and Glenn Gould's strange, dissonant moans.

The phone rang and she picked it up while lowering the volume on her CD player. It was her mother.

'How did it go, darling?' she asked, in a tone Alice recognised well. It was one she adopted when she felt the need to disguise an underlying anxiety with a veneer of brightness.

'Fine, Ma. Just fine. The couple both said that Stevenson was the one to let the cat out of the bag, not me. One or other of them must have changed their mind recently, otherwise we wouldn't both have been subjected to investigation, charged and so on. But, thank God, they both told the truth today.'

'That's terrific. So you're in the clear now? Completely exonerated?'

'I am. A clean slate, again. I got a nice text from Alistair and the DCI is delighted, apparently.'

'I expect you and Ian celebrated tonight?'

An innocent enough inquiry, and one that should have been straightforward enough to answer, but was not. Alice was well aware of her parents' view of her lover, and it would only be compounded if she told the truth. To them, he appeared overly detached, selfish and unnaturally self-sufficient. Not sufficiently protective of her. So if she said, 'He's gone out for a meal with friends,' she would, to lessen the impact, also immediately have to add, 'but I was asked out too,' and then go on to explain why she had declined to go. And that, in turn, would be complex, involve telling more than she might wish. It would be so much easier just to spout a small, white lie.

'He's not back yet,' she said. As the words left her mouth, she realised that even they would be insufficient for her parents. Why had he not thought to return early at the end of such a day? But it would have to do.

'So late? But you'll celebrate together later?'

'Yes.'

—

At 11.30 Ian Melville opened the bedroom door and found the light still on. He smiled at Alice, got into bed and snuggled up close to her. He was wearing a white tee-shirt with his scarlet boxers and he smelt strongly of beer. From his expression it was clear that he still remained unaware of the significance of the day.

'Good evening, you,' he said, slightly tipsily, putting a cold arm around her and looking to see what she was reading with feigned curiosity.

'Good evening,' she replied evenly, keeping her eyes fixed on the print.

'So,' he said, 'what did you do with yourself after we left?'

That bloody 'we' again, she thought.

'I ate my supper . . . read for a bit, you know, nothing out of the ordinary.'

'Sorry about Cici,' he said, scratching behind one of his ears. 'I know you don't find her easy, but she doesn't mean anything. Honestly. She's all right with a paintbrush, but not so good with words.'

'I wouldn't say that. She seems able to express herself pretty well to me.'

'You know what I mean,' he hiccupped. Disagreeing, Alice did not feel the need to answer, and continued trying to read her book.

'What's the matter?' he said, slipping his arm out from under her shoulder and linking it behind his head with the other one. 'This isn't about Cici, is it?'

'No, it's not. Today was my disciplinary hearing.'

'Christ! So it was.' He closed his eyes and then opened them again, looking at her with an expression of remorse. 'I completely forgot about it. How did it go? I'm sorry I didn't ask. Why didn't you say something?' He leant towards her, exhaling his beer-heavy breath in her face.

'I couldn't with bloody *Cici* about the place.'

'You could have done something – I don't know, taken me to one side. Got me into the kitchen with you. You could have got it across somehow!'

'No. You should have remembered,' she said hotly, turning her back on him and switching off the light. Something inside her head was thumping and the back of her eyes ached. It was too late, too late at night for this discussion.

'Alice, I'm sorry. I am so sorry,' he said, and then, having waited for an answer and received none, he too turned so that she could feel the curve of his warm spine against her. Usually, hearing such an abject apology, she would have replied that it was all right, that it did not really matter and rolled over to face him, to look into his eyes and put her head close to his, touch his forehead with her own. But in her mind's eye she saw Celia's feline smile, heard the little laugh he had given to soften his chastisement of her, and so she said nothing.

3

On the pavement, the woman watched disconsolately as the bus rejoined the stream of traffic, realising as she did so that her plans, such as they were, would have to be changed. Fate had intervened and there was no point in struggling against it. As she stood still, pondering what to do next, she felt the sharpness of the January air cutting her cheeks and she realised, belatedly, that she was not dressed for a walk. All she had on was her lightweight yellow anorak, a thin cotton jersey and her jeans. Her footwear, too, was not ideal, as she had chosen it that morning with an eye to fashion rather than practicality. She was wearing her red open-toed sandals, ill-fitting and with narrow cork heels, not the other pair, those comfortable trainers.

Setting off, unsure where to go or what to do, she peered into the faces of the pedestrians she met as if they might know where she was meant to be heading and direct her. After about ten minutes walking along the main thoroughfare, a sign saying 'Braid Road' caught her eye. She looked round blearily, taking in the prosperous villas on either side of it, each fronted by a well-kept garden, and at the imposing, red sandstone church near the corner. The name meant nothing to her, and she stood still for a moment, wondering whether to retreat back into Morningside or to carry on up this unknown street.

A passer-by, seeing the woman's mouth moving as she talked to herself, hurried onwards, afraid that he might be accosted by her. She, unaware of the impression she was making and still having made no conscious decision, began traipsing uphill. Her mind was as blank as a sheet of paper, one foot moving in front of the other as automatically and unthinkingly as her lungs were drawing in the cold air.

Finding herself at the brow of the hill, she surveyed the scene in front of her, uncertain, once more, whether to carry on or turn back into known territory. On her left was a road marked Hermitage Drive and, to her right, another, Braidburn Terrace. Carrying straight on and heading downhill would be the easiest option in these shoes, she decided, so she set off on her descent, carrier bag swinging to and fro against her calf, heedless as to where she would end up. It seemed wise to keep walking in this weather, try and generate some body heat. The exercise might help to dislodge her headache too.

After a further few minutes she noticed a low wall on her left with an opening in it. A line of parked cars led up to it, and some of them looked quite flash, she thought. If it was the entrance to a park she would go in and take a shufti. Her time was her own, and she liked parks. The modest side entrance bore a sign, 'Hermitage of Braid and Blackford Hill Local Nature Reserve', and she walked through. As she entered, a flock of about twenty rooks rose upwards, cawing their alarm at the intruder before dispersing into the treetops and regrouping.

Running parallel to the wide path was a swift-flowing burn and, entranced by it, she followed its course as it led her into a more densely wooded area. Struck by the loveliness of the place, she stood still, deliberately breathing

41

in more deeply, as if the air in the park might be healthier, fresher, unpolluted by car fumes. By good luck, she marvelled, she seemed to have wandered into a miniature Highland glen within the Lowland city. As she looked up, the crowns of countless leafless trees appeared silhouetted against a cloud-free blue sky, and light streaming between their branches fell and danced on the undergrowth below them. Where she was standing the terrain was relatively flat, but looking eastwards it began to rise on either side of the path, turning into small hillocks and undulations, and in places the bare rock of cliffsides was exposed, a few stunted ferns or rowan trees clinging to the cracks. Everywhere, the sound of running water could be heard, as if from a living organism, drowning out the usual hum of the traffic.

While she was within the confines of this park, she mused, the bustling metropolis of Edinburgh might as well not exist. A bomb could have fallen on the city, not that she would have cared. In fact, it would be no bad thing.

In the distance she could make out the outline of a grand mansion and, instinctively, she began to move towards it. A cyclist, with a dog trailing behind him on a long lead, passed her, and far off she could hear the excited, high-pitched shouts of children as they played somewhere deep in the hills.

The house, when she reached it, did not disappoint her. Situated in its dell, it seemed ludicrously romantic, with its bay front and corner turrets and, best of all, the walls crowned by battlements. The burn coursed behind the building, twisting and turning, eventually transforming itself into a torrent and powering its way between moss-clad boulders towards a small waterfall.

Still gazing straight ahead as she walked, absorbed by the sights before her, she did not notice a deep puddle on the path and stepped clumsily into it with both feet. The water was icy, and she looked down in despair at her sodden tights and mud-covered sandals. A metal bench had been placed by the waterside, and with a sigh she plumped herself down on it, now feeling almost intimidated by the discordant cries of the rooks as they circled above her in the darkening sky. Maybe they would launch an attack on her eyes, like in that Hitchcock film, *The Birds*? Fat chance, and anyway, she would give them what for. They would wish they had never hatched. Pluck them.

She put down her carrier bag on the muddy ground and crossed her legs. While she was getting her breath back, listening to the crows, she was entertained by the passing joggers as they forced themselves onwards, lungs pumping out white steam, mud spattering their Lycra-clad buttocks. Some seemed to be racing, and innocent pleasure could be derived from watching the discomfort of others.

Fortunately, she had, she laughed to herself, long since dropped out of the human race. Without thinking, she started to turn the wedding band on her finger, and when she became aware of what she was doing she shook her head. All in all, it was just as well those cash people had refused to take it. True, the money would have been useful, it was always useful, but the ring was part of her past. All reminders of it should not be lost. In her mind's eye she could still see Archie's trembling hand as he fitted it over her slim finger, looking her in the eye shyly as he did so, unable to stop grinning even though they were in the Kirk. And it was bloody gold all right, not a curtain ring, better stuff than the engagement one, for all its diamond solitaire. More carrots or whatever they were called. That place in Gorgie had not demanded any bills or anything else to take it, they had been only too eager to convert it into cash for her. No questions asked, they did what they said they did. The Leith branch had airs and graces above its station.

Feeling strangely unsteady on her feet, she rose and trudged onwards through the woods until the scenery changed again and she found herself in what seemed to be a tract of open countryside. Through it, the burn flowed onwards, but it was wider now, spreading out on either side of a gravel bank and becoming more sluggish. The place seemed somehow familiar, like a landscape she remembered from childhood. It was a vast area with reeds dotted in amongst the sour grass, and pancake-flat, like the hinterlands of the village she had grown up in. There was nothing ornate or fancy about that childhood place, just like the people who had lived there.

The sun had begun to set and a light drizzle was falling, soaking her head and shoulders. Feeling cold, she pulled the ends of her jacket collar together and kept on walking, putting one sodden foot in front of the other, humming 'Clementine' to herself, still in good spirits and enjoying her unexpected rural break. Everyone else seemed to have left this part of the park and she meandered off the main pathway, heading upwards on what looked like a sheep-track, and after a short climb found herself in a wide gully. On either side of the path were low thickets of bare, wind-twisted bushes.

When the weather suddenly took a turn for the worse, she hunkered down in front of them, seeking shelter from squalls which seemed to have risen from nowhere and now lashed at her, constantly changing their direction. As she backed into the bushes, trying to keep dry, a thorn pricked her backside and made her squeak like a baby. It was not a comfortable place to be in. The ground was damp and hard as metal, and in her squatting position her close-fitting trousers cut into her flesh.

All the same, taking advantage of the minimal cover, with nowhere better in sight, she decided to eat her crisps there. Tasting one and finding she had no appetite, she sprinkled the rest of the packet on the ground, picturing, as she did so, Saint Francis in his brown robes and sandalled feet as he fed the woodland creatures. The empty Tesco bag blew away, inflated like a balloon and rose into the air, dancing jauntily before impaling itself on an overhanging branch.

As she continued to squat, her belly began to feel uncomfortable, unnaturally distended, and she was aware of a painful pressure on her tight bladder. If she moved, she could actually hear the liquid splashing inside her. Drops of rain coursed down her wet face and her hair clung to her scalp, no longer providing any warmth for her head.

Her mind drifted back to the events of day before, scorched onto her brain and unforgettable. How could he do such a thing to her? Oh, if he could see me now, she thought, and then she shouted it out loud, consumed with an overpowering anger, unable to contain it any longer. Gradually, her voice tailed off into a prolonged moan, expressive only of her despair.

The very sight of me would paralyse him with horror. Kill him stone dead. I thought I was beyond hurting, cauterised, invulnerable, until I met him.

Tears came to her eyes and she tried to wipe them away, but found it difficult because her hands were numb with the cold. It was as if she was wearing thick gloves; her fingers no longer seemed to have any sensation, as if they belonged to someone else. A few minutes earlier, her whole body had started to shiver uncontrollably, and now, worried about herself, she rose unsteadily to her feet, determined to leave the place and return to the warmth of the city.

As she lurched forward, she stumbled and fell, twisting her knee on the way down. Breathing more rapidly, and aware of that fact, she raised herself onto all fours and began to crawl out of the gully. Her headache seemed worse, a thumping pain in her right temple, every time her knees made contact with the ground.

Behind her she heard something which sounded like a twig snapping, and shuffled round to see what was there. But nothing was visible. Teeth chattering like castanets, she forced herself onwards, but heard, once more, something behind her. She was sure of it, frightened by it. The sound was like breathing, heavy human breathing, coming closer all the time. It was followed by a light, tinkling laugh which echoed in her head. Ungainly as a wounded beast, she twisted round on all fours, her head poking out in front of her, determined to face whoever was playing these pranks on her. Please God, please, please God, it would be kiddies. The ones she had heard earlier.

'Who's there?' she demanded in a gruff voice, her tongue feeling oddly swollen in her mouth. A pile of dried leaves rose in the wind and hit her in the face and, frantically, she batted them away with one hand, temporarily blinded by them. On its own, her other arm could not bear her weight, so she collapsed, face first, chin hitting the ground, buttocks high in the air like those of a devout Muslim in a mosque.

'Who's there? Who's there . . . please, please?' she begged, terrified now, desperate to see whoever it was who was following her, tormenting her. Feeling weak, she managed to get to her feet and started to limp away from the sounds, the eerie laughter. Her hair flapping into her eyes made them sting and water, and she clenched and unclenched her jaw, forcing herself onwards, trying to ignore the knife-like pain in her knee.

Another noise filled her ears, this time like the hissing of a snake, and she looked up and saw a figure standing in front of her. It seemed huge, looming over her, and she knew in her bones that it intended her harm. Without thought she tried to escape from it, flinging herself into the nearby thicket, fighting her way through the jagged hawthorn and blackthorn bushes, feeling nothing as their thorns ripped through the flesh of her head and hands. Startled, a bird flew up at her, again hitting her squarely in the face, and she screamed, unable to contain herself, horrified by its feathery feel.

From some place deep within the thicket came a strange scrabbling sound, as if something, or someone, was clawing its way through the undergrowth to get to her. To get at her. Hearing it, she quickened her pace until her damaged knee gave way, and she fell forwards, exhausted. She had reached a clearing at the edge of a rock face, and a hundred feet below, the burn shone like polished steel in the light of the newly-risen moon. In the silence she remained motionless, breathing shallowly in an effort to keep quiet, terrified that the sound of her teeth chattering might give her away.

For five more minutes she remained where she was, unable to stop the shivering that racked her body, but alert, listening for any of those horrible sounds. None came. Whatever it was that had been pursuing her had, finally, gone. It had given up. She let out a sigh of relief, newly conscious of her own thumping heartbeat. And then, both behind and in front of her, she heard the familiar, tinkling little laugh.

4

The first to wake the next morning, Alice slid from under her lover's outstretched arm and edged quietly out of the bed. In the dark her hand scrabbled on the bedside table searching for her watch. Finally she found it, carried it into the kitchen and turned on the light. 7.32 a.m. Christ almighty! Neither of them had remembered to set the alarm and now she would be late for work. But all was not lost, she thought. If she drove instead of walking as usual, she could still make it on time.

In the cold bathroom she hurriedly threw on those of yesterday's clothes that she could find, and then brushed her teeth using the disgusting sweet, striped stuff that Ian insisted on buying. She made a mental note to beg him once more to get something else. Or, conceivably, to do the shopping herself, for a change.

The bread bin contained only a single, stale croissant which she scanned for mould. Finding only a patch the size of a pinhead she ate the croissant with some raspberry jam, mould and all. Gulping down the last of her tea she set off down the tenement steps towards the street, confident that she would make St Leonard's by eight-fifteen. Halfway down she remembered that she had neither closed the front door of their flat nor given Ian a farewell kiss. Rattled at having to use up more precious minutes, she turned round and tore up the two flights of stairs and rushed, panting, back into the flat.

Unthinkingly, she clumped along the bare boards of the corridor leading to their bedroom and flung the door open. Despite the racket, Ian remained asleep. A miracle, she thought, or, and more likely, the effects of last night's drink. Light from the corridor outside illuminated his face, and for an instant she gazed at the slumbering man, touched by his vulnerability. Time stood still. His dark hair lay in curls over his forehead and his long lashes were visible against his unnaturally pale skin. She bent over him and planted a light kiss on his cheek, but he did not stir, only groaned slightly and flicked his head with his hand as if brushing away a fly. Amused, she closed the door as quietly as possible and tiptoed back towards the front door.

He would have no recollection of any kiss bestowed by her, remain unaware until the evening that she bore him no grudge and was, almost, but not quite, ashamed of starting their quarrel. What did it all amount to now? The hearing had been abandoned and she was free of it. So what the hell? What did it matter if he had forgotten all about it? If only that ghastly Cici had not been there they would not have argued because, apart from anything else, she would have been unable to keep in her good news, would have blurted it out the minute she had seen him. Then their evening would have ended very differently. Probably, in bed together with only a bottle of wine between them. No. There was no doubt about it; that woman was a menace.

Alice crossed the street to her car and turned the key in the ignition, but as soon as she had edged it out of its parking space she became aware that something was wrong. The steering wheel felt unnaturally heavy between her cold hands, and the cobbles appeared to have grown overnight, become rougher, larger and more uneven. Even the sound made by the wheels as they rolled over them seemed different, louder, and punctuated by an occasional heavy clunking noise.

Just before she reached the junction with Broughton Street, she stopped, clambered out of the vehicle and made a quick inspection. The tyres on the driver's side appeared entirely normal but as she walked round the car she noticed that the passenger-side rear tyre was flat, its hubcap unnaturally close to the ground. Examining it, the front one looked soft too. For the moment nothing could be done. She would simply have to park the sodding thing back in the space she had just vacated, leave an explanatory note on the windscreen for any over-eager wardens and get it fixed that evening. Thinking about it, there was a spare in the boot, and with luck Ian would give her a hand. He was better with jacks.

With the clanking noise getting louder by the second, she reversed slowly in the direction of her space, hoping that the axle would come to no harm. Looking in her mirror, she saw a red VW Golf slide into the very slot at which she had been aiming. The man got out of his car and walked away, apparently unaware or unmoved that he had just stolen her space.

She looked at her watch, 8 a.m., and then at the unbroken line of parked cars on either side of the street. All the residents' parking spaces were occupied, and so, too, were those reserved for ticket buyers. The only empty ones were marked by double yellow lines.

At a snail's pace she drove onto the double yellow lines and parked the useless vehicle. As she locked the door she caught sight of a deep scratch on the driver's side extending the full length of the car, and any thought of

51

leaving a notice for the wardens left her mind. Someone had used a screwdriver or penknife on it. The bastard! They would have to get a lock-up sooner rather than later.

Now sweating before the labours of the day had even begun, she started to jog up Hart Street and, cursing to herself, felt the first few drops of rain fall on her unprotected head.

In the Hermitage, Simon McVicar stopped at the little ford to catch his breath, listening to the thin winter birdsong which was just audible above the roaring noise made by the burn. His lungs hurt. No doubt, he thought, the pain was attributable to all the cold air he had been sucking so forcibly into them. Or, maybe, he was simply a little unfit? Bent double, his head dangling down, he could feel his spare tyres being compressed against each other, and in his skimpy new running shorts his pasty legs looked rather too solid, with no taper to the ankles.

Feeling suddenly self-conscious about his appearance, he looked round, hoping desperately that he would see no one from his work. In his normal clothes he appeared, in his own eyes at least, as a reasonably trim figure, but in this kit every imperfection was accentuated. Concluding that in motion they would be less obvious, he straightened up, took another deep breath and set off jogging down the wet tarmac path once more.

A little while later he was trotting past Hermitage of Braid House, his legs feeling shaky and heavy as lead. Briefly he wondered about stopping again and taking another rest, when a man, far bulkier than himself, drew level. Glancing sideways at him, he decided that his fellow jogger must be at least ten years older than he was and appeared to be carrying an extra couple of stone or more. The brute had a neck like an old bull. This was no athlete. To be overtaken by such a figure would be beneath him, undignified to put it mildly. The man looked like a slob, someone who had let himself go completely. Probably a couch potato ordered out by his spouse.

So, without his rival realising it, he decided he would match him pace by pace, prevent him from drawing ahead. Determined to keep in front, he lengthened his stride and attempted to breathe in a more regular, rhythmic fashion. The moisture now running down his brow trickled into his eyes but he ignored it, occasionally shaking his head in an attempt to get rid of it. By the time they reached the raised bridge he was scarcely able to breathe, and unpleasantly aware that his heart was racing in his no longer flat chest. The tubby man seemed to be gliding along effortlessly, the only sign of exertion being his complexion, which seemed slightly ruddier than before.

Gasping, and now desperate to stop, McVicar decided to simulate a trip. Taking a break for an injury was perfectly legitimate, he decided. So he stopped dead, and with what little wind he had left, let out a mild expletive, looking angrily at the ground as if intent on punishing the rut or ridge responsible for his stumble. Standing on one leg and rubbing the ankle of the other, he attempted to convey to any passers-by and to his oblivious competitor that he had only come to a halt because of his injury. But without a backward glance, his former running mate powered onwards, as unaware of the faked accident as he had been of the scarlet-faced man who had recently been huffing and puffing beside him.

McVicar wandered over towards the burn, its waters now brown from the overnight rain, and tossed a twig idly into it. He watched as it was carried away, twisting and turning in the swirls and eddies, occasionally submerged but always bobbing up again. When it finally disappeared from view, he set off once more, still heading in the direction of the Blackford Depot. If he was ever going to get into his best suit again, this pain would have to be endured, otherwise a diet of lettuce leaves lay ahead of him. Of course, rabbit food and exercise together would be the most efficient combination, but life was not worth living without chocolate and red wine. The odd latte, too.

Seeing a little-used path peeling off on his left he decided to take it, thinking that the sight of unfamiliar scenery might occupy his mind and make him forget about the raw ache in his lungs. A grass surface would be springier too, less damaging to his no longer young knees.

For a very short while, the new sights did seem to supply him with a burst of energy. But the soaking ground seemed to go on sloping ever upwards, forcing the puff out of him, and there was no plateau in sight. Forcing one weighty leg in front of the other, trying not to groan, he felt a slight twinge of pain in the left side of his chest. Fearful that he was on the verge of a heart attack, he stopped abruptly, intent upon resting, preventing any further damage.

A large boulder resting on the rabbit-grazed grass caught his eye. He walked slowly towards it and sat down on its smooth surface. After a period of immobility with his head between his knees, the pain in his chest disappeared and he decided that it must have been heartburn. This time. He stood up, relieved that he had done no permanent damage. He had quickly reached the decision that a new suit would be in order, with him alive inside it. No point in being a slim corpse. Thinking about things realistically, no one's figure remained unchanged throughout their late teenage years, or even their early twenties or thirties. If for any reason he could not find a suit he liked in M&S then he would simply wear his kilt to the wedding instead. After all, he was not at the last hole of the straps yet and a judiciously-placed sporran would camouflage any slight pot-belly.

A movement, seen from the corner of his eye, caught his attention. A stoat in its white winter clothing was standing on its hind legs and, intrigued by the sight, he lumbered slowly in its direction, his wet trainers squelching with each step. Instantly, the creature darted off into the nearby thicket, but he continued towards the spot it had occupied, keen to get one more look at it. He peered into the thicket and saw, sticking out of the bushes, a pale, outstretched human hand. He blinked in disbelief. Disgusted, his first instinct was to move away from it, to back away from it and forget all about it, but he was, he reminded himself, a responsible adult. A fully qualified actuary, no less. Heavens, if *he* shirked his civic duty, what hope was there for the rest of society?

So, against all his instincts, he crept towards the hand, keeping his eyes on it in case it moved or twitched. Bending to look more closely, he allowed his gaze to travel upwards. A discoloured arm was attached to the hand, and beyond that he could make out the profile of a yellowish face. The edge of its mouth appeared to have been nibbled away by some beast, exposing all of the back teeth in the upper and lower jaws and a vast expanse of pale pink gum. The missing area of flesh curved upwards like a crescent moon or a clown's exaggerated smile.

Without his mobile, Simon McVicar did not know what to do. So he did the first thing that came into his head and released a piercing scream. When nobody responded to it, he let out another one, higher this time, and saw, to his relief, the portly jogger running towards him.

‘Nobody told me that yesterday,’ Alice said, in between gasps for breath. While Simon McVicar was standing motionless by the dead woman, screaming for help, she had been tearing up the stairs of St Leonard's Police Station, taking them two by two in her haste. Arriving sweaty and twenty minutes late, she was informed by an unconcerned DI Manson that she was supposed to be at Gayfield Square, helping out the short-staffed SART boys again.

‘Nobody said!’ she exclaimed.

‘Well,’ he replied nonchalantly, ‘they should have.’ His feet were resting on his desk.

‘But “they” whoever “they” are, didn't and as a result I nearly killed myself trying to get here on time . . . and I live just round the corner from Gayfield Square,’ she persisted, suspecting that he was the mysterious ‘they’.

‘Are “they” responsible for your lateness, then, Sergeant?’ he replied, deliberately baiting her and watching her already high colour rise with indignation.

‘No,’ she conceded, ‘but I would have been on time at Gayfield Square.’

‘But you didn't know you were to go to Gayfield Square, did you?’ he said, twisting her tail for the pleasure of it, then turning a page of his newspaper and dropping it onto his desk with a smile as broad as the Cheshire cat.

'No – but if my car . . .'

She did not have time to finish her sentence as DCI Bell marched into their room. Immediately DI Manson removed his feet from the desk and caught the little woman's eye, keen to get her attention and prevent it from straying to his open newspaper.

'What are you staring at?' she demanded sharply.

'Nothing.'

'Where's Alistair?' she snapped, her gaze resting on the copy of the *Scotsman*. The two police officers shook their heads; neither of them had any idea where he was.

Since she had failed to be promoted to Superintendent, Elaine Bell's scant store of patience seemed to have dried up completely. Had almost anyone rather than DCI Ranald Bruce pipped her at the post she might have reconciled herself to remaining at St Leonard's, but his success stung, like vinegar dripped onto a recent wound. He was, in her view, grossly over-promoted already.

She, of course, was blind to his political skills, although they were the real secret of his success and the key to her own failure. An early morning phone call from him had set her nerves jangling. Preoccupied, now replaying their conversation in her head, she heard herself admitting that he would be indeed a 'new broom' as he had described himself. Silently, she had added the observation that he would be ideally suited to the role, being made of wood from the neck upwards.

'Fine, fine,' she said, her mind still on other things, 'he'll be late as bloody usual. Well, he'll just have to go and fill in at Gayfield instead of you, Alice, and you can go to the Hermitage with Eric.'

'Right.'

'But what's happened there?' the Inspector inquired,

stretching his arms high above his head and then standing up.

'Didn't I tell you? No? A couple of joggers have found a body in the undergrowth there. One of them phoned half an hour ago. It's a woman . . . oh, and she's half-naked. She may have been raped.'

The bulky and inexperienced WPC stationed at one of the boundaries of the crime scene signalled with her arms, revolving and then crossing them like an uncoordinated windmill. She was trying to attract the attention of two CID officers heading uphill. As they deviated from their original course, turning towards her, a stooped, bird-like figure peeked out from behind her billowing raincoat. The smaller woman's posture betrayed her great age, and she, too, was gesturing at them, frantically flapping a hand to hurry them along. Both women knew that it was point-less to shout, their voices would be lost in the roar of the gale raging around them. The storm had blown in across the North Sea and was running amok up the east coast, spinning weathercocks, splintering slates and smashing up yachts in harbours as far apart as Coldingham, Musselburgh and Arbroath. Before dawn it had taken possession of the city and was busy playing with the inhabitants, turning their umbrellas inside out and rattling their chimney-pots.

'You go, Alice,' DI Eric Manson shouted, peeling off, heading instead in the direction of a small group of men that he had just spotted in the distance. They were clustered in a small circle, the majority of them down on one knee, their heads close together like young children absorbed in a game of marbles. Everything about them suggested that they were with the body.

Suddenly one of them rose, chasing a piece of paper as it bobbed in front of him, caught in an up-draught, his hands outstretched as if beseeching the elements to return his property.

As Alice drew closer to the large policewoman, the old lady dodged in front of her human windbreak, almost blown off her feet as she did so, but determined to get her say in first. One hand was clamped over her crocheted yellow-ochre bonnet, and from the other swung a nylon dog lead. It was blowing to and fro in the strong gusts as if weightless. Her head, which shook constantly, was sunk deep into her shoulders. Looking up at Alice like a tortoise from inside its shell, she blinked and said dolefully, 'Teazel – Teazel's gone off! I'll need to get him back. I'm very sorry.'

'Where did he leave you?' Alice asked, leaning towards the woman and trying to project her voice over the noise of the wind.

'I don't know. I lost him a while back, some place before the raised bridge. But he always races on. I think he may be in there,' she said, pointing at the sectioned-off area, the blue-and-white tape that marked it writhing like an eel in the shifting gusts. Then she added pensively, 'He shouldn't be, should he? But dogs don't know the law, do they? They can't read and write. But I'm very sorry, officers . . . for your . . . all your trouble.'

'That's the problem, you see, Sarge,' the large WPC said slowly and unnecessarily. 'He may be in there, disturbing things, mucking up the evidence. What should we do?'

'I've been shouting for him,' the old lady volunteered, adding, 'she gave it a go and all, didn't you, love? But it's hopeless.'

'Yes,' the WPC agreed, and as if to prove the point she bellowed out, 'TEAZEL! TEAZEL!', her words disappearing into nothingness, carried away by the next blast which rushed past them and blew their hair into their eyes. Looking desperate, the old lady joined in, adding her cracked treble to the chorus and scanning the horizon with her bespectacled eyes.

'Come on, Teazel, ye wee devil!' she implored, suddenly losing patience with her pet and whirling the lead in her hand as if it was a lariat and she was about to lasso a recalcitrant steer. From behind a trio of distorted hawthorn bushes a few hundred yards away, the missing Border terrier appeared on the skyline. Seeing them, he bounded towards them as if overjoyed at finding them again. His tail wagging furiously, he leapt up onto his owner, leaving muddy pawprints all over her grey raincoat and all but bowling her over. Only the policewoman behind her saved her from falling. Dangling from the dog's mouth was the limp body of a long-dead rabbit, its skeletal legs terminating in over-large furry paws. The old lady bent down and, with surprising dexterity, removed the corpse from her pet's jaws and clipped the lead back onto his collar. Then, nodding, but saying nothing more, she set off hastily in the direction of the big house. The dog followed jauntily behind her.

'Did you get her name?' Alice asked, watching them as they hurried away.

'Yes. She's called Irma Goodbody.'

'Where does she live?'

'Christ, I forgot all about her address,' the WPC said, a look of panic on her face.

'Better catch her then. Off you go. We'll need a full statement. She may have seen something useful.'

Nodding, the sturdily-built policewoman jogged after the pair, her arms flailing as she battled to keep her balance on the uneven ground.

'Over here, Sarge,' a man's voice shouted. Turning and catching sight of the speaker, Alice went to join him. He was standing on a muddy footpath, holding the fringed ends of his tartan scarf over his ears, determined to stop his earache from getting any worse. The path on which he stood zigzagged between clumps of dead bracken. In the nearest clump lay a light yellow anorak. Part of it was covered by the dark, slimy fronds of the plant and as she got nearer one of the wet sleeves broke loose with a sound like the crack of a whip. In the strong breeze it blew freely, waving cheerily at them as if it had a life of its own.

By the time Alice had reached the man her shoes were sodden, but she was feeling pleased to be there, out in the fresh air, glad to have stumbled across this oasis of countryside hidden in the heart of the suburbs, murder or no murder. Whoever it was who had failed to tell her that she was supposed to be starting her working day in Gayfield Square with the SART boys had done her a favour. But for that she would be traipsing in and out of the pawnshops in Leith, inhaling exhaust fumes and dodging the gobs of chewing gum that studded the pavements. Instead, here she was, outside, exploring this unexpected find of a place. She made a mental note to tell Ian all about it later – he would love it and so would their dog. A walk here would be a treat, making a fine change from the tamer, more familiar landscapes of Arthur's Seat, the Meadows and Inverleith Park. In this wilderness, there were acres of proper woodland, tangled undergrowth and a reed-fringed burn meandering its way through its own marshland.

A photographer, following behind Alice and conscientiously videoing the scene from every angle, failed to notice a rabbit burrow and put his foot in it, tripping over and falling to the ground with a thud. A heartfelt obscenity issued from his lips. Immediately he inspected his camera lens, wiping a smear of mud from it with his sleeve.

'Are you OK?' she asked him, and when, still prone, he nodded, she pointed at a couple of empty cans near his feet. They lay on a patch of burnt earth, their ends touching the soot-blackened stones of a makeshift fireplace.

'Did you get them?' she asked, and then, spotting a nearby Scene of Crime Officer, she waved at him, summoning him to come over and plot their location.

'Have you found anything else?' she asked the SOCO as he hunkered down on his knees trying to get a closer look at them. Neither can was rusty; a crumpled one had contained beer and the other, cider.

'More rubbish, you mean?' he replied, his kneecaps now waterlogged, sounding unimpressed by her find. Rising stiffly, he added grudgingly and as if it was of as little significance, 'A high-heeled shoe. It's probably hers. I can't think who else would be leaving their footwear about in a place like this.'

'Can you show it to me, once you've finished here?'

'Aye,' he replied, picking a fragment of dried heather out of his green paper suit. 'It's fairly close by her. We found it maybe ten metres or less from the body.'

A lone red leather sandal rested upside-down on a patch of flattened grass. After a good look at it, Alice moved towards the group of men assembled at the edge of a thicket of squat, bare bushes. DI Manson, one side of his raincoat open and flapping in the wind like a loose sail, was bent double, inspecting the body.

'That's what you get in the countryside,' he said for her benefit, hearing her approach. His lips were pursed and he was shaking his head in disgust.

'What d'you mean?' she asked, bending down beside him to get a better look at the woman. They had had this argument of old. In his view nature was red in tooth and claw, and to be despised. Man and his works were placed above it, had to control it.

'The wild beasts have been at her,' he replied, gesturing at the corpse's savaged mouth with a wave of his hand.

'They didn't kill her though. That'll been one of us city dwellers,' Alice replied.

'Don't start with any of your . . . your . . . animal rights nonsense, Sergeant,' he said testily. 'I'm not in the mood.'

Alice looked at the dead woman's face. Both of her eyes were closed and one side of her mouth curved upwards in a grotesque lop-sided grin. Something had widened her smile. A small, yellowish bruise extended from below her hairline over her right temple, and her wiry grey hair was matted, with twigs and leaves protruding from it. Scratches, as straight, deep and well-defined as claw marks, disfigured the front of her nose and a semi-circular area of flesh was missing from an earlobe.

Slowly, Alice's eyes travelled down the body. The only clothing remaining on it was a black bra and it looked ill-fitting, unnaturally loose, as if it had been undone. Her mud-encrusted jeans lay a few feet from her bare legs, and her exposed kneecaps looked red and raw, contrasting with the pale flesh of her torso as sharply as blood spilt on snow. A pair of black pants, with grimy, clay-coloured fingerprints all over them, encircled an ankle. Raised, angry-looking abrasions were visible on her naked arms, and below her bloodied elbows her hands were dirt-smeared, her fingernails black as a navvy's.

'This place gives me the creeps,' DI Manson said, looking round and shivering theatrically to underline his distaste for it. Straightening up and catching sight of the rooks circling above him, he added, 'Look! Bloody vultures! You don't get them in the city centre either. Remind me not to die in a place like this.'

'Have you spoken to Professor McConnachie yet?' Alice asked. With all her attention focused on the woman's disfigured face, she had hardly registered his dig.

'Yes,' the DI replied, jangling the coins in his trousers pockets noisily as he searched for his lighter. Finding it, he tried unsuccessfully several times to light his cigar. Eventually, a colleague held his hands up to shield the flame.

'What did he have to say?'

'He's still mulling things over, but he reckons that we should treat it, for the moment, as some kind of sexual homicide. He's not happy about the bruise on her head. She may have died from the blow that caused it, or hyperthermia or both. Or something else altogether. He can't say yet. He needs to open her up first.'

'Have we any idea at all who she is?' Alice asked, finally dragging her eyes from the disfigured face and turning towards the Inspector.

'Nope. All we know is that she's been food for the beasts.'

'We've nothing to go on at all?'

'No. Nothing.'

Manson drew on his cigar deeply, hoping that the inhaled smoke would, somehow, warm him. After holding it in for a few seconds, he partly exhaled, filling out his cheeks like a hamster before releasing a few puffs through partly opened lips. 'There was nothing in her clothes except a few coins, and no handbag's turned up either. You'll need to speak to the two joggers as soon as possible. They're both in a squad car together.' He added, 'One or other of them followed the ferret and found her.'

'The ferret?' Alice said incredulously. 'That seems unlikely. After all they don't usually roam wild, they're domesticated.'

'A ferret – a weasel – a sodding skunk!' he interrupted her, now blowing a stream of blue smoke forcibly through his lips. 'How the hell do I know? What does it matter? As you said yourself, Sergeant, whatever it was didn't kill her. So we don't really need to identify the brute right now, do we?'

—

Watching inside as drops of rain started to run down the windscreen of the car only to be blown straight across it, Simon McVicar made plain his reluctance to leave the shelter of the vehicle. He appealed to the female sergeant; he had on his running clothes and nothing else, and they were thin and wringing wet. Surely he could be interviewed in the warmth, inside the car? Outside, the air was turning arctic and it had begun to drizzle. He would freeze in the wind, he protested.

Patiently, Alice explained again to both the witnesses that they each had to be seen on their own, either outside the car or in the station, she did not mind where it was. Calculating that the trip to and from the station, plus the likely waiting around, would rob him of a full morning's work, Simon McVicar finally capitulated and stepped out onto the damp ground. The wind slammed the car door shut behind him.

Standing a few yards away from the car, he felt vulnerable in his scant, clinging kit, exposing his goose-pimpled legs to the world. He was also consumed with anxiety. Upset. It all seemed to him, in some ill-defined but real way, inappropriate. 'Out of order', as people said. Those assisting the police in a murder enquiry, he thought, should be properly dressed, not clad in over-tight, skimpy shorts. So clothed, he felt sure he lacked solemnity and weight. In a word, dignity. To compensate for this perceived deficit he became pompous in his speech, determined to prove to the detective that he was a man of substance, someone to be taken seriously, not some kind of unemployed gym-bunny.

'I understand that you found the body?' Alice began.

The man's hands, which hung loosely by his side, had begun to tremble. 'Correct, Officer. I was the unlucky one,' he answered, opening and closing his fists in a deliberate attempt to stop them shaking. He was aware that she had noticed the movement.

'Can you tell me what happened?'

'Certainly. Very shortly after I had departed from the main path I stopped for a while to . . .' he hesitated briefly and then continued, 'admire the view. At that moment in time I saw a stoat, an ermine, and I followed it. As a result of following it I chanced upon the lady.'

'Had you ever been to the place where you found her before?' Alice asked.

'No, I've never been here before. This is my first time and I can assure you,' he added bitterly, 'my last.' He edged closer to the police vehicle, now leaning against it in an attempt to protect himself from the wind which was whipping about his unprotected legs.

'When you found the lady, was she dead?' Alice asked him.

'How d'you mean? What d'you think?' he said in disbelief, his voice quavering, outraged, sounding as if he was on the verge of tears, 'Have you seen her? She's been eaten, for pity's sake! Of course she was already dead!'

'When you found her was there anyone else about? Did you see anyone else nearby?' Alice persisted.

'No,' McVicar replied, 'I was completely on my own. All alone – not a soul in sight. I shouted for help. I'd not got my mobile with me so I shouted for help instead, for assistance. Dan, the fellow in the car with me, heard me and came to see what the matter was. He phoned . . .' As if he had run out of air, the man's voice petered out and he suddenly covered his face with both hands, hiding his eyes and breathing in and out steadily and deliberately.

'I've never seen a dead body before,' he said quietly, bowing his head as if in shame.

'I quite understand, Simon,' Alice said, putting an arm around him, 'and it must have given you an awful shock. I have, too many times, but not many like her, thank God. Do you think you could help me with just one more thing?'

He nodded his head, shoulders hunched, his hands still protecting his face from her gaze.

'Do you know what time it was when you found her?'

'No. I left my watch at home and, to be honest, I've lost all sense of time. The best I can do is – and it's just an estimate – I reckon I found her an hour ago or so. I don't know what the time is now.'

Once he was back alone in the privacy afforded by the squad car, Simon McVicar began to weep, accidentally releasing a single, loud heartfelt sob. Appalled and ashamed at his own reaction, he wiped his tears quickly away with the bottom of his damp white singlet and blinked hard, trying to prevent any more teardrops from forming. But they continued to cascade down his cheeks, and he knew why. The dead woman had looked, at first glance, horribly like his own mother, and on first seeing her, his heart had missed a beat. Suppose it really had been her, lying in the dirt with her pants about her ankles? Assaulted, raped. No, murdered. It was too unbearable to consider. He must, must, *must* get the lock on her back door fixed, this very day, and he must tell her only to walk the dog in broad daylight and in public parks. Snib the windows too. Take her mobile with her at all times. Jesus! No one was safe in this city.

How had this happened? Today had started like every other day in his life, every other ordinary day, and now, somehow, whether he liked it or not, violence had sidled up to him and, against his will, made his acquaintance. Kissed him. Raped him too, if you please. If only, he rued, I could put the clock back, I would get up and go straight to work, omit the morning run, and never place myself within a country mile of Hermitage of Braid.

The traumatised man's temporary running mate, Dan Purvis, had been whiling away his time in the police car playing 'Snake' on his phone. In his full-length, breathable tracksuit, the cold did not trouble him. He was a butcher by trade, used to refrigeration rooms, and had manhandled enough lifeless animal flesh in his working days to blunt the sensibilities of a Sunday school teacher. Seeing the dead woman he had not recoiled from her, but had bent down closer to get a better view. When he had had his fill of the sight, he had, finally, responded to his companion's repeated, hysterical requests and called the police. While waiting for them to arrive he entertained himself by making calls on his mobile phone. The first

person he spoke to was his wife, and he described everything in Technicolor detail to her.

'Somethin's been gnawin' at her face, I reckon.'

'A dog, mebbe?'

'Naw, hen. Somethin' wi' wee, jaggy teeth.'

'A rat?'

'Aye. Could be.'

As he was nattering away to her, an inspired idea
had struck him and he rang off with scant ceremony. Of
course, it was obvious! They could profit from this stroke
of good luck, and there was no time to waste. Immediately, he called one of his drinking pals from The Jolly
Beggars, a journalist, to see if he was interested in his
story. The next five minutes had been spent in haggling
over a fee for his world exclusive. Now standing outside
the car, he confirmed to the police sergeant that there
had been nobody other than himself and McVicar in the
vicinity of the corpse.

'To be honest, I thought it was a woman screamin',' he
said bending down to peer through the car window at the
man weeping inside. Having gawped unashamedly for a
few seconds, he continued, 'From the screams, I thought
a lassie was being raped or somethin'. She, I mean he, was
screamin' blue murder.'

'Do you know what time it was when you first saw the
body?'

'No, but I can find out,' he said, drawing his mobile
phone from the pocket of his tracksuit. While he was
finding the call log, Alice, suddenly suspicious, asked
him, 'Did you call somebody when you were with the
body?'

'Yes, I called yous.'

'Anyone else?'

'Aha. I called my wife, and she called me back. Let's see, 8.52 . . . so I must have found the man at about 8.30, 8.40 or so.'

'Did you call anybody other than us and your wife?'

He looked up, mobile still in his hand, and met Alice's direct gaze. He would have to tell her. They could easily check, and he would be in trouble if he had lied.

'Yes, I did. I called a pal of mine, a journalist with the *News*.'

'And what, precisely, did you tell him?'

'It was no big deal, Officer,' he said defensively, putting the phone back in his pocket before continuing, 'I just told him what I'd found, like. A dead woman with chunks bitten off o' her by a rat and wi' her breeks off an' everythin'. Like she'd been raped. That's all.'

'Did you . . .' she asked, still holding his gaze steadily, 'take a photograph of her with your phone?'

He shook his head, but she did not believe him. He was just that type.

'Sure about that?'

'Aye. I'm quite sure about that. Simon Vicar or whatever his name is, him greetin' in your car, stopped me, if you really want to know. He pushed me out of the way just as I was takin' my shot. Said it wasn't "respectful to the dead" or something. So I've got no photos. If you don't believe me you can check my phone, see all my other ones – my wife, my kiddies . . .'

'Is this where you usually run? Were you here yesterday too?'

'No. I come to this place about once, maybe twice a week at the most, but not where she was. I don't like it up there. Young lads go and light fires there, shoot themselves up, spray graffiti on to the rocks. I went there

70

once before, last winter, and a couple of the wee bastards showered me with stones. I've not been up since.'

———

DI Eric Manson dropped the evening newspaper on to his desk and then, as if in pique, scrunched it up into a ball and flung it into the wastepaper basket.

'Irresponsible shite,' he muttered to himself, standing up and stretching, raising his arms high above his head and taking a long, dog-like yawn.

'At least you knew he'd done it, Sir. Told the papers, I mean. It didn't come as a complete surprise, as a bolt from the blue you might say,' DC Elizabeth Cairns remarked, putting down the phone, leaning back in her chair and taking a sip from her mug of tea.

'And your point is?' the Inspector asked. His hands were now clamped to the back of his head and, as he stretched again, his shirt came adrift from the waistband of his trousers, revealing a sliver of hairy flesh.

'Well, it reduced the shock value, I suppose,' the Constable said brightly, pushing her gold-rimmed spectacles up the bridge of her nose and smiling at him.

'And you, what exactly have you found out, Defective – sorry, Detective – Constable? What do you know?'

Feeling now that she had somehow inadvertently edged herself into the limelight, the policewoman sat up straight, trying to look alert, and said, 'That description, Sir, the one we circulated, it hasn't produced any response yet. Not a proper one at least. Someone I know in Torphichen Street thought they'd recognised it and gave me a name. But I checked it out and I'm quite sure it's not her. It turned out to be a hooker down Leith way, someone called Michelle Vincent? But she's still alive and kicking. In fact, she's up in the Sheriff Court today for another breach of the peace.'

'Michelle Vincent?' DC Galloway said, looking up from his computer and laughing. 'It'll not be her for sure. I could have told you that, if you'd asked me. She's a bottle blonde, sometimes a redhead, been a purple head in her time, even. She'll not go grey until she's nailed into her box and six foot under.'

The door to the Murder Suite opened and Alice Rice came in, shedding her coat as she walked and rubbing her hands together, trying to restore life to her cold, numb fingers.

'What news from the outside world?' Eric Manson asked, seated once more at his desk and looking at her expectantly.

'About the dead woman? Well, she wasn't lying in the bushes yesterday afternoon, it seems. I spoke to a couple of dog-walkers, regulars in the Hermitage, and they were there at about 3 p.m. and saw nothing. They let their dogs off the lead near where she was found, and if she'd been there I reckon they'd have found her, wouldn't they? Sniffed her out. The dogs, I mean. I described her to the walkers and neither of them recognised her from my description, and no one DC Stark's spoken to did either. He's drawn a complete blank with the other dog-walkers and the cyclists too. One jogger remembered seeing her yesterday and then his companion reminded him that they hadn't been jogging in the place yesterday. He struck me as a bit of an attention-seeker anyway, thrilled to have a bit part in the drama, volunteering to come into the station and assist us with our inquiries. A time-waster, really.'

'That's it?'

'Pretty well,' she nodded. 'Someone claimed to have seen a man in a yellow anorak out for a walk yesterday, but I don't think that can have been her. She didn't look like a man, did she? Not with her long grey hair and her red sandals. Yellow's a colour not often worn by men, but it can't have been her, can it?'

'No,' DC Cairns said, wrinkling her nose, adding a few seconds later, 'men don't look good in yellow – none of the ones I know, anyway.'

The Inspector, seeing that Alice was about to take a seat, added, 'I wouldn't sit down if I were you, Alice.'

'Why not?'

'Because you're straight off and out again, and you can take DC Cairns with you.'

'Where am I off to?' Alice asked evenly, her suspicions already aroused.

'Guess? You can phone a friend if you like . . .'

'To the bloody Cowgate.'

'Exactly. The post mortem has been scheduled for 4 p.m. I've a meeting with the DCI and Superintendent Bruce then, so you'll have to go instead of me.'

'But what's the point? We don't know anything about the woman yet. Wouldn't it be better to wait until we at least know who she is? Reschedule it? If we knew who she was it might explain what she was doing in the park. If the pathologists need a history, and they always do, we can't give them one this time. Couldn't it wait a few days?'

'4 p.m., Alice. Anyway, once they've got their cleavers out, perhaps they'll be able to give us something for a change. I don't suppose that crossed your mind?'

'What? A bout of vomiting, from all their repulsive smells?' Alice said truculently, bowing to the inevitable with ill grace and collecting her coat.

5

'Female, Caucasian . . .' Professor McConnachie said, speaking into his hand-held Dictaphone, bending over the naked corpse and adding, 'age – late fifties, early sixties, something like that. Long, frizzy grey hair, shoulder length . . . detritus in the hair consisting of leaves and twigs.' He stopped for a moment, pressed the *record* button on his Dictaphone once more and then looked beadily at the machine.

'Forget to press the right button, Prof?' the mortuary technician asked.

'No, but there's no red light going on, Brian,' he said, gazing at the small man and holding the machine out towards him.

'Bust, is it then?' Brian asked unconcernedly, in his Liverpudlian accent, making no attempt to take the Dictaphone from the outstretched hand.

'No,' Professor McConnachie said patiently. 'Not bust, Brian. It has no battery left. No juice. Could you get me another one, please?'

''Fraid not, Prof. We've no batteries left in the drawer. I've ordered more but they're not likely to arrive for a couple of days.'

'A Dictaphone?'

'Yes, it's a Dictaphone,' Brian answered, sounding slightly aggrieved, annoyed that his intelligence was being questioned.

'Another Dictaphone? Perhaps you could see if you could get me another Dictaphone, then?'

'Oh. Right you are,' the technician replied, putting down the cloth that he'd been using to wipe the corpse's knees, taking the machine and disappearing through a door.

'So, Alice,' the Professor said, 'can you tell me anything about this woman? I spoke to Eric earlier, but at that stage he knew nothing.'

She shook her head. 'We've been asking all over the place, but so far we haven't turned up a thing about her. She's a complete mystery. We're hoping that you may be able to help us this time.'

'So she's a dead-end, then,' the technician said, laughing to himself as he handed the Professor a new Dictaphone. He returned to his wiping with renewed vigour.

'Blue eyes,' the Professor said, opening one of the woman's eyelids with his gloved fingers. He leant over her head and added, 'A haematoma . . . say, five centimetres long by five wide, extending from the hairline down the right temple.'

DC Cairns sidled up to the Professor to get a proper look, and as she was craning over the corpse her head almost banged into his balding skull. He gave her a warning look.

'Remains of a strawberry nevus on the right cheek,' he continued.

'Where?' she asked, undeterred by his forbidding expression.

'There – on the cheekbone,' he said, pointing at a small, reddish mark in the shape of a starfish. 'Seen it? OK for me to go on?' he added sarcastically, but as if it was a straight question the DC nodded her head.

His mouth close to the Dictaphone, he pressed on. 'Animal damage to the angle of the mouth, on the right, and to the right earlobe.'

'The stoat?' Alice interrupted him.

'Could well be. That or a rat, I would hazard, from the small bore of the teeth. Rats would always be at the top of my list.'

Picking up the woman's right arm and then moving on to inspect her left, he continued, 'Abrasions on the posterior surfaces of both forearms . . .'

'She's been crawling, pulling herself along on 'em, I reckon,' the technician observed.

Throwing the man a glance to silence him, the Professor carried on with his dictation. 'Abrasions on the anterior of both kneecaps and on the dorsal surfaces of both feet. A significant degree of livor-mortis down the back to the thighs . . . with contact pallor on the buttocks and shoulder blades.'

Bending over, he examined the woman's abdomen and said, as if to himself, 'An old surgical scar, maybe six inches wide, probably as a result of a Caesarean section.'

DC Cairns nodded her head and reiterated, 'Yes, a Caesarean section,' as if she was confirming his opinion. The Professor stopped his dictation for a moment, annoyed, and looked crossly at her. But, as before, she appeared unconcerned by his reaction.

'You've had one, have you, Constable?' he said.

'No,' she replied artlessly.

He shook his head, astounded by the apparent thickness of her skin.

'No signs of injury to the external genitalia or to the breast or thigh areas,' he continued, then he tapped the technician on the shoulder and said, 'swabs, please, Brian.'

Once the swabs had been brought, he made an announcement to those assembled around the body: 'Everyone got everything they need? Photos, jewellery, measurements and so on? Because I'm ready to open her up.'

Acknowledging their nods with one of his own, he said in an American accent and as if he was in a cheap drama, 'OK, I'm going in!'

So saying, he made a large T-shaped incision on the woman's body, extending from her shoulder tips to her pubic bone. Once it was complete, he wiped his brow with the back of his gloved hand. The bloody scalpel was still clasped in it. As the intestines were being removed the smell in the room became overpowering, and Alice looked over at the Constable to see how she was faring. But she was absorbed, watching the Professor's every move, seemingly quite untroubled by the noxious stench around her. He seemed finally to have warmed to her, won over by the deep interest she was showing in the proceedings, and he even began addressing some of his remarks to her.

'My, my . . . that does tell us something,' he said, smiling at her and pointing a gloved finger at an organ, now exposed, within the body cavity.

'What is it?'

'Her liver. If you put the state of it together with her fairly emaciated condition, I reckon that she must have been a pretty heavy drinker. Look at it – grossly enlarged – and lots of fatty changes too.'

After examining the lungs and the heart, the pathologist then removed the stomach from the collection of extruded innards, emptied it of its contents and cut into it to inspect its inner surface.

'What are you doing now?'

'Give me a second,' he sighed, then murmured again into his machine. 'Examination of the stomach lining revealed the presence of Wischnewski ulcers.'

'What did you say?' DC Cairns asked, determined not to miss anything.

'Wischnewski ulcers.'

'My dad's got ulcers,' DC Cairns exclaimed excitedly, craning over to get a better look.

'Not like these ones, he won't,' the Professor said, looking at her. 'They only appear when someone's become hypothermic. They're a characteristic finding in cases of hypothermia.'

As the dead woman's skin was being peeled from her face by the technician, Alice looked away. She then set herself an impossible task. To conjure up in her imagination a pebbled beach with low, translucent waves crashing onto it and simultaneously to try to take in the significance of anything said by the Professor. She heard the words 'subdural blood' and forced herself to look at him, deliberately avoiding any sight of the flayed face. Catching her expression of complete incomprehension, he added, 'There's blood under the dura – blood on the surface of the brain, if you will, only apparent at post mortem.'

DC Cairns nodded sagely.

'She had a bruise on her right temple,' Alice said. 'I saw it. It was highly visible. You mentioned it earlier too.'

'I did, but that was an old one, fairly superficial too. This is on the other side, the left side, and it . . .' he hesitated before speaking into his Dictaphone again, 'is about four by six centimetres in diameter.'

He pulled on the woman's neck in order to tip her skull over and drain the blood from it into a measuring vessel.

'Mmm,' he said, holding it up, 'about 75 to 100 milli-litres of blood. From its appearance it looks quite fresh as well. That could well be the fatal injury.'

Once the procedure was completed, the Professor removed his mask and helped himself to a drink of water.

'What do you think, Prof?' Alice asked him.

'I am still cogitating . . . trying to put everything together in my mind. The external findings don't suggest that she'd been raped. No marks of violence in the genital area. We'll have to wait for the results from the swabs, combings and so on, but if she was raped, it doesn't look as if brute force was used to overpower her. Could have been the threat of a knife, I suppose. The ulcers tell us that she was hypothermic and she seems to have had a fatal, or possibly near-fatal, subdural haemorrhage. Oh, and I'm pretty certain she was an alcoholic. Again, we'll need to wait for the results from the blood, urine and vitreous humour, but I'd bet my own money on it, just looking at that liver.'

'A suspicious death or natural causes?'

'I can't say for sure, but she could well have been attacked. If so, it would have been by a blow to the head – striking the left temple. Or it could have been caused by a fall, of course. I can't tell at present. Ideally we need her history. And I don't know whether she died from the subdural or the hypothermia or both. She's rather more prone than most to a subdural, being an alcoholic.'

'So what should I tell the DI?'

'Tell him, for the moment, just for time being, to treat the cause of death as the subdural. We have to exclude an attack, the worst-case scenario. The best case is a fall. Everything may well change as more information comes to light. Hopefully we'll get something useful from the lab results – if not, from you lot.'

———

The traffic on the Cowgate was at a standstill. Workmen in hard hats at the St Mary's Street junction and at the Grassmarket end were supposed to be controlling the cars, but neither of them was allowing any vehicles to pass. As a result, there was a lengthy hold-up, with horns blaring and engines revving but no movement.

As they walked back to the station, turning at the lights uphill onto the Pleasance, Alice said to DC Cairns, 'You did well. I take it you've been to a post mortem before?'

'No,' the Constable replied, 'I've never. But I've seen far worse than that.'

'Where on earth? Were you a pig stunner in an abattoir or something?'

'No, but I worked as a nurse for a while. An awful lot of things happening to the living are much worse than that. The dead don't feel a thing, do they? So they're all right. You don't need to worry about them.'

'Still, there are the foul smells, the sounds, you know, the saws, the ripping and tearing . . .'

'It's water off a duck's back as far as I'm concerned. It would probably mean nothing to you too if you'd had to watch people crying out in pain, people screaming – and that's just a hashy catheterisation. A post mortem's a cakewalk in comparison, a party.'

'Why did you give up nursing?' Alice asked.

'Because,' she replied in a matter-of-fact tone, 'I never grew a second skin. And you need one for that job. Oh, and the pay. It wasn't too hot either, sweeties, not to mention the hideous uniform they force you to wear.'

'We shouldn't be here – in the pub,' DC Galloway said, and then he tilted his glass of IPA towards his mouth and took a large gulp.

'I don't see why not. There's nothing more we can do tonight,' DC Littlewood replied. He was using the coasters on their table as cards, propping them up against each other in an attempt to make a house. Just as he was about to complete the third storey, DC Cairns pushed up her spectacles and blew hard on them, causing the entire structure to collapse.

'You shouldn't have done that,' he said peevishly, looking at her in disbelief and then gathering the coasters up to try again.

'If you do it again . . .' he threatened, but his voice was drowned out by a loud roar as the pub erupted with joy, men now rising from their seats and punching the air as Hearts scored their first goal against St Mirren.

'Anyway,' Alice said, once the noise had died down, 'it's late and the Inspector knows we're here.'

'How did you manage at your first post mortem?' DC Littlewood asked the bespectacled female constable. He had given up on the card house and was now curious about the new recruit from Torphichen Street.

'Fine,' she replied breezily. Her second glass of gin and tonic was already half empty.

'You didn't throw up, then?' he asked, impressed, a couple of crisps in his hand.

'No.'

'I did,' he said, his mouth now half-full, and added, 'but I'd had a heavy night before and it was first thing in the morning. I'd have been all right otherwise.'

''Course you would!' DC Galloway said sweetly. 'Like you were the last time. Not.'

'Want another one, Sarge?' Tom Littlewood asked, pointing at Alice's empty glass.

'No thanks,' she replied, finishing the dregs. 'I'd better be going home.'

She stood up and walked towards the door, but before she reached it she found herself face to face with Eric Manson. He looked exhausted, colourless.

'Everything all right, Sir?' she asked, surprised to see him in the pub and worried suddenly by his haunted expression.

'Yes, Alice. But I need to speak to you . . . outside, if that's OK with you?' She nodded, feeling uneasy, further disconcerted by the uncharacteristically nervous tone in his voice. Something really must be up. He followed her out onto the High Street and they stood close together by the door of The Thistle as she waited for him to speak. A couple moved past them and as they went into the pub the sounds of rowdy conversation leaked out from it. A drunk staggered through the doorway, bumped into the Inspector, winked and sniggered, 'A fine night for it, eh?', as if he and Alice were about to kiss.

Watching the man meander down the pavement, Manson still said nothing. Alice asked him: 'You said you needed to speak to me, Sir?'

'Yes, I did,' he answered, but again he said nothing. She waited a few more seconds, her impatience growing. The air was freezing, and Ian would be back by now, waiting for her.

'Well, I'd best be getting home then, eh?' she said, looking at him, trying to prompt him to speak, and then, when he did not, turning towards the Tron Kirk, ready to go.

'It's about Ian,' he said.

She stopped in her tracks and turned back to face him.

'What about him?' Her heart already racing, her words came out too fast, in a rush.

'He's been in a car accident. He was hit this evening by a car in Stockbridge.'

'He's all right?' she said.

He said nothing.

'Tell me he's all right?' she repeated, pleading with him.

'I can't.'

'Tell me –' she implored him.

'He's dead. They took him to the Infirmary but he was dead on arrival.'

6

The next morning Alice awoke in a strange bedroom and for a single, blessed second, wondered where she was. As her eyes roamed around the room, the realisation that she was in her sister's house was accompanied by a physical sensation of dread, of fear almost, as the fact of Ian's death hit her once more. Feeling tears forming behind her eyes, she deliberately looked up at the ceiling, blinking them back, and tried to concentrate on the whiteness of it, the strange pattern made by the single hairline crack, anything to distract her from this new, unwanted reality. But a voice in her head, unbidden by her, repeated insistently: 'He is dead. He is dead. He is dead,' chiming like a bell.

'Alice?' It was her sister, Helen, standing outside the door.

'Yes?'

'Would you like some breakfast?'

No. That would be the truthful answer, but it was not worth saying. Sometime she would have to get up, sometime she would have to face them all, and now was as good a time as any.

'Thanks. I'm just coming.'

'I'll just bring it in then, shall I?' her sister asked, and, without waiting for an answer, barged her way sideways through the door and into the room. She bore a tray, laid for breakfast, and on it was a small vase of snowdrops. As if Alice was an invalid, she placed it in front of her, resting it on the blue duvet, and then bent over her, plumping up one of the pillows, ready for her sit up and lean against them. Then she sat down on the bed and looked intently at her sister.

'Thanks,' Alice said, looking down at the toast and boiled eggs and feeling no hunger for any of it. The meal seemed about as appetising as her own bedclothes.

'Did you sleep all right?' Helen asked.

'Fine. Thanks.' Her answer sounded oddly formal, Alice thought, and added to the air of unreality that enveloped her, that she could not shake off. Everything that mattered had changed. The world was no longer the same. Yet the rules of grammar were being adhered to, food was being brought at the normal time of day and their exchange had been a model of polite triviality. But she, or the she that she recognised, no longer existed. She had become hollow, no longer had any substance. There was now a huge gap in her where once her heart had been.

'Do try and eat something,' Helen said.

When Alice made no move, her sister took matters into her own hands, knocking the top off an egg with a knife and then buttering the two slices of toast.

'They were laid yesterday, so they'll be as fresh as can be,' she said.

'What?' Alice said, bemused, her mind somewhere else.

'The eggs.'

'What about them?'

'They were freshly laid, yesterday.'

'Were they laid by your hens?' Alice asked, trying to sound interested, but feeling her chin tremble as she said the words.

How the hell had this happened? How could they possibly be talking about the identity of the hens that had laid the eggs when Ian was dead? Simply pronouncing his name in her head made the tears swim in her eyes.

Because that was all he was now. A name in people's mouths, a memory in their minds. As insubstantial as air. There was no flesh, no body to touch any more, no eyes to look into, no voice to hear. He, as she had loved him, was no more.

'Yes,' she heard her sister's voice as if in the distance, 'and I'm pretty sure they are both from the Black Rocks. I got them as pullets, on point of lay, and I think that these two are a couple of their first efforts.'

'Really?' Alice answered, trying to infuse her voice with interest, but finding that she was quite unable to think of anything else to add. Mechanically, she lifted her spoon and sank it into the yolk, watching her sister watching her.

—

The kitchen, when she entered it, seemed to be alive with noise. Sam, her four-year-old nephew, was racing around the wooden table on his bicycle, stabilisers squeaking on the wooden floor. He was naked except for a pair of trainer pants, and his dog, a blue-eyed collie, was tearing after him and barking loudly. Quill, Alice's mongrel, was in hot pursuit of both of them, and he, too, was barking. The boy was shouting their names, egging them on in their pursuit of him and howling like a wolf.

Helen had her hands in the sink, washing pots and pans from the night before, and her younger child, Angus, was sitting cross-legged at her feet. He was watching the TV, a wide-eyed look of wonder on his face, singing out loud and occasionally bursting into high-pitched laughter.

Walking into the room, Alice felt overwhelmed. Everything happening in it was happening too fast, it was blurred with speed, and the colours were too vivid, the sounds too loud. When she spoke, her voice sounded oddly heavy, leaden, like someone else's.

'Hello, Sam.'

'Out of the way! Get out of the way!' he shouted at her, missing her by inches as he careered past, the dogs straining to reach him.

'Sam!' Helen said crossly, but he took no notice of her.

Rolling her eyes heavenwards, she took off her rubber gloves and, on his next circuit, stretched out to catch him as he whirled past her again. At her second attempt, she managed to grab his bare shoulders and slowly draw him towards her. Once he was still, the dogs, too, came to a halt, and Quill, pink tongue lolling from his mouth, wandered over to the water bowl for a drink.

Seeing that the bowl was empty, Helen took her hands off her older son, and the instant he was free he pedalled away to start his circuits of the kitchen table once more. The dogs, seeing that the game had begun again, rushed back to join in. One of them tripped over the television flex, pulling the plug from the socket, and instantly a loud wail came from Angus, who found himself sitting in front of a blank screen. Tutting irritably, Helen picked him up. The child turned his head away from her, wriggling in her arms, desperate to return to his seat on the floor and resume his viewing.

'It's all right, Helen,' Alice said, putting the tray down by the sink. 'I liked it as it was.' Helen looked at her doubtfully, so she added, 'Honestly, just as it was.'

Before Helen had a chance to respond, she had to leap out of the way to avoid being run over by her son.

'Are you sure?'

'Sure.'

Helen bent down and put the plug back into its socket and the TV flashed into life. There were gurgles of joy from her younger child, already enraptured by the picture on the screen. Alice picked up a red-and-white dishcloth and began to dry one of the newly-scrubbed pans. Her sister returned to her place at the sink, yellow gloves on once more, as she attacked a blackened oven dish.

'Pete left it in the oven overnight to "roast" peppers,' she said with a rueful sigh. Alice nodded but said nothing. After a while Helen spoke again. 'Would it help to talk?'

'Not really,' Alice answered, cutlery in hand, her eyes on the children. But in the minutes of prolonged and uncomfortable silence that followed she felt the need to say something. Helen seemed to expect it.

'I haven't get my own mind around it yet, Helen,' she began. 'It's hard to explain. It's like something I've only half seen, something glimpsed. One bit of my brain knows exactly what it saw, but another bit of it, the hopeful bit, goes on insisting that it was not that at all. It tells me that it was something else. And that's the bit that I want to believe. The hopeful bit, the bit that says that there's been a mistake and he's not really dead, that someone else was run over, not him. And then I can believe that he'll come walking through the door at any minute. Every time I think I've accepted his death, believe it, the hopeful bit of my brain upsets everything, saying I'm wrong. I know he's dead, of course I do . . .'

'What happened?' Helen asked, leaning her head against her bare forearm and rubbing her itchy forehead on it.

Alice breathed out. She did not want to talk to anyone about it, had a superstitious fear of putting into words the circumstances of his death. Describing it, talking about it, meant that it was true, that she accepted that it had all happened and in that way. In the process of telling it, he would become a story, a tale to be told, someone to be spoken about by others, but who no longer said anything himself.

'He was in Stan's Bar in Stockbridge,' she started, hesitating before forcing herself to go on, listening to the sounds coming out of her mouth as if they were being made by someone else. 'I don't know who he was with exactly, Cici told me their names but I didn't know any of them. Some of his studio pals, apparently. I phoned her to find out what had happened . . . because she'd been with him. She said that he was knocking back the drink a bit and became argumentative, so she decided to leave. He left at the same time, and as he was crossing the road, dawdling a bit, he was hit by a car. Simple as that. They took him –'

She stopped, aware that tears had forced their way into her eyes again. 'Well, not him any more... his body . . . to the Infirmary, but it was too late. DOA. Dead on arrival. I saw him.'

'What happened to the car driver? Was he hurt?' Helen asked, slipping another plate into the rack.

'I don't know. It was a hit and run,' Alice replied, tired with the effort of speaking. 'Eric didn't tell me and I forgot to ask. I'll be told as soon as they get him.'

'Quiet you two! Ssshh!' Angus demanded, putting his finger to his mouth to silence them and adding, 'I can't hear the telly!'

Seeing her sister's appalled expression, Alice wordlessly put an arm around her shoulder. She did not mind what the boy had said, would have preferred to remain silent herself. But to admit this sounded too unfriendly, and she did not have the energy to work out how to phrase it as tact required. It would be difficult to tell Helen that the children's complete indifference to her predicament seemed preferable, at present, to her own obvious concern. Their self-absorption meant that they required nothing of her, had little interest in anything she said. Her tears did not have to be hidden from them because they would not notice them even if they were coursing down her face. Their own inner worlds were so interesting, so vivid and engaging, that little of anyone else's impinged upon them. So she did not have to make any effort with them, nothing needed to be hidden or explained. Thankfully, the part she played in the drama of their lives was so small that they would not notice her absence from the stage. Yet they were company. In contrast, Helen's sweet sympathy demanded a response.

'Aunt Alice?' Angus said, rising from his place on the floor and toddling towards her, the lip of an empty beaker trailing behind him along the tiled floor.

'Yes?'

'Why are you here?' he asked, frowning, looking at her and attempting to drain the last drop of juice from his beaker.

For a moment she was not sure what to answer. Did he know? Should she allude to Ian's death or simply gloss over it? Angus knew him after all, had referred to him as 'Uncle Ian' on their last stay. But maybe she was supposed to palm the child off with some innocent lie? Such as, 'I'm here because I like it here.' Or perhaps his parents had a policy of not shirking the 'big issues' as they arose? What did the boy know of death?

'Well,' she began, feeling the need to say something and catching her sister's eye, in the hope that she would provide some kind of guidance on the appropriate answer. But before she had begun to formulate anything, the boy yelled, 'Prank Patrol!' and rushed back to the TV set.

Later that morning, Alice went alone to feed the chickens. Her nephews, too busy wrestling with each other, had declined to come with her and she was relieved to be on her own. The silence outside was like balm. The henhouse was set in a small paddock surrounded by laurel bushes, and the morning sun danced and sparked on their shiny, dark green leaves.

She threw the birds their mix of grain and layers pellets and then went into their house to see what they had laid since the previous day. A few of the straw-lined hen boxes contained clutches of pale brown eggs but in one a hen was sitting, surveying Alice with an unblinking, malevolent gaze. A couple of eggs lay touching her feathered breast and Alice stretched a hand out to collect them. A sharp peck to her wrist made her look up, meeting the bird's outraged eyes. Its stare left her in no doubt that any further attempt to rob it would be met with the same treatment, so she retreated, turning her back and leaving.

As she leant against the dilapidated little hut she gazed at the small flock as they pecked feverishly on the ground, the sun reflecting off their glossy, green-black feathers. Sparrows hopped between the scaly feet of the fowl, ducking and dodging in search of missed morsels. A loud crowing behind her made her come to and she whirled round. A huge cockerel, his red crown flopping over one eye, charged at her, flinging himself at her legs with his sharp spurs uppermost.

Instinctively, she moved aside to evade his attack and her manoeuvre worked, the cockerel missed his target and ended up somersaulting in the dirt. While she was still gazing at her floored assailant, a memory bubbled to the surface, of the last occasion on which she had entered his domain. It was five months earlier, in the height of summer, with the cow parsley blooms fading and the air heavy with the hum of bees. They had gone together to the hens. She was supposed to be feeding them and Ian planned to sketch them as they scratched about, beaks agape, in search of grain. As soon as she had entered the hen-run, the cockerel had launched a surprise attack on her, charging without warning from a space below the hen-house, wings flapping and spurs to the fore. But he had been stopped in his tracks by a tin pencil case flung at him, bouncing off his head and causing him to run off, squawking, to the shelter of his harem. When Ian had picked his case up, he had brandished it at the cowering bird, muttering, 'Next time, rooster – you'll be coq au vin.'

The memory was so vivid, so strong, that she could see his smiling face in front of her, hear the laughter in his voice. And she did not want to. Trying to think about other things, she walked back towards her sister's house. It was an old, stone-built farmhouse set on the side of a hill. Normally the beauty of the place moved her. It seemed to be being gradually reclaimed by the earth, with ivy, clematis and climbing hydrangea covering its walls, fringing its lower windows, their tendrils curling upwards into the metal gutters. Majestic lime trees surrounded it, sheltering it from the prevailing wind, and, in the summer, the scent of its flowers was heady, drowsy bees working in its shade. She took its existence as proof that harmony could be achieved between the works of man and nature, each enhancing the other. Even in the winter, on the coldest, darkest days, something of its essence usually touched her, but not today. It was as if she was no longer able to truly see; everything was there just as it had been before, but the sight of it left her cold. A veil seemed to have been placed between herself and the world.

'Aunt Alice . . . phone!'

Sam was standing beside her, and seeing that she did not move, he immediately shouted at her, 'Come on, come on. Chop, chop!'

Obediently she followed him back to the house, and as she entered the kitchen her sister handed the phone to her, soundlessly miming the words, 'Ian's mother.'

The noise in the room had not abated but was, if anything, worse. A radio was now in competition with the television, the dogs were barking and the washing machine was whirring on spin-cycle. So she walked into the nearby study and closed the door.

'Hello,' she said.

'Alice?' Mrs Melville asked, apparently not recognising her voice.

'Yes.'

'How are you, dear?'

'I'm all right, thanks. And you?'

'I'm fine too. But I need to speak to you about Hamish.' The old lady's voice sounded firm, as robust as ever.

Slowly, Alice closed her eyes, then, sighing to herself, she covered them with her left hand. In her grief she had forgotten all about the child, Ian's son. He lived with his maternal aunt and her partner in Roseburn Terrace, on the top floor of a tenement close to the Water of Leith. The boy's mother, who had had a brief affair with Ian, had died a year earlier and Ian had learnt of her death and the boy's existence simultaneously. Since then they had both been trying to get to know him, seeing him once a fortnight, and if allowed, more frequently. He was now aged four, curly-haired and sturdy, with a gap where one of his front milk teeth had been knocked out in a fall.

'Right,' she said, feeling ashamed, shocked by her own thoughtlessness. Maybe it was true that blood was thicker than water. Mrs Melville, despite her bereavement and over seven decades spent upon the earth, had not forgotten the boy, overlooked his very existence.

'Does he know yet?' the old woman asked.

'I don't know, but I wouldn't think so. I haven't told him. If you haven't either, I can't think who would have done.'

'That's what I thought. But it does need to be done . . . and his aunt, Rachel, needs to know too.'

'Shall I do it? Would you like me to do it? I could go and see her today if you like. Let Rachel know.'

'Yes. The sooner the better, I think, but I'll come too. I want to see Hamish and to speak to Rachel about him myself. Whatever has happened to his father, I'm still his granny. I'll leave the arrangements up to you, if you don't mind, and perhaps we could meet there. In Rachel's flat?'

As she was searching for a parking space in Roseburn, Alice saw Mrs Melville getting out of her car. She looked frail, more bent than usual, and seemed to be having difficulty fitting her keys into the lock. Succeeding, and looking up, she caught sight of Alice and waved her over. They greeted each other wordlessly, instinctively putting their arms around one another, holding tight as if afraid that if they did not they might lose one another as well. Both were determined not to cry, aware of the contagion of tears and each unwilling to set the other off. Red-rimmed eyes would only further upset the boy. Unusually, the old lady took Alice's hand in her own, gripping it firmly and only releasing it once they were inside the tenement.

They climbed the four flights of stairs at a snail's pace, stopping every few minutes for Mrs Melville to rest her legs and catch her breath. Once they came to the immaculately-painted, green front door she held onto the banisters, attempted to straighten herself up and said, 'Are you ready, dear? Shall we go in?' Her face was white, almost bloodless, but her expression was firm and resolute. Alice nodded and knocked on the door.

The woman who opened it, Rachel Ford, was tall and gangly, with washed-out blue eyes and a pale, freckled complexion. Her finely-lined face looked anxious as she ushered them in to her sitting room. It had a single window overlooking the river and was furnished with a couple of old-fashioned armchairs and a grand piano, which dominated the room. As they were sitting down she said in a high, slightly tremulous voice, 'I've not told him.' She sounded defensive. Mrs Melville leant forward in the over-soft armchair into which she had sunk, using the arms to pull herself closer to the edge of the seat.

'Would you like us . . . me or Alice, to tell him?' she asked.

'No.'

For a moment there was complete silence. Mrs Melville smiled benignly at Rachel Ford but said nothing, as if waiting for her to explain herself. Her tactic worked.

'I've tried to. I've begun once or twice but I can't do it,' Rachel said, shaking her head and looking them both in the eye before continuing. 'I'm sorry. I'm the one who had to tell him when Paula died and I can't do it again. It was too awful.'

'But he should know, shouldn't he, dear? It is important that he knows, isn't it? Not least because otherwise he won't understand why there are no more visits from Ian.'

There was another long, pregnant pause. Finally Rachel said, 'Yes, he should know. He's entitled to know.'

'Very good. Then I'll tell him for you, shall I? I'm his granny, I can do that,' Mrs Melville said, levering herself up from the deep armchair and adding, 'don't worry, Rachel, children are surprisingly resilient . . .'

She hesitated for a second, and continued, 'and he was just getting to know his father. Don't worry, it'll not be like the loss of Paula.'

While the old lady was out of the room, Rachel Ford turned to Alice and said, not unkindly, 'Would you like to keep seeing him, Alice? Obviously, everything's completely different now that Ian's dead, there's no connection between the pair of you, but you can see him occasionally if you'd like to.'

It had been spelt out to her. With Ian alive, the child had been in some definite sense 'theirs'. He did not live with them and saw them only once a week or so, but he formed a large part of their dreams, their plans. One day, when he knew them better, had come to love them, he might live with them. They rarely discussed the prospect but both knew that it was there, secretly rejoiced in it, and cherished the possibility. But he had never been, in any sense, 'hers', and Rachel was underlining this simple truth. Without Ian she had no right of any kind to a relationship with the little boy, no tie that would be recognised as continuing in his absence. If she saw him at all, it would be on sufferance.

'But frogs don't croak, granny – they go "Gribbit! Gribbit!"' the child said. He was perched in his grandmother's arms holding a bean-bag frog in his hands and tapping her on the arm with it to emphasise his point. Seeing Alice and Rachel in conversation, the old woman winked at Alice to let her know that the deed had been done.

'Alice!' the boy said, struggling to get free of his grandmother and running towards her. Now, standing directly in front of her and looking up into her face, he demanded, 'Where's Quill? Why's Quill not here with you?'

'He's busy,' she said, lifting him onto her knee, 'he's hard at work today.'

'At work? Is he in the Police too – a police dog?' the boy asked excitedly, his eyes shining.

'Yes, but he's of a higher rank than me, he's an Inspector. Inspector Quill.'

'Inspector Quill!' he repeated, savouring the words, before stomping back to where his grandmother was sitting and backing himself into the space between her knees. Leaning against her he said mournfully, 'Granny's not got a dog, only got a cat. Macavity the Mystery Cat.'

'He's called the Hidden Paw,' the old lady said, sweeping his dark hair out of his eyes and then taking him in her arms.

Over the following days Alice walked a great deal. It seemed to help. She had no desire to speak to anyone about her loss, but wherever she went she talked to herself, trying to resolve things in her own mind. Late one afternoon she set out from the house and, after continuing eastwards for an hour, found herself at a nearby loch. It had frozen over, and she stopped there for a while, taking a seat on the broken-down jetty that abutted the thatched boathouse. Still lost in thought, she swung her legs idly to and fro, over the edge.

In the distance, a swan, its brilliant white plumage making the ice surrounding it look grey and dirty, swum round and round in small circles within its tiny black pool, trying to prevent the only remaining water from icing over. As she watched the bird, the contrast between the white of its feathers, the black of the water and the blue-grey of the ice registered in her brain. She gazed at the scene, pleased by the sight and thankful that something of it had penetrated the veil that surrounded her at last, and touched her. It was odd. She had been there last year with Ian and because of that she had had to force herself onwards, expecting to find it desolate in his absence. But his absence was no more marked, no sharper, there than anywhere else.

Sitting on the rotten wood of the jetty, she looked down at the snow-melted surface of the ice all around her and noticed masses of small tracks on it. Some had been made by the elongated toes of a bird, a heron perhaps, and some by rabbits, showing the characteristic scuff where they had kicked off. Running across the middle of the loch was a single set of fox prints. Each one of its four paws was perfectly aligned.

Without thought she stepped out onto the ice, a sudden zinging sound as it took her weight making her hesitate momentarily, then she began following the fox's tracks. They meandered across the smooth expanse, leading her to a bank of dead reeds at the far end of the loch. Below them lay a small pile of feathers, and a few grains of wheat, with droplets of blood spattered among them.

I must tell Ian, she thought, and then, catching herself, she cursed the workings of her own mind. It was so lazy, following the old, known tracks like a tram, refusing to adjust to new roads, and crashing time after time.

Forced to contemplate his absence anew, the pain was almost unbearable and she shouted out loud, railed against everything, including him. How could he have done it? How could he have left her on her own without him? She might live another thirty or forty years without seeing his face again, without touching him.

Already, she could not conjure up his likeness at will, had to rely on an image from a particular photograph. 'He is gone,' she repeated to herself, 'he is gone and will never come back.' She tried to force her brain to reshape itself, to stop making her relive the horror of loss endlessly.

Drained, she knelt down on the ice, her hands covering her face, and listened in the silence for him. For something, anything, some tiny sign that he was beside her still. In the scarlet-streaked winter sky, silhouetted against the fading light, a pair of mallards flew overhead, their wings beating in unison, the movement audible in the heavy air. It was nothing more than a couple of wild ducks returning to the roost but it was enough to remind her that life was going on, the world was still spinning on its axis.

As she looked upwards, straining to see the black dots as they disappeared into the distance, she heard a single crack, and the next second fell forwards, plummeting through the ice. Gasping, breathless with the shock of the cold water, she flailed about, and her hands, unexpectedly, found solid ground. Next the top of her head touched it, and she realised, still falling forwards on her knees, that she was in the shallows.

Suddenly, as she pictured herself, kneeling in water less than a foot deep, shards of ice splintering around her as she desperately sought a sign from above, the preposterousness of her position struck her and she laughed out loud, at the bathos of it all. Still doubled up, unable to stop hooting with laughter, tears coming to her eyes, it struck her that Ian would have loved the whole scene. Because, thankfully, there had not been an ounce of sentimentality in him.

7

'Are you OK?' Elaine Bell asked. The DCI was busy in her office, her eyes fixed on her computer screen and her right hand scribbling simultaneously, but the solicitousness in her tone was heartfelt. She was fond of her sergeant. But she was also short-staffed and in the middle of a murder investigation. Crucially, she had to tread carefully, mindful of the legal pitfalls awaiting her. If she allowed an employee to return to work too quickly, or too slowly, and a complaint of stress at work or some such thing followed, she might find herself in hot water.

'Fine.'

DCI Bell looked up from her screen to peer into her subordinate's pale face, trying to assess whether her brief response could be taken on trust or not. Exhausted, at the end of a long case, she had seen Alice look a lot worse, she decided.

DC Elizabeth Cairns bustled into the room holding a sheaf of papers, and before she had off-loaded them onto the desk, she was sent packing, unceremoniously, with a dismissive wave of a hand.

'I'm not sure whether to believe you or not, Alice. Are you still staying with your sister?'

'Yes.'

'Perhaps you want to stay there a little bit longer? Need to, even?' the DCI continued probing, watching carefully her sergeant's reaction to the question and adding, 'I don't know. On the other hand, maybe it would help to have other things to think about?'

Alice nodded, and, still feeling her way carefully, Elaine Bell said, 'If you'd like to come back, we could certainly use you here. Progress has been pretty sluggish. We still haven't discovered the identity of the body in the Hermitage. You could pick up where you left off.'

The telephone rang. Unreasonably annoyed by its unseemly intrusion into their delicate conversation, the DCI snatched it up.

'DCI Bell,' she said, then paused briefly before continuing, 'Yes, Sir. The lab's confirmed that. Yes, I appreciate that. Of course, but there are a few hundred thousands or more of them in Scotland, aren't there? Plenty of women, too, I'm sure you'll find. Yes. Yes. I will, as soon as possible, naturally. I will . . . Sir,' she added with distaste. Putting down the receiver she said '*Superintendent* Bruce,' stressing his rank sarcastically and unconsciously folding her arms over her chest.

'Have you tracked down the driver yet?' Alice asked.

'The driver?' Elaine Bell inquired, bemused, still sufficiently riled by the phone call to have forgotten everything else.

'The one who ran down Ian?'

'Sorry – sorry, Alice. Of course. My mind was on other things. No, we haven't, I'm afraid. We're still looking. But you should know . . . a witness says that he had a good drink in him before he crossed the road.'

'Of course he had, he'd just left a pub,' Alice replied, uneasy, not sure exactly where this exchange was heading.

'"He'd had more than enough" was what she actually said. She also reported that he pretty well launched himself onto the road without looking properly.'

'Not Ian. I don't believe it. He held his drink well. He wasn't stupid or mad. What exactly are you trying to tell me?' Alice asked, suddenly distraught, looking her superior directly in the eye.

'I'm telling you – that it was a hit and run, we know that, but . . . he may have been partially responsible for –'

'You said there was a witness?' Alice demanded.

'Yes. A witness.'

'Who? How many have we found?'

'Only one, so far. I'm not sure I can tell you the name off-hand – but Celia Something or other . . . We're still looking for the other two. They're on holiday together somewhere in Ireland.'

'There must have been plenty of people in the pub?'

'There were.'

'Do they say that? That he launched himself – without looking?'

'No,' Elaine Bell said, now trying to pacify her, 'they don't say that, but they weren't there. Only Celia and the other two actually witnessed the accident. I'm only telling you because . . . you need to know that it has been suggested. If you're coming back here – well, you should know that. That's why I'm telling you now. You can see her statement, if you like.' The DCI frowned, annoyed with herself for weakening, attempting to justify herself.

'I do. She didn't say that to me when we met up.'

'I didn't know you'd spoken to her. All I can say is that's in her statement. Maybe, talking face to face with you, she wanted to spare you any un . . .'

'Unlikely,' Alice retorted, cutting in. 'Anyway, the toxicology report will settle it.'

'It will give us his blood-alcohol count, certainly.'

'Thank you, Ma'am,' Alice said stiffly. 'I'll start first thing tomorrow, if that's OK with you?'

'That is OK with me,' Elaine Bell said, keeping her eyes on her subordinate's face. 'One other thing . . .'

'Yes?'

'Just before you went off, they released Brian Riley. I only got the news today.'

'Riley?' she said in disbelief.

'Riley.'

Alice shook her head, stunned by the information. The name was only too familiar to her, the man too. A vicious-looking face, freckled as a bird's egg and topped with carrot-coloured hair. Riley seemed to function in life without conscience or empathy, and twice she had helped to ensure that he was returned to prison in Saughton. He was also responsible for a recurring nightmare of hers. It had been triggered by her discovery of his last victim, his own wife, in horrific circumstances. Less than six months earlier, she had found the woman on the floor of their kitchen in Muirhouse, still curled in the foetal position to protect herself from further attack by him, with dark, arterial blood spurting from a knife wound in her thigh. More was flowing freely from a gash to the stomach. A carving knife lay beside her.

While waiting for the ambulance, Alice had made a makeshift tourniquet from her own scarf but it had come loose. Fastening it a second time she had gone to look for the ambulance, and in her absence Mrs Riley, herself, had undone it. By the time she returned, the woman had lost consciousness, and lay, like an island, surrounded by a sea of her own blood. In the dream, Riley stood laughing beside her, pointing at the dead woman and guffawing, inviting her to appreciate the joke. Looking at him and then at the knife, she heard herself, in the dream, beginning to chuckle.

'He's back home in Muirhouse,' DCI Bell said.

'How did that happen?' Alice asked. 'The jury found him guilty, they were unanimous. With his record, he should have been put away forever.'

'I know. But, unfortunately, in the judge's charge to the jury he went over the top in hinting at Riley's guilt. So, he's out again, thanks to the appeal court and silvery tongue of Mr Thriepland QC. Frankly, I don't know how some of them sleep at night.'

Back in Broughton Place, Alice unpacked her rucksack. Quill was to remain with her sister for a couple of weeks, enjoying himself in the country and in the company of another dog, and the flat felt unnaturally empty, unnaturally quiet. Everywhere she looked there were reminders of Ian. Each one hurt. His toothbrush sat next to hers in a mug in the bathroom, his dirty socks were on the chair by the bedroom window and his favourite cup, unwashed and with a rim of coffee, had been stacked by the sink. With all his belongings there, it was as if he had walked out of the flat to buy a bottle of wine and would be returning in ten minutes. But ten minutes passed, and the next ten minutes and then the next until it was midnight.

As she got into bed, the familiar scent of his body arose from the warmed sheets and she wept, exhausted, feeling anew the rawness of it all, the impossibility of solid flesh and bone and the life within him disappearing into nothingness. One minute there had been a man, one like no other, talking, laughing and loving; and the next, simply cold, meaningless, indistinguishable matter. Lifeless flesh. It was impossible to take in.

And Elaine Bell's news went round and round in her head, tormenting her. Suppose he had 'launched' himself into the oncoming traffic, was it because he had been unhappy, heedless of what might happen to him, or because he was drunk and did not know what he was doing? But why would he have been so drunk? He normally took no more than he could handle, two or three pints at most, so why should he have drunk so much more on this occasion? Could it be because of their stupid row, when she had been so cold and unrelenting towards him, annoyed by his forgetfulness, jealous of Cici? But she had kissed him the next morning, and there had seemed to be all the time in the world to make peace.

And, surely to God, she had not been that cold towards him, that bad? It had only been a trivial falling out, not some kind of cataclysmic break-up with harsh, unforgettable words exchanged. And he had drunk the bloody stuff, she had not made him do it. It was not her fault. That way lay madness. Work alone would keep it at bay, fill her mind with a million other things and leave no room for grief. Concentrating on the job would keep her sane, it would be her salvation, she could lose herself in it.

———

The next morning she was the last to arrive in the office.

'Hello, Alice,' Eric Manson said, pulling out her chair for her to sit on. It was something he had never done before; she knew it was his way of showing his sympathy for her, and extraordinarily eloquent in its way.

Today, everyone was reacting differently to her. As she had climbed the stairs to the Murder Suite, a couple of constables she knew, thought of as friends rather than simply colleagues, had passed by her, saying nothing, averting their eyes from her in their embarrassment, unable to think what to say. But one man, a civilian employee, only recently stationed at St Leonard's, stopped her in the corridor and immediately expressed his sorrow at her 'sad bereavement'. Facing him, she found herself temporarily lost for words, worried that she might loose control, but she managed to mumble something about her gratitude for his 'kind words'. In her own ears, her answer sounded odd, artificial and clichéd, but she meant what she said, and his directness of approach had given her some slight comfort. Best of all, now they both knew where they were.

At lunchtime DC Littlewood appeared at her desk. In one hand he held his own meal, sushi followed by a fresh fruit salad, and in the other he held the food he had, unasked, chosen for her. A small Scotch pie, a packet of crisps and a can of Irn-Bru. Handing them over to her, he nodded shyly and said, 'Comfort food, Sarge. I know your tastes,' before continuing to his own desk.

She spent the early hours of the afternoon familiarising herself with everything that had happened in her absence, and occasionally DC Cairns or one of the other members of the squad would explain something, often correcting each other, occasionally arguing passionately.

'I see we had a call from a bus driver, Derek Burnett, doing the Braid Hills route. Why have we not followed him up?' Alice asked no one in particular.

'Because, Sarge,' DC Gallagher said patiently from his desk at the back of the room, having responded to a few of her earlier inquiries, 'the woman was found in the Hermitage, mind? The bus doesn't go anywhere near that place – there's not a stop anywhere near it.'

'So what? She could have walked there. She could have walked some distance from a stop.'

'Aye,' he said, thinking as he spoke, 'aye, sure enough, she could have, I suppose, but no bus ticket was found on her.'

'Quite. But no bag was found on her either, no wallet, no keys, nothing. The absence of a ticket, alongside the absence of all those other things, is hardly conclusive. I'm going to arrange to see the man, he might have something to tell us.'

The bus driver, an unshaven, fleshy man with forearms like hams, was watching television when Alice and DC Elizabeth Cairns entered his living room. He did not turn it off and kept half an eye on the screen. On it a football match was being shown, although, in their honour, the volume had been slightly turned down.

'This woman, the one you called us about, what was she wearing?' Alice asked him. His wife, who had shown them in, resumed her seat, picked up her newspaper and retired behind it as if it might make her invisible.

'I cannae mind now, but like what they said in the paper. She was dressed that way. A wee bit shabby-like.' He glanced in the direction of the two policewomen and then his eye moved on, looking for somewhere to put his plate and the remains of his pizza.

'Where did she get off, which stop?' Alice asked him, trying to catch his eye, prevent it from returning to the screen.

'No bloody stop. I threw her off.' He hesitated and then bawled at the TV, 'Come on! Come on, wee man, get it into the back of the net!'

'Why did you throw her off?' DC Cairns asked, the excitement in his voice drawing her eyes to the match too.

'Eh?' Having risen half out of his seat, he appeared not to have heard the question. After a second he sat down again heavily.

'Why did you throw her off the bus?' she repeated.

'Goal! It's a goal! One–nil and only another minute to go!' he shouted, jumping up from his chair, ecstatic. 'See that? Did you see that?'

Lowering her paper, his wife looked at him, and shook her head slowly, muttering under her breath, 'Big bairns, men, the lot o' them.'

The instant he returned her gaze, annoyance on his face, she dipped back behind the paper again.

'Mr Burnet,' Alice said, raising her voice to get his attention, 'can you tell us why you threw the woman off your bus?'

'Oh aye,' he said, taking a sip from his can of lager, 'I threw her off because she was annoyin' everybody, greetin' away tae herself. She called me names an' all. Then she done it.'

'She done it?'

'She wet herself on my bus. The filthy bitch.'

'Whereabouts did you throw her off?'

'Eh . . . somewhere at the end of Morningside Road, before it changes into Comiston. I dae ken exactly, see I made a special stop for her, like. Tae get her off.'

A Cairn terrier came into the room and immediately sprang up on to the man's lap, getting a couple of affectionate pats on its rump as it settled down.

'Can you tell us anything else about her?'

'Like what?' he asked, his eyes fixed on the screen again.

'Well, what she looked like, what she sounded like, that kind of thing?'

'That was a bloody foul!' he shouted, gesticulating wildly. 'Has the ref no eyes in his heid? Yellow card, ref. Come on, book him! The wee cheat took a dive!'

'The woman?' Alice began again.

'Aye,' he answered, briefly coming to as if from a dream and looking at her. 'I cannae mind what she looked like. No' bonny, that's for sure. I knew when I phoned yous but I've forgotten now. She was old, middle-aged anyway, and she had that big red blot on her cheek. And I can tell you one other thing for free – she stank.'

'Of?' DC Cairns asked excitedly, pressing the bridge of her glasses onto her nose.

'She'd peed herself, what d'you think? Perfume?'

'Her voice,' Alice said. 'Did she have any sort of accent that you recognised? Was she Scottish, for example, English, Irish or whatever?'

'She didnae sound a bit like you do, hen, that's for sure. Proper, you'd call it, maybe? Right posh or English, I'd say. No, she talked like me. Scottish.'

He hesitated for a second, then hit his fist on the arm of his chair, screaming, 'Red card, this time! It should be a red card now. Get him off the park, ref, right now!'

Startled by the blow, the dog, its tail now between its legs, looked up at its master and then launched itself onto the floor. Once there, it scuttled behind its mistress's legs for shelter, whining from the safety of its hiding place.

'Are there any regulars on that route? Any passengers whose names you know?'

'What d'you mean?' the man asked, unable to take his eyes off the screen. A penalty was about to be taken and he was hunched forward, tense, mentally readying himself to take the kick.

'Aye,' his wife answered, looking first at him and then at the two police officers. 'He's mentioned them to me. There's a pair of twins always get off at the same stop, right at the end of Morningside. Done it for years. He calls them –' she hesitated, trying to remember, 'the something or others . . . Derek, what d'you call them?' She folded her paper tidily on her lap.

'Who?'

'They twins – you know, the ones who dress the same. What's their name?'

No answer was forthcoming.

'Derek,' she said crossly, 'what's their name?'

'Aaaw, Jesus!' her husband sighed, his head now in his hands. 'Why d'you let that plonker take it! An open goal and he's nowhere near it . . . send him back to Czechoslovakia or wherever you bought him from! What a tosser!'

'The name, Derek,' his wife insisted.

'Eh . . .' the man said, coming to again as the final whistle was blown, '. . . Fitz. The Miss Fitz. The misfits, see?'

'That's their name – Fitz?' his wife chipped in, trying to help.

'Aye. They're no' though.'

'Not what?' DC Cairns asked.

'Fit – if you get my drift.'

He laughed, stretched his arms above his head, jubilant at his team's win and now relaxed and prepared to talk. 'She was trouble, that one. A barefaced troublemaker, if you know what I mean. When I told her to get off, she showed me her ticket as if it entitled her to stay – she

111

stayed sitting, never even apologised. Said she couldn't help it.'

'What did you do?'

'I tore the ticket up in front of her face. Into wee pieces and dropped the bits onto the floor. I can put anyone I want off my bus, for cheek, violence, anything. I'm allowed, it's my bus.'

'Where was her ticket for?'

'Eh . . . I'm not sure. I think it was Fairmileheid. But I couldn't swear it.'

'Anything else you can remember about her?' Alice inquired.

'Like?'

'Anything at all.'

'No.'

'What about the flowers?' his wife prompted, picking up the dog and cuddling it.

'What about them?'

'He gave me flowers, in cellophane. Pretended they were from him, didn't you, Derek? Is it coming back to you now? But I seen the ticket. He said they were from Lisa's but they weren't, they were from Flora's Flowers. He didn't even know what they were. Eventually I got it out of him, didn't I, Derek?'

By way of reply the man shrugged his shoulders, grinning widely.

'The woman had left them on the bus . . . that's right, isn't it, Derek?'

—

Alice first became aware of a new, strange sensation, a prickling feeling at the back of her neck, as she was hurrying down Leith Street on her way home. She looked behind her, suddenly convinced that someone was following her, watching her. She was sure of it. Rain was falling hard about her, smashing onto the pavements and overflowing the gutters, pouring out of the black sky.

She glanced back up the street again, searching for the person, but everybody seemed to be on the move, desperate to reach shelter. Her wet hair fell over her eyes and she shook her head, instinctively trying to shed the water and see better. But it was useless, and with the rain still cascading down, her vision became blurred once more.

To cap it all, as she waited to cross the east end of York Place, she was suddenly deluged with water. A pool had collected by the pedestrian crossing, deep enough to overflow onto the pavement, and a bus ploughed through it at speed, careless of the nearby pedestrians, soaking them, leaving only waves in the brown puddle where it had passed. Among the sharp intakes of breath from the other people at the crossing, she cursed angrily and out loud.

Again she turned round, still trying to see who was following her. The other pedestrians were now crossing the road, rushing to take advantage of the green man. In seconds she was the only one on the pavement. She wiped her eyes, and then scrutinised the streets in all directions, but no one stood out. All the shoppers, students, traffic wardens, commuters, schoolchildren and others appeared to be on the move, striding purposefully towards some destination or other. Nobody was standing still, mirroring her movements or lack of them, waiting to take a cue from her before moving on. It must be all in her head, she decided, an overheated fancy, her imagination working overtime. Stress could, she knew, play strange games with the mind.

But the odd physical sensation would not go away, and it felt real enough. She turned to look behind her several more times as she made her way down the hill, unable to shake off the conviction that someone was tailing her. Her body would not lie. Deliberately taking a diagonal course across the mouth of Broughton Place she thought, for a second, that she had caught a glimpse of a man stopping for a moment to watch her. But when she turned round to get a proper look at him he had gone, merged into one of the small groups of people still braving the downpour. It was ridiculous, she told herself, this fear – childish, irrational and unjustified.

She looked up at the windows of her flat and, seeing them unlit, thought for a single second that Ian must still be busy in his studio. Then it came back to her, how things were, that she was on her own. Glancing up Broughton Street for a final time, she pushed open the door of the tenement.

8

When Muriel Fitz opened the front door of the spot-less villa in Nile Grove that she shared with her twin sister, the smell of boiling marmalade billowed out like a sweet cloud. Warning Alice what to expect, she led her into the kitchen. There, the other twin, Margaret, the youngest of the pair by ten minutes, was perched on a three-legged stool, scooping out the insides of Seville oranges into a large pan. On the stainless steel hob, the mixture was bubbling and frothing like hot lava.

'We'll have to carry on, I'm afraid, as we're mid-boil. I hope that's all right with you, officer?' Muriel said in her brittle Morningside accent. Showing Alice to a chair, she immediately re-armed herself with a wooden spoon and dipped it experimentally into the brew. Both women were dressed in fawn cashmere polo-neck jerseys and match-ing fawn flannel slacks, and to protect their good clothes each wore an oilcloth pinny, tied tight at the waist. A large railway clock ticked in the background, its pendulum swinging steadily below it. In the heat, the sisters' cheeks had reddened and Muriel had her long, straight grey hair scraped back into a neat ponytail. Margaret had elected to cover her head with a floral shower cap, a few thin wisps of her fringe escaping from it.

'On the phone, Miss Fitz, you told me that you remem-bered the woman I described?' Alice said, watching them as they rhythmically dipped their spoons into the softened pulp and dug it out. She had no idea which of them she had spoken to earlier or, for that matter, which of them would answer her now.

'We do. We certainly do. She was a memorable individual,' Muriel replied, and Margaret looked up briefly, nodding her head to communicate her agreement with her sister's comment.

'Can you tell me what you remember about her?'

Muriel caught Margaret's eye, and seconds later and as if something had been decided between them, she began to speak.

'She appeared to be – how can I put this politely?' She hesitated. 'Deranged. Wandered.'

'Or drunk,' Margaret added, gathering a handful of the hollowed-out orange skins together and beginning to slice them up with an oversized butcher's knife.

'Yes – or intoxicated,' her sister conceded, looking at Margaret and remarking, 'not too coarse, mind. We don't like huge bits, do we?'

'No, but I don't like it like Golden Shred either,' Margaret replied, continuing to slice exactly as before.

'How did she behave?' Alice asked, enjoying the smell of bitter orange from the boiled pith and peel.

'Not well,' Muriel began, her wooden spoon now raised like a conductor's baton. 'First of all she was talking to herself. Weeping away, too. Muttering incessantly to herself. She seemed to think . . .'

'That someone wanted to sit next to her!' Margaret chipped in delightedly, finishing her sister's sentence and banging her knife heavily on the chopping-board for emphasis.

'Margaret!' Muriel said coldly, gesticulating with her spoon, 'I thought we'd agreed –'

Her sister nodded, and a contrite expression passed fleetingly across her flushed face.

'As if anyone would choose to sit beside *her*! She was sobbing to herself, making awful faces at anyone who came near her. Growling, once, like a tiger or a lion, or a madwoman, when she thought someone was going to sit next to her. People were moving away from her seat in droves. We certainly did. And . . .'

'And,' Margaret said, standing up, unable to restrain herself any longer in her excitement, 'imagine. She called the bus driver "a twit"!'

'A twat, actually,' Muriel corrected her, nudging the final batch of pulp off the chopping board and into the steaming pan.

'Twit. Twat. It's all the same,' Margaret shot back peevishly, seated once more, her knife pointing at her sister.

'I think, dear, that you'll find it's not,' Muriel replied, adding menacingly 'and we agreed, didn't we, who would speak?'

'Why,' Alice intervened, ignoring their bickering, 'did she call him a twit or a twat or whatever it was?'

'A twat. Because,' Muriel replied, 'he had braked sharply and we were all thrown about the bus. At the lights at Holy Corner, he misjudged them badly. You know what those drivers are like, careless, in a word, slapdash. Everyone was flung about like so many sacks of potatoes, and she banged into the seat in front. Most likely she got a whiplash.'

'In front,' Margaret repeated, nodding her head excitedly.

'Anything else about her that either of you remember?'

'To be frank, and we began by sitting directly behind her, she was a bit . . . high? Unwashed, if you know what

I mean. She was drinking something or other while she was actually on the bus. I couldn't see what it was. Cheap sherry, I daresay. Lost all self-respect, I expect. Living homelessly in the Grassmarket or wherever those sort of people live nowadays. Of course, it's come up a lot lately, hasn't it?'

'I saw what it was!' Margaret said, giving her twin a smug glance.

'You did not!'

'I did, really, dear, I did. When we were moving, after she'd banged into the seat in front, I saw her empties. It was beer or lager, you know, that sort of Tennent's stuff in tins. There were three or four empty ones, lying beside her on her seat.'

'If you say so,' Muriel replied, sounding unconvinced.

'You have my word.'

'Whereabouts did she get off the bus?' Alice asked.

The sisters eyed each other and, having reached another unspoken agreement, Margaret replied breathlessly, 'No, she did not. She did not get off the bus. Well, not voluntarily, at least. She was forced off it!'

'Why?'

'Because . . . because . . .' Margaret paused for a moment, searching for the right expression, 'she'd spent a penny . . . right there, on the bus seat! We'd already moved after she called the driver a twit, but you couldn't miss it. The driver, "Redface", we call him . . .' she hesitated once more, like a timid child checking the policewoman's reaction to their nickname, 'Redface manhandled her off the bus.'

'He did no such thing!' her sister said in a shocked tone.

'He did, Muriel, he did!' Margaret protested, looking fearfully at her sister.

'No,' Muriel said, arming herself with oven gloves and taking the bubbling pan off the hob, 'you mustn't exaggerate like that to the police, dear. Not the police. Redface never laid a finger on her. That would be an assault, wouldn't it, officer? A crime. No, he just sounded very, very cross, looked like a big angry bull, and that was enough!'

'Where did she get off?'

'Ah . . . just before our stop. At the end of Morningside Road. We get off by Hermitage Terrace, then it's a short walk home,' volunteered Muriel.

'How long would it take to walk to the Hermitage from the end of Morningside Road?'

'At a brisk pace, no dawdling, say, fifteen minutes?' Margaret replied, looking at her sister for confirmation.

'No dawdling, ten minutes,' Muriel said, 'at my pace, anyway. Now, jars, Margaret. Where have you put them?'

The grounds of the Salvation Army Hostel on Ferry Road betrayed the fact that the Victorian edifice was no longer in domestic use but had become an institution. Branches of trees had grown, unchecked, across its lower windows, obscuring the view and blocking out the light, and the lawn, once an even green sward, was now ragged and punctuated by untidy yellow tussocks. A faded blue plastic frisbee rested on the face of a broken sundial and the flowerbeds and the lawn had merged, sprigs of leggy privet invading them both.

The place felt desolate and unloved, and that first impression was only confirmed by the men and women mooching about by the front door, some seated on a bench talking to each other, one or two standing alone, most with cigarettes in their hands. Tracksuits, T-shirts and denim, in one combination or another, were worn by them all and the staff of the hostel were distinguishable from the residents only by the identity cards hanging around their necks.

As the police car with the two policewomen inside it crunched over the sparse gravel, one of the smokers, a squat woman with a pitted complexion, flicked her cigarette end in front of its wheels. Her eyes remained fixed on the spot, spellbound, until the car had run over the butt, as if crushing a dog-end was an exciting spectator sport.

The hostel manager's writing desk was cluttered with papers, and on top of her computer sat a couple of spindly Spanish dolls, their tiny, pea-sized heads adorned with black mantillas. As she bent to pick up a red biro from the floor, breathing noisily, she confirmed that she did not recognise the woman from the description that DC Cairns had given her over the phone. Waddling across her office in her scuffed trainers to circle a date on the calendar, she explained that she had been working in night shelters in Aberdeen for the past year and had only very recently relocated to the capital. So she was not yet familiar with all of their regular service-users. Such things took time, they would appreciate.

'Have any of your service-users gone missing from the hostel over the last few weeks?' Alice asked.

'We call them "lifehouses" nowadays – like lighthouses. Gets rid of the stigma, you see.'

'Sorry, anyone gone missing from the lifehouse?'

'Some. Some always do,' the woman replied, ruffling her crew-cut hair with her hand as she talked. 'But we've not heard anything bad from the hospitals, or from you lot, about them. As you know, our residents come and go as they like. Sometimes they depart in a hurry, leaving all their possessions behind. Sometimes they come back and collect them. Often they don't.'

'Have any of your female residents gone missing within the last two weeks?'

'Aha. Two, but I doubt either of them is your lady. They're both young, under twenty-five. One's gone down to London and I've no idea where the other is at present. She's got a mum in Port Seton, but they fell out. She might have gone to stay in her house, if they've made up again. Your best bet, to get your lady recognised, identified or whatever, is to speak to the residents in the TV room.'

Eager to get on with her own tasks, she added, 'Come on, I'll take you there. I need to see Ruth anyway.'

They followed her along a grand corridor with doorways every few yards. Its scarlet-painted ceiling had a heavy white egg-and-dart cornice, and their footsteps echoed off its marble-tiled floor. The characteristic clicking sound of snooker balls emanated from the first room they passed. The next room had been turned into a kind of laundrette, and a couple of overweight women in T-shirts and leggings leant against its doorway, chatting as they watched the small procession pass.

'I need to speak to you, Ruth,' the manager said in a slightly threatening tone, nodding at one of them as she walked by.

'Okey dokey,' Ruth replied, raising a middle finger behind the woman's retreating back and smiling slyly at the passing police officers.

At the end of the corridor, the manager opened another solid wood-panelled door for them and immediately turned round to go back, saying nothing, now preoccupied with thoughts of her imminent confrontation with Ruth.

In one corner of the room, a woman lay on a settee, moaning. Her face was turned to the wall, and she was wrapped from the waist down in a coarse grey blanket. Loud rap music blared out from a huge television screen ,and a female and two male residents in the room were talking to one another, one of them striding about as he did so, his arms waving constantly as if he was engaged in some kind of dance. Twitching and constantly jerking his head from side to side, he was as lean as a whippet.

'Would you mind,' Alice said, moving to the centre of the room and raising her voice to be heard above the racket, 'having a word with us?'

'Who's she?' the female resident, Donna, asked DC Cairns. As she spoke, a half-smile transformed her heavy features. Behind her thick glasses her light blue eyes appeared huge and owl-like, and they shone with genuine curiosity. Buttresses of thick yellow plaque separated all of her lower teeth.

'Police,' Alice said, but seeing an instantaneous expression of alarm on the faces of the residents, she quickly added, 'but we've just come here for information. We're not after any of you.'

'Just as well,' the whippet snapped, shaking his head. 'This is our house. This is where we live, like. None o' us invited yous in. You'll no' have a warrant either.'

'Shut it, Ronnie,' his companion said, wagging his finger in the boy's face. The man was in his sixties and had a massive, leonine head that dwarfed the rest of his body. Like the girl, he was now smiling at the two police officers and had drawn closer to them.

'No, you shut it, Rab,' Ronnie said, head jerking to and fro as he began pacing up and down again. After one circuit, and as if irritated by the noise, he turned off the TV.

'What do you want to know?' Rab asked Alice, ignoring the boy, and looking DC Cairns up and down so hungrily that she felt the need to fold her arms in a vain attempt to stop his gaze stripping her further.

Alice gave them a description of the dead woman and they all listened intently to her words, gradually clustering around her, but saying nothing. From a corner of the room the swaddled woman let out a series of animal-like whimpers.

'Ssshh!' Ronnie castigated her, blinking rapidly in his annoyance, and when she continued to moan, grabbed a lighter from his pocket and threw it at her.

'Your woman sounds a bit like Moira,' Donna said, 'or maybe Cathy?'

'Aye,' Rab agreed, 'could be Moira. She's got that kind of frizzy hair and she had that red mark on her cheek and all. But Cathy's not got anything like that on her face, has she?'

'No,' Ronnie said, joining in, 'she's not.'

'Do you know where Moira is? Where she lives – or lived?'

'No, I don't bloody know where she is,' Ronnie said, flicking his thumbs and index fingers rapidly over each other and looking annoyed, ''cause that lot done it to her, didn't they?'

'Did what?' DC Cairns asked, following him with her eyes as he set off around the room again, arms lashing the air.

'Made her homeless! When she was here she couldn't give a receipt for the vouchers for clothes they gave her, because she'd spent the money, so they kicked her out, didn't they! Taff told me all about it.'

'She'd spent the money on clothes?' DC Cairns asked, trying to follow the boy's meaning.

'No. No' on clothes . . . on cider, beer, maybe. But they made her homeless. That's the point.'

'She'd gone against the contract,' the girl said primly. 'No drink, no drugs inside here. That's the rule.'

'Did any of you know her well?' Alice asked.

'No' really, but Taff does,' Ronnie said, brushing an imaginary fly from the side of his face.

'Where would I find him?'

'He's no' well. Got cancer of the lungs or the liver or something. He's on that radiotherapy. He'll probably be at the drop-in centre in Cromarty Street. He likes that place for his breakfast – you get a great breakfast there for fifty pence. Egg, sausage, bacon, black pudding and beans.'

'Miss,' the girl said, sidling up to Alice, grinning widely and displaying all of her coated lower teeth, 'you're a policewoman, eh? I got my exams. I'd like to be a policewoman an' all.'

'Aye,' came a low, slurred voice from the bundle on the settee, 'that'd be right, Donna. Then you could arrest yourself, eh? Ya thievin' junkie bastard!'

———

They headed off through the mid-morning traffic to the drop-in centre, taking a left along Ferry Road and catching the lights onto Inverleith Row, making speedy progress until they were forced to idle in a queue at Canonmills. Ten minutes later, the North Bridge was clear and they turned down the Royal Mile past the round tower of the

Scandic Crown hotel and into a small, dark side street with metal bars guarding all of its lower windows.

The centre had a shield-shaped red sign swinging listlessly above its doorway with 'The Salvation Army' written across it in white lettering. A woman, holding a couple of carrier bags in one hand and smoking a cigarette, flattened herself against an oversized grey wheelie bin so they could pass up the steps to the building.

The door was open. 'This place is like a beauty parlour,' DC Cairns whispered, wonderment in her voice. 'I think I'll have a bikini wax while I'm here.'

Overhead spotlights flooded the centre with a mellow, tinted light, illuminating newly-painted beige walls and reflecting off a flooring of shiny beige tiles. But a brightly-coloured poster on the wall proclaiming 'Jesus Christ is Lord' dispelled any illusion that tanned beauticians in close-fitting white nylon might be found there.

There was no answer at the first door they tried, but when they knocked on the second, marked 'Grace Shelley: Senior Project Worker', it was opened by a rather startled-looking woman. As Alice explained why they had come, she seemed to relax, chattering easily before, finally, giving them the benefit of her opinion.

'Take it from me, eh? Taff will probably not talk. Our service-users generally don't.'

'I expect you're right, but could we, at least, see if he's here? Then find out if he is prepared to talk to us?' Alice asked.

The woman nodded, and they followed her out of her office, waiting as she locked its door then, meticulously, tried the handle. Upstairs in the Meeting Room about eight people were seated on plastic chairs, one of whom was an old man. He was unshaven and wore a black baseball hat with its peak low over his eyes. He was leaning over a round table, sketching with charcoal, his tongue poking out as he concentrated on his picture. By his hand lay a plate with the remains of a bacon roll on it, and a can of Sprite beside it. On the wall behind him was printed in capitals 'THE ART GALLERY' and twenty frames had been painted onto it awaiting pictures. But there were no pictures and all the frames were empty.

At a nearby table sat a young woman, her thick tresses of auburn hair held in place by a gold Alice band. Her long, crossed legs pointed towards the old man.

'What you doing here?' she demanded in a hostile tone, seeing the two women, 'You inspectors? You come to inspect us?'

'They just want to know if Taff's here, love,' Grace Shelley said, smiling at the girl as if to reassure her.

'No' now,' the old fellow mumbled, blending one of his charcoal lines with the heel of his palm, the blackened cuff of his shirt dragging over the paper.

'I've checked the register,' DC Cairns said quietly in Alice's ear.

'Any entry for him?'

'Yes. His name appears between "Lad" and "Minnie Mouse" and it says he arrived at ten o'clock. There's no time given for when he left.'

Overhearing her, Shelley asked, 'Anyone know where Taff's gone?'

Nobody answered, and looking at Alice she shrugged her shoulders, turning as if to leave the room.

'Anyone here know a middle-aged woman called Moira?' Alice asked, more in hope than expectation.

At first her words were met with silence, then the girl said, unnecessarily loudly, 'No!'

Having made her contribution, she got up and sidled past the policewomen, keeping her eyes on them as if they were snakes and might strike at any moment. Her departure from the room was followed by the sound of her high-heeled boots clattering down the tiled stairs. Apparently oblivious to the noise, the old man's head remained bowed, his nose almost touching the paper as he continued working, cross-hatching his drawing with small, cramped strokes.

'Excuse me,' DC Cairns said, getting closer to him in case he was deaf, 'but do you know Moira, Taff's friend?'

'Aye,' he said, brushing the charcoal dust aside with his sleeve.

'Can you tell us anything about her?'

'What do you want to know?' he asked. He tipped the peak of his baseball cap upwards, looking, for the first time, directly at his questioner.

'Anything, anything at all.'

'Fine,' he said glancing at his pale, watch-free wrist as if to check the hour, 'I think I've the time, and I could do with a cup of coffee.'

Twenty pence having changed hands through the kitchen hatch, he sipped at his cup of milky coffee, continuing to draw but, occasionally, deigning to answer their questions.

'Where does Moira live?' Alice asked.

'No idea. I've not seen her for over a month and I've only ever met her in Candlemaker Row.'

'What do you know about her?'

'Just a wee bit . . . a wee, wee bit. When I first met her, maybe three years ago, I'd heard her called "Sister Moira". She'd just lost her flat in Craigmillar. People liked her, she was kind, took her pals in. She'd share anything she'd got with you, everyone said that. I think she'd been a nun before or something, a religious person, maybe.'

'Does she have a surname?'

He shook his head. 'No more than I do. We don't ask questions of people – unlike you lot.'

'Anything else you can tell us?'

'Aye. She liked her drink, and she'd a nice singing voice. Knew Rabbie Burns' stuff backwards and all the old hymns. She'd belt out "Jerusalem" at the drop of a hat.'

Walking down the stairs, with Grace Shelley leading the way, Alice asked her why the 'art gallery' was bereft of pictures.

'Goodness knows, it's not my fault,' the woman sighed, threading her bead necklace through her fingers. 'It's not through lack of trying. I read in the *Evening News* about an artist having an exhibition and it said he'd been home-less for a while, before he hit the big time. So I phoned him up and he seemed excited about the idea of having a gallery for the homeless, happy to help with it, but he never showed up. Then a woman, a teacher at the Art College who I'd found out about, seemed willing to get involved, but she never turned up either. So I don't know what's wrong. It can't be the gallery itself, because they've never even seen it.'

'What about the old chap upstairs?' DC Cairns chipped in, 'couldn't he do something? He seems keen.'

'Did you see his pictures?' Grace Shelley asked, sound-ing taken aback by the suggestion.

'No. He was leaning over them too much.'

'Just as well! He only does women, huge, stark-naked women, and I'm not sure that all of our service-users would appreciate that. Besides, we're supposed to be a Christian organisation . . . not a knocking shop.'

In the Murder Suite DC Cairns sat back in her chair, took off her gold-rimmed spectacles and rubbed her tired eyes.

'Have you finished your list?' Alice asked, catching sight of her.

'Yes, I've done it.' She picked up a piece of paper and began reading it out loud. 'The Sisters of Notre Dame, no. Sisters of Mercy, no. Sacred Heart and the Carmelites, no. Poor Clares, no, Dominicans . . . blah blah. None of them seem to have had anyone called Moira on their books, so to speak, in the last twenty years, or within living memory at least.'

Alice nodded. 'She could have changed her name, I suppose, like "Lad" and "Minnie Mouse". She might have adopted Moira as a name when she went on the streets?'

'Yes, I thought of that, too, but there's no one who fits her description either. Her hair may not always have been grey, but she'd probably have had that birth-mark forever. Mr Burnett, or Redface or whatever the twins called him, said she sounded Scottish, so I've restricted myself to convents in Scotland.'

'Me too, and I've done no better than you with my lot, including the Servites, the Benedictines and the Carmelites. Not forgetting, of course, the Order of Perpetual Indulgence, open brackets, Scotland, close brackets, "A worldwide order of queer men and women of all sexualities" as I discovered when I rang them in error.'

'Maybe she wasn't a nun at all, maybe she was a nurse – "Sister" Moira. It's just as likely,' mused the constable. 'Not because she was one, a Sister, I mean, but simply to mark her out as having been a nurse.'

'If she was, what's the quickest way for us to find out about her?' Alice asked, yawning, unenthusiastic about starting to pursue a new line of inquiry while the earlier one was still incomplete.

'Easy. The Nursing Register, but it's unlikely she'll still be on it.' The constable hesitated, pondering, and then added, 'I've got it – genius that I am. The Nursing and Midwifery Council will still have her details. They'll know all about her, if she was ever one of theirs.'

The emailed reply from the Council was not long in coming. It disclosed that they held details of four Moiras, one currently registered as a midwife and who had qualified in 2007; one who was now a Community Practitioner Nurse Prescriber living in Kent and Medway, and one who was recently deceased. But the remaining one, Moira Fyfe, seemed promising. She had qualified in 1975, been a Charge Nurse up until 2003 and, in that year, had been struck off the Nursing Register. Her last place of work was listed as the Royal Hospital for Sick Children in Sciennes Road, Edinburgh.

9

With a steaming mug of tea in her hand, Alice spoke to the Clinical Nurse Manager at the Sick Children's Hospital. The woman's tired voice hinted at the pressure she was under, and twice she stopped, mid-conversation, to speak sharply to someone in her office.

'Moira Fyfe,' she said, returning her attention to her call. 'That's a while ago, back into the mists of time. I qualified with her, but after that I moved down south. If you want information about her, accurate information rather than just tittle-tattle, I'd speak to one of her old colleagues. There'll still be a few of them around. Ginny Baird is the one I would try. She's a Charge Nurse on the Neo-natal ward, and like me, she goes back to before the Flood, but, to the best of my knowledge, she's spent her working life here.'

The hospital cafeteria was busy, most of its seats taken and a low buzz of conversation filled the air. As they entered, a trim figure, dressed in a dark blue tunic and matching trousers, came forward to greet them. On a tray she carried a bowl of soup, a packet of sandwiches and a bottle of fresh orange juice.

'Do you mind if I eat while I talk to you? We're run off our feet at the moment,' she said, leading them to a table by the ladies' toilet and not waiting for an answer.

'Anything you can tell us about Moira Fyfe?' Alice said, getting down to business straight away and drawing up a chair opposite her. DC Cairns, feeling hungry and also determined to waste no time, left the table quickly, returning with two plates of chips, beans and sausages and laying one in front of her colleague. She herself had not eaten since breakfast and had no intention of missing lunch.

'I worked with her for . . . twenty, twenty-five years,' the Charge Nurse said, dipping her spoon into the mushroom soup and stirring it, deliberately dunking the croutons into the thick liquid.

'What happened in 2003 when she was struck off?' DC Cairns asked, her mouth full.

'Don't I know you from somewhere?' Ginny Baird said, screwing up her eyes and looking hard at the constable.

'No.'

'Your face seems familiar. I think I do know that face.'

'I don't think so,' DC Cairns replied haughtily. 'Maybe you've seen me in the supermarket or somewhere like that? Never mind that now. Could you just tell us about 2003, please?'

'I'm sure I do . . .'

'No, really.'

'It was awful – a tragedy. Earlier that year, in the January or the February, Moira's husband died unexpectedly. They'd no children. Well, no living children at least. They'd had a son but he passed on when he was still a baby.'

'What happened to her husband?' Alice asked.

'Isn't that terrible, I was her friend, but I can't remember. A heart attack, something like that. Something very quick, very sudden. He was there one minute, gone the next. She got a dreadful shock.'

'Go on, please.'

'After her man's death she took to the bottle. They were that close, the pair of them. I don't think she could cope on her own without him.' The nurse sighed heavily, raising a spoonful of soup to her mouth but continuing to speak. 'She'd come in late, stinking of drink, and for a time we tried to cover up for her, but things got out of hand. It was dangerous, in a job like this. Eventually, the union stepped in and tried to help her, the occupational health people even got involved, but it was all hopeless. She couldn't stop herself, she was that lonely.'

She shook her head and, finally, drank a spoonful of the soup.

'So what happened then?' Alice persisted.

'It was an accident waiting to happen . . .'

'And?' DC Cairns said, pushing her spectacles back up the bridge of her nose and looking at the woman earnestly.

'I do know you,' Ginny Baird said, returning her gaze, studying her features, trying to place the policewoman.

'No, I'm sure you don't. I must have a rather ordinary face, I think, because this happens to me all the time. So, could you just carry on with the story, please?'

'She was supervising a senior student who was giving a subcutaneous injection of insulin to a twelve-year-old child. A girl, I think. The student got the dosage wrong, trebled it, and Moira didn't notice. In the old days, that would never have happened. She'd have been onto it in a second, but she was half cut. The girl died and the student gave up nursing for good. It was all Moira's fault, of course, and she took the blame for it.'

'After she was struck off, what happened to her?' Alice asked, spearing a chip with her fork.

'Everything fell to pieces as far as I remember.'

'What do you mean?'

133

'Well, the parents of the girl sued the hospital and her. They got a lot of money through the courts. With no job, she had no money. She fell behind with her mortgage payments and I think she sofa-surfed, or whatever it's called, for a while, until her friends could take no more of her. She was with me for a short while, but my husband kicked up after she nearly set the house on fire with a chip pan. The next thing I knew she was living in some kind of hostel.'

'You continued to keep in touch with her, did you?'

'Not really. We kept up for a little bit but . . .' she hesitated, shaking her head, 'I don't think she wanted to see me, or anyone else much, any more. Not from her old life. She kept saying that she was getting treatment, counselling and so on, but if she was, it didn't seem to be working. I don't think there was a day she didn't think about that wee girl.'

'When did you last hear from her?'

'In 2005 or 6. A while ago now. It was embarrassing. She asked me for money. She was living in some kind of supported flat, somewhere in Niddrie or Craigmillar, that sort of area. Niddrie Drive, Niddrie Avenue, maybe, somewhere or other down there. She turned up here, at work. She was pretty far gone, stinking of alcohol, and she had a pal with her, a Welsh bloke she called Taff. They were both talking loudly, laughing too much, but he had an edge about him. To be quite honest, he scared me. I gave her a tenner, just to get rid of them, and I've not seen her since.'

'Is this her, the woman you've been talking about?' Alice said, taking a photograph out of its brown envelope. It had "Mortuary" stamped on the back of it.

'Jesus H. Christ!' the woman said, staring at the stark black-and-white image and returning her sandwich, untouched, to its plate.

'It is Moira Fyfe, isn't it?' Alice asked.

'Oh yeah. It's her all right, but she looks – old, bloody awful. She's only about my age, you know. I've never seen her with grey hair, but yes, it's her all right. Poor thing, she looks as if she's been battered.'

As they were leaving through the canteen swing doors, Alice asked the constable whether she had ever worked in the hospital.

'Oh yes,' she replied airily.

'So Mrs Baird probably did recognise you?'

'I certainly recognised her, but I wasn't letting on. I had my hair dyed black then, when I was a student, so that may have confused her. I couldn't let her know though, could I? I couldn't help her to recognise me.'

'Why not?'

'Because,' the young constable said, striding onwards, 'I'd have no authority left, would I? Don't forget, she used to tell me what to do – in another life – but now it's me asking her the questions and,' she giggled at the thought, 'she's the one who's got to answer.'

With the woman's full name it proved easy. A few well-placed calls from the hospital car park established that Moira Fyfe had been living at a hostel in Bread Street immediately before she died.

Her room there, number 14, was small and windowless, more like a monk's cell than a bedroom. The worn trainers of its current occupant lay at the end of the narrow bed, and a dark blue, pinstriped jacket with elbow patches hung from a coat-hanger on the back of the only chair. On a wooden table lay a cigarette lighter and a broken plastic razor.

'This was her room?' Alice asked, looking round and thinking how austere it seemed despite still being occupied. The air stank of Dettol. The manager, Jack Imrie, a tall, thin man with intense, deep-set eyes and a gold stud in one nostril, nodded his head but said nothing. The owner of the jacket stood behind him in the open doorway, and he, too, nodded as if the question had been addressed to him.

'Have you still got her stuff?'

'We will have it. We keep it for about 28 days. It'll probably be in the storeroom.'

'Can we see it?'

'No problem, I'll take you there,' the manager answered, gesturing to the resident that he could return to his room and then closing the door quietly behind him.

Moira Fyfe's entire worldly possessions fitted in to a single, scuffed holdall. A couple of changes of clothes, a pair of trainers, a few toiletries, a coloured photograph of a bearded man holding a baby and a worn, bedraggled, red toy elephant with one button-eye missing.

'That's it?' DC Cairns said, in a tone of disbelief.

'She's got more than some,' the manager replied, bundling her things back into the bag and then searching in a cupboard for the book they would have to sign to take them away.

'When you last saw her, on the night of the 13th of January, how did she seem?' Alice asked.

'She was much as usual. Maybe a wee bit more crabby. After she got back from A&E she calmed down and went off to bed. I didn't see her the next morning. My shift was over.'

He pointed to the line on the form where the signature was to be written.

'Why did she have go to A&E?' Alice asked handing the biro back to him.

'There was a scuffle between her and another woman. Nothing much, but she fell over and complained afterwards that she felt dizzy. Our procedures leave nothing to chance, so one of the staff went with her in the ambulance to the Infirmary. They didn't keep her in or anything, but even then they didn't get back until after midnight.'

'Who's her GP?'

'She went to the one-stop shop near the St James' Centre. She's one of Susan Shaw's patients.'

'Why didn't you report her missing?'

'Because,' he said, closing the book with a snap, 'that's not the way it works, is it? Our service-users come and go as they please, free as birds, with or without their things. We'd never be off the phone to you otherwise, and, mostly, wasting your time.'

'What are you doing in here?' a female voice inquired. A little woman with sparse, frizzy black hair and the pencilled-on arched eyebrows of an aged chanteuse had entered the storeroom. She was looking intently at the two police officers as if they were unauthorised intruders.

'It's OK, Maggie,' the man said, going over towards her, 'they're with me.'

'Maybe they are, Mr Imrie,' she said hotly, 'but I'm supposed to be in charge of the store. Not you. No one should be in here without my say-so.'

'Have you checked that out?' she inquired of Alice, touching the sleeve of the navy jacket she had on and adding, 'I happen to know that one of our other residents had her hopes set on it.'

'No, I haven't,' Alice replied, 'but I don't need to – you see, it's mine.'

'Not until I sign it out, it isn't, young lady,' the woman corrected her, looking down at the policewoman's feet and adding, 'I see you've not helped yourself to any of our new shoes, yet, at least.'

—

'Well done, Alice,' Elaine Bell said, taking a seat on the edge of her sergeant's desk. She crossed her arms and looked out of the window, staring across at Arthur's Seat and the dark clouds gathering around the summit.

'I'm getting her records from Doctor Shaw, and once we've got them, Professor McConnachie can take a look at them, see what he makes of them.'

'Fine. So, in summary . . .'

'In summary, her name was Moira Ellen Fyfe and she was aged 59. Her last known address was at the Friends of Galilee place on Bread Street.'

'She's a down-and-out,' DC Cairns added, uninvited, from the far end of the room, leaving her seat and coming to stand beside her colleague.

'Forensics haven't reported yet, so we still don't know if she was sexually assaulted,' Alice continued, 'but when she was discovered she was partially undressed. No possessions were found near her, and a pair who travelled on the bus with her reported that she was drunk before she got off the bus. The Prof told us she was an alcoholic. She was covered in scratches, particularly on her hands and arms, as if she had been running from somebody . . . trying to escape from somebody.'

'So, it's still a murder hunt?'

'Of course it is, she'd been practically stripped, Ma'am!' DC Cairns blurted out, shocked that there could be any doubt about the matter.

'Alice?' the DCI asked, pointedly ignoring the constable. The sergeant nodded. 'Yes, for the moment. We've got statements from as many of her friends, colleagues, or whatever you'd call them, as we could find in the hostels, drop-in centres, settlement flats and so on. For all the use they are. With the exception of that man.'

'Yes, except for bloody Taff, of course,' DC Cairns interrupted.

'Taff?' the DCI said.

'Apparently he was her best friend,' Alice replied, 'None of her so-called pals have been exactly falling over themselves to talk to us, and even if they do it's difficult to tell how reliable they are. But one name, his name, keeps popping up. Otherwise it's pretty hopeless. Three people at number 194 claimed to know her just to get a cup of tea off us, drank it down and then immediately confessed to their "mistake". Another one assured us that Moira died last winter, and yet another had a theory that Taff was her son.'

'OK. You can go home now, Liz,' the DCI said, jerking her head in the constable's direction. The young woman collected her coat from the back of her chair and then waited, looking towards Alice who was busy logging out of her computer. When the constable made no further move to leave, DCI Bell said impatiently, 'Off you go, Elizabeth.'

Taken aback by her insistence, the constable said, 'I'm just going, Ma'am. I was waiting for Sergeant Rice.'

'No, on you go,' the DCI said, deliberately catching Alice's eye to let her know that she was to wait behind. Once the slightly puzzled constable had left the Murder Suite, DCI Bell stood up and, looking out of the window again, she stretched.

'It was just to let you know we've found the car.'

'Where was it?'

'In a back-street garage in Fountainbridge. The lab are pulling it to pieces now.'

'Do we know who was driving it?'

'No,' the DCI said, 'not yet. It's yet another unlicensed banger. It probably rose, like Frankenstein, from some scrapyard or another. But it's . . .' She turned to face her Sergeant.

'Thanks, Ma'am,' Alice said before she could finish the sentence, rising and walking towards the door, suddenly desperate to escape. Whoever had killed him, Ian was dead and she did not want to talk about it, be reminded about it right here and right now. Finding out about Moira Fyfe had, like some wondrous drug, staved off all thoughts of him. But his death was not just another case to her, and the wound was still too raw. She did not want to be overwhelmed, to break down in front of her Chief Inspector, and she could already feel the tears beginning to well up. The slightest sign of fragility and she might find herself jobless and hopeless. She knew what would fill that particular vacuum, and dreaded it.

'Alice!'

'Yes, Ma'am?' she replied, her head still turned away from her boss.

'Are you all right?' Elaine Bell asked, coming towards her.

'Fine, thanks,' she said, nodding, still heading for the door but then briefly turning and forcing her features into a smile.

———

In her flat, Alice spent a couple of hours sorting through Ian's possessions, throwing out rubbish, putting his clothes into black bags, separating their books and stacking his ready to be stored in the cardboard boxes that she planned to acquire from the friendly assistants in a nearby wine shop. Some objects defeated her. A photograph album, once hers alone, had become a joint possession, recording their life together, and it was filled with images taken by him. A derelict boat in Dunbar harbour, a close-up of the prickles on a thistle, the golden eyes of a half-submerged frog, so many things she would have overlooked without him beside her with his keen eye. Should the album go to his mother, or his son, or could she keep it?

It fell open on her lap and she looked down at a large photo on the left-hand page. It showed Ian in their kitchen. He was grinning widely, naked to the waist, his bottom half clothed in a strange grey-and-white woollen garment. It had a wide waistband which he held out daintily on either side. Memories of the day she had taken the picture flooded back. They had returned from a weekend away, cold and hungry, their clothes wet from an ill-judged, rainy, seaside walk taken on impulse, on the way home. Finding no trousers in the clean laundry basket, or in any of his drawers, he had simply improvised and worn a favourite sweater as trousers. Amused at his own appearance in the mirror he had posed for her camera, his legs one in front of the other in a flat-footed balletic pose.

Looking at the photo, she smiled. She would keep it and the rest of them for her and her alone. No captions would be necessary, because the album had recorded their life together.

———

The ringing of her mobile woke her. She had fallen asleep in the armchair. In the dark she searched the room frantically for the phone, almost tripping over one of the piles of books. But when she picked it up, no voice was forthcoming. In the silence she said 'Hello' several times, but still no one spoke, no one answered her. She checked the call log as she wandered, still half-asleep, to her bedroom. *Caller unknown*.

Three hours later, at 2.30 a.m., her phone went again. This time when she picked it up she heard her own name, followed by the first few bars of a tune. The music was faint, and had an ethereal quality to it. Still drowsy, she could not place it. She listened for over a minute, and hearing no voice, turned the phone off.

Later, as she tossed and turned, trying to get back to sleep, she realised what the tune was, but the knowledge gave her no relief, no further slumber. In the silence, and frightening herself as she did so, she hummed the melody once more, hearing in the dark the first few solemn bars of Beethoven's *Funeral March*.

At five o'clock her mobile rang again and, at first, she ignored it. Then, worried that it might be a work call, she picked it up.

'Alice?' It was a stranger's voice.

'Yes?'

'You shouldn't have done it . . . I'm waiting for you.'

Before she could say another word, the line went dead.

10

Strange snippets about a life, Alice thought, could be gleaned from reading an individual's medical records. From among the dry details, something of their personality always emerged.

The medical notes in the file for Moira Fyfe, née Sykes, began, as expected, at the very beginning, with her own birth. The event had taken place at home and was straightforward, but the presence of the strawberry nevus on her cheek seemed to have been a worry from the first. It was noted by the GP to be 'large, red and diffuse', and a drawing showed it covering her right cheekbone.

At the age of four, she was described in a letter of referral to an orthopaedic surgeon as 'a high-spirited wee girl', having crashed her tricycle into her grandparents' cold frame and broken her right wrist. Her teenage years were sparsely documented, with entries only for prescriptions for acne, reference to a bout of glandular fever and to a spell in hospital following a fall from a roof. When later she was attending the Family Planning Clinic, a letter spoke of 'Moira Sykes . . . this delightful young nurse', and another alluded to 'this charming young woman'.

In the 1980s three separate miscarriages were recorded in between more mundane complaints: bouts of flu and tonsillitis and, in an isolated case, a spell during which she suffered from tennis elbow. An operation note detailed the birth of her son by Caesarean section. His death, too, appeared, albeit indirectly, with a psychiatrist speculating as to whether it had been the catalyst for the episodes of depression she later suffered.

In 2002 an irregular italic hand noted the death of her husband, 'her black mood' and 'suicidal ideation'. Thereafter, the record was sprinkled with prescriptions for Prozac, and the clinical notes often mentioned her depressed state, the adjective usually favoured to describe this being 'low'.

Less than a year later, when she had attended for an 'ulcer-like pain', the GP had added to his clinical comments the observation, 'smells strongly of alcohol'.

From then onwards the signs of Moira Fyfe's decline into alcoholism could be read clearly enough: a succession of falls, injuries from a fight with a 'friend with whom she had been drinking', an unexplained injury on her right hand and marked, continuing weight gain followed by an equally dramatic loss. By 2006 she was noted as suffering from 'acute pancreatitis', developing into 'chronic pancreatitis', and by 2008 'Type-2 diabetes – alcohol induced?' had been added to the list.

A second folder, which contained a copy of the records from the Royal Infirmary, proved to be the most valuable because, amongst other paperwork, were documents concerned with two separate attendances at A&E in Little France. The first visit arose from an assault that she had been subjected to while 'dossing' in Warriston Cemetery. In this incident, her nose had been broken and she had lost a tooth. But it was the sparse entry for the second visit that caught Alice's attention and made her heart beat a little faster. It was a clinical note dated 13 January 2010 and was short and to the point: 'Attendance following a fall in the hostel. Alcohol +++. C/O a head injury on the left temple. O/E external bruising, yellowish, on R. temple. Fairly bright and alert. PERLA.'

'Anything interesting?' DI Manson inquired, standing behind her and peering over her shoulder. Deep in concentration, she was startled by his sudden appearance.

'Possibly – it's hard to tell, it's in their usual code. But at the PM, Professor McConnachie found blood on the woman's brain resulting from an injury to the left side of the head. He wasn't sure whether she died from its effects or the hypothermia or both. But it was that collection of blood which made him think she might have been hit on the left temple.'

'So?'

'An A&E entry for the 13th of January records an injury to the left temple. So there may have been no blow . . . meaning, she wasn't hit. Everything could be explained by a fall in the hostel two nights before we found her.'

'No blow?'

'Exactly. No blow. They told me at the hostel about the fall but I didn't realise she'd hit her head.'

'What's PERLA?'

'No idea.'

Looking into her eyes, he said, 'You all right, pet?'

She nodded.

'Really? You're a bit pale.'

'Really, I'm fine,' she answered jauntily, turning away, knowing that any other answer would disconcert him. Kind as he had been, he was not a natural Good Samaritan, nor her natural confidant. Anyway, it was too bloody dangerous to say anything else; her fitness for the job depended on her being 'fine', and without her job she would fall to pieces. Whatever happened, and that included harassment by a nuisance caller, she must not be taken off the investigation.

'Good. Glad to hear it. Has the Prof seen these records yet?'

'No. I was just looking at them first, so that . . .'

Turning away, he interrupted her, too keen to get on to wait. 'Have them sent over to him the now and then go and discuss them with him, eh, pet? He'll sort it out for us. That PERLA and so on.'

━

Professor McConnachie was seated at his desk, three foil cartons in front of him and a pair of wooden chopsticks poised above his favourite, beef in black bean sauce. As Alice drew up a chair he popped a morsel of meat into his mouth and said, 'I prefer them, don't you? More authentic, I always think.'

When she looked blank, he waggled the chopsticks at her. She nodded noncommittally, watching as he deftly plucked a battered prawn from another container and put it between his crooked, ivory-coloured teeth. Steam from the hot food misted the edge of his glasses, and a pink drop of sweet-and-sour sauce was running down his blue-and-yellow striped tie.

'So, have you changed your view about the cause of death?' she asked.

'Not really,' he said, clacking his chopsticks together before plunging them back into the beef.

'But what about the accident in the hostel? We didn't know about that before. Wouldn't it explain the injury to the left temple?'

'Yes, it would. But that's always been my position. Nothing in the copy records you've provided me with has made me change my mind on that issue.'

'But we didn't know about the fall,' she said, perplexed.

'Correct. What I'm saying is that I've always thought that the subdural haemorrhage was likely to have been causative of her death. Whatever caused it – fall or blow. It and the hypothermia, probably.'

'You'd agree then that she may not have been hit by anyone in the Hermitage?'

'Mmm,' he nodded, unable to speak due to his mouthful of food. After he had finally swallowed it, his prominent Adam's apple bobbing up and down as he did so, he added, 'Aha. I accept that the fall in the hostel can account for the subdural collection, that's what I'm saying.'

'What about the other stuff? The bruise on the right side of her head, her undressed state, the scratches to her legs and arms?'

'With the benefit of the PM, it was only the subdural that really bothered me. Not the other bruise – it was healing, superficial. I thought she'd been hit on the left side. If there was someone after her, chasing her, then that would explain the scratches and so on, an attempt to get away through a thicket or some such thing. Likewise, he might have been responsible for the undressing. But, you'll have heard that no foreign DNA was found on her, or at least none suggestive of any sort of assault, sexual or otherwise.'

'So what are you saying? Can we close the case?'

'Uh, uh. Not so fast,' he said, extracting a piece of gristly meat from his mouth and looking at it askance.

'This is beef?' He wrinkled his nose. Placing the morsel to one side, he wiped his chopsticks on a paper napkin and put them back in his desk drawer. Then he continued. 'As far as I'm concerned, everything except the fatal injury may now be accounted for by the hypothermia, but I'd still like to know why she died from the bleed – it caused her death, after all.'

'How d'you mean?'

He extracted a crumpled linen handkerchief from his trouser pocket, and as he unfurled it a paperclip flew out onto the table. Unperturbed, and folding the handkerchief in four, he dabbed his lips with it.

'She went to hospital, didn't she, so why didn't they pick it up? I think this new information muddies the waters further.' He stopped speaking as he looked at the pink goo on the linen, wiped the drip from his tie and then put the handkerchief back in his pocket.

'The woman was in their hands, so to speak,' he carried on, 'precisely because of the fall, and yet they failed to pick up the bleed. Why didn't they find it? It must have been there, to some extent at least, when they saw her. So, why wasn't she X-rayed or CT-scanned? Did they even check her on the Glasgow Coma Scale? There's nothing about that in the notes. The Triage Nurse's assessment seems to have been done in indecent haste, judging by her hurried scrawl. Ms Fyfe was an alcoholic for heaven's sake! We know she'd had a skinful earlier. So how could they properly assess her mental state? How could they tell what might be attributable to the effects of alcohol and what might be attributable to the effects of the fall?'

He shook his head and began carefully to reseal the cartons with their white cardboard lids. 'Always enough for two,' he said. 'I'll take it back for my wife to eat tonight. I think you'd best speak to Elaine . . . to DCI Bell. I don't think the file can be closed on this one just yet. In fact, if anything, I think we may well be on our way to a Fatal Accident Inquiry.'

———

'Oh, I will consider it. No, never been there, Sir. I'm not sure if the club even allow women onto their hallowed turf, do they? At any rate I think we have to undergo ritual cleansing or something first?'

Elaine Bell tried to keep the fury she felt out of her voice. Fortunately, the Superintendent seemed to think that their phone conversation was over, and hearing the click at the other end, she dropped the receiver as if it was red-hot, murmuring under her breath, 'Arsehole!' To be subordinate to, patronised by, that man, a golf-playing mason and worshipper of authority (however bone-headed it might be), was not good for her health. No doubt he had only mentioned Muirfield in order to rattle her, to deliberately provoke her. A social at a place that did not admit women! But the red rag had done its job, because she could feel the veins pulsing in her forehead, and her vision seemed to be altering subtly with each heartbeat.

Conscious that her GP had warned her that her blood pressure was now 'dangerously high', she brought the portable blood-pressure cuff from her desk drawer and applied it to her left wrist. Automatically it inflated itself, tightening on her flesh and constricting her blood vessels. The dial began flashing. After the requisite thirty seconds she examined it. 200/125. With a reading like that, she was heading for a stroke! Now on the edge of panic, she deflated the cuff and quickly applied it to her right arm.

Once more she felt the thing activate itself, gripping her arm like a small boa constrictor. 125/40. How could one account for two such different readings from a single heart? What could they mean? Hypertension followed by hypotension, a positively catastrophic fall in her blood pressure. Surely by now she should have fainted or something?

On the other hand, perhaps the kit was unreliable? That might well explain it. It had, after all, cost under a tenner at Superdrug. Perhaps she should take it back and return to alternative medicine, to the infusion and the gemstones. A lapis lazuli for blood pressure, wasn't it? One from the pack she had ordered online was still in her desk drawer. As she raked through it, pushing aside the various cold remedies that cluttered it up, the door opened and Alice Rice's face appeared.

'Can I speak to you, Ma'am?'

'Yes, come in,' Elaine Bell replied, taking the gemstone surreptitiously out of the drawer and clasping it tightly in her hand, at the same time concealing it and yet allowing it to begin to exert its miraculous powers.

'What's the Prof's view then?' she asked, knuckles white around the stone.

'He thinks she died as a result of the head injury that she got when she fell in the hostel.'

'Splendid. So we've finally unravelled the mystery. It's no longer a suspicious death, just an everyday tale of a down-and-out having a drink in the Hermitage, who dies as a result of the delayed effects of a fall the previous night. What about the bruise on the other side of her head?'

'It's old and trivial, apparently. It wasn't the cause of her death, he says. He thinks she probably got it a few days beforehand. The fall caused the bleed.'

'Another one bites the dust!' said Elaine Bell triumphantly, now openly rubbing the stone with its small gold chain between her fingers. She wanted to slip it round her neck as soon as possible. Already it seemed to be exerting its benign effects on her circulatory system and she felt calmer, her nerves no longer jangling. Muirfield, indeed! It was a joke. A bloody joke!

'Professor McConnachie thinks we may need an FAI.'

'What? Why on earth?' Elaine Bell said, suddenly apprehensive again, her grip tightening once more on the stone.

'Because he's concerned that the hospital failed to pick up the subdural haemorrhage, didn't do enough tests and so on.'

'Oh for God's sake! Do we know anything about that?'

'No, we haven't had a chance to check it out yet. He's only just raised the possibility, after all. I'll need to find out more about the accident at the Bread Street Hostel, speak to the nurses, the doctors who saw her at the Infirmary and then go back to him.'

'Right, on you go then. No time like the present. Once you've done that, we'll wash our hands of it, pass the papers on to the Fiscal Service and see what they have to say. At least it'll be off my desk.'

She put the lapis lazuli pendant around her neck and countered Alice's curious glance with a single raised eyebrow. It worked. No question was forthcoming from her sergeant.

The air in the Bread Street Hostel was chilly. The few old-fashioned, cast-iron radiators in the building were unequal to their task, incapable of making any real impact on rooms with lofty ceilings and large Victorian windows.

Alice, shivering in the cold, waited in the manager's office for about ten minutes as, one by one, various members of staff wandered in, looked at her and then marched straight out again. None of them, she noticed, questioned the presence of an unaccompanied stranger in the office, free to peruse any sensitive information lying about on the desk.

Eventually, someone who had come in to collect a phone directory asked who she was waiting for.

'Maureen McKee.'

'Right. Mr Imrie's away hunting for her the now.'

As more people passed through the office, Alice stared idly out of the window at the grey slate roofs of the tenements opposite. A pigeon, its dull, damp feathers puffed out, strutted up and down the zinc-clad spine of the nearest building. Out of the grey, sunless sky another one arrived and immediately the resident pigeon began courting it, advancing towards it and then retreating, head bobbing up and down, as if performing a well-rehearsed dance routine.

It was, she thought, as if spring had unexpectedly broken into winter. The second bird nodded its head, responding to the other bird's display. And from nowhere, the thought of Ian's death, his eternal absence, hit her, ambushed her anew.

Determined to prevent herself from crying, she fixed her gaze on a prayer-card pinned to the wall. If she could focus the whole of her attention on that, it should drive unwanted thoughts away, for the moment at least. Silently, she read it to herself.

In the light of God's mercy
In his almighty Love
Slimmers are precious
To Heaven above.

What about naturally thin people or unrepentant fat people, she wondered. Are they, too, not precious to God? Then she looked hard again at the card and saw, with her now dry eyes, that it said, 'Sinners are precious'. She laughed.

'Is it me you're wanting?' an Irish voice inquired. When Alice turned round she found herself face to face with a small, plump woman with a high complexion and bushy, low-set eyebrows which partially obscured her pale blue eyes. She, like the rest of the staff, was dressed for comfort, in baggy tracksuit bottoms and a loose-fitting T-shirt. The slogan on it read, 'JC's the Coolest Cat'.

'Are you Maureen McKee?'

'I am she,' the woman replied, beaming as if pleased to be asked, chewing her gum and showing no obvious uneasiness despite the fact that a policewoman wanted to interview her. Perhaps, Alice thought, she was not a car driver, and therefore had a clean conscience? Or, more likely, someone had already told her what the police-woman wanted to talk about.

'I understand that you were in the room when Moira Fyfe had her fall?'

'Moira Fyfe. Aha.' The woman smiled again, sitting down and clasping her fingers together around a crossed leg, bending confidingly towards her inquisitor.

'Could you tell me what happened?'

'I could, I could, I certainly could. Moira had come back in that evening. She smelt of the drink, and another of our service-users, Linda, had a go at her. The pair of them didn't get on. She accused Moira, outright, of having stolen her money to buy the booze. It happened in the TV lounge. Like I said, Moira was the worse for wear and she lost it. Launched herself straight at Linda, but luckily Linda seen it coming and dodged to the side. Moira toppled over, and on the way down she cracked the side of her head on something.'

'Is Linda still living here?'

'Aha.'

'What did you do when Moira fell?'

'I left her there. She was OK where she was on the floor. I went and filled in the Accident Book. You have to do that before anything else, I was trained for that. Later, I put the ointment on her head. She'd no bruise there or nothing like that, but that's what you're supposed to do. Procedures like. Tiffany took Moira to her room to gather some stuff.'

'Tiffany?'

'Tiffany's another member of staff here. She'd been watching TV with the residents before I came in. I went with Moira to A&E.'

'In an ambulance?'

'No, in my own car. The manager told me to take her in it. Moira was mouthing away all the time, shouting out loud, saying that she didn't need to go. I said to her, "And what would you know about that?" "Everything," she said, "everything!" As if she did know, as if she was a doctor or something!'

'Did you wait with her in casualty?'

'No. Well, not when they seen her, like. She got taken into a wee room by the nurse on her own, for privacy's sake.'

Maureen coughed, holding her hand across her mouth.

'What about when the doctor saw her? Were you with her then?'

'Em . . .' She continued coughing, her eyes watering, her colour rising so that even her neck became dark with blood. She sounded as if she was choking. Simply looking at her made Alice feel breathless.

'Are you all right? Do you need some water or a pat on the back?'

'Em . . . no,' the woman spluttered, gasping for breath and adding weakly, 'it's nothing. I just swallowed my gum.'

After a few moments of silence and when the woman's breathing had returned to normal, Alice repeated her question: 'Were you with her when the doctor saw her?'

'I was not.'

'Did she tell you what happened to her when she saw the doctor or the nurse? What they said to her?'

'No . . .' The woman coughed once more, attempting this time simply to clear her throat. 'She said it had all been a feckin' waste of time. She knew there was nothing wrong with her, that she'd get a clean bill of health. Then she fell asleep in my car and snored like a pig.'

———

Linda Gates, Moira Fyfe's accuser, looked about fifteen years old but claimed to be twenty-four. Alice found her in the pool room, waiting her turn, her gaze fixed on the table and her cue held like a staff beside her. She was so small that the tip of it was a foot above her head. While she waited she whispered to a friend, periodically licking the chalk off her fingers. She did not conceal her reluctance to talk, rolling her eyes heavenwards, and seemed to believe that denying everything, however trivial, would protect her and allow her to return to the game more speedily. Accordingly, she denied knowing Moira Fyfe, denied accusing her of anything and of having been involved in any confrontation with her. Faced with the other witnesses' accounts of events, she simply maintained that they were all lying, and when Alice questioned her as to why they might be doing that, she replied hotly, 'Because they're bitches!' When her opponent in the game of pool guffawed at this response she shouted angrily, as if it was some kind of proof of her innocence, that she had no money to steal, so why would she be accusing anyone of stealing something she'd never had.

Alice decided to try one more time. 'So, despite the fact that you lived in the same hostel as Moira Fyfe for months, and two separate witnesses saw you accuse her of having stolen your money, you're maintaining that you never even met the woman?' she asked, trying to sound incredulous. But she knew the answer she would get. It would be more remarkable, after the stream of denials, if Linda Gates had conceded that she knew her.

'Aye, that's right. See, I never leave my room, do I?'

At this remark her opponent on the table laughed uproariously, twirling his finger at his temple to convey to everyone in the room his view of her sanity, or lack of it. Glaring at him, Linda stamped to the door and slammed it behind her.

II

The alarm clock silenced, the Reverend Duncan McPhee yawned, stretched and then leant over and switched off his electric blanket. A good nine hours achieved, he thought, pleased that he had not had to resort to a pill. While still under the duvet, he mumbled his devotions to himself, confident that God would hear him.

Steeling himself to face the cold, he lumbered out of bed and across the room to open the curtains. In the bathroom his ablutions were perfunctory, the only deviation from normal routine being his use of a lather of mango-scented soap instead of Gillette foam. The can was empty.

Returning to his bedroom, he took his black clerical shirt off its hanger and buttoned it up, then looked blearily into his cuff-link box for his studs. Disentangling them from the catch of his grouse claw kilt-pin, he affixed first one and then the other to his dog collar and shirt. His black trousers took more of an effort as the dry-cleaning process appeared to have shrunk them. Finally conceding failure, he gave up in his attempt to do up the second button.

'Thought for the Day' on the radio caught his attention, and as he listened to it, he began to fume inwardly. More self-pitying drivel, of precisely no universal significance, from that tiresome, rambling rabbi. If the fellow had nothing to say, as was clearly the case, why on earth was he being pandered to by the BBC and provided with a platform to peddle his trite nonsense from? Could it be simply for old times' sake? What other possible explanation could there be? Surely, licence payers, such as himself, were entitled to a bit more for their money than an anecdote about burning the toast, impatient words to a partner followed by heartfelt penitence. If there was much more of this so-called religious twaddle, the militant atheists would win the day and the slot would be scrapped. They were playing into Dawkins's hands.

After he had breakfasted and fed the dog, he strode into his study feeling ready for the day's work. His diary lay open on his desk, and reaching for his spectacles on the cord around his neck, he read the entry for Tuesday 8 February. A funeral, and for a second his heart missed a beat. Who on earth was Matilda McEwan? Then he saw in brackets the word 'Parish' after her name and breathed easily again. Not a member of the congregation, so Jim would be dealing with that one.

Further down the page, in blue biro and in his own neat hand, there was another entry: 'School Assembly – Garstone Secondary – 2 p.m.' That would be a doddle. He would use the usual text, so all that he needed to do by way of preparation was to find the appropriate prop. The Tate & Lyle syrup tin with its picture of the dead lion and the bees, and Samson's riddle printed on it, 'Out of the strong came forth sweetness'. And if, God forbid, Juliet had finally thrown out the tin, then he could rely on his old standby, the Old Testament tale of the Burning Bush, the image of which was on his lapel badge, and the significance of the Call. That sermon too, known by heart, required no further thought, and as the headmistress had suggested spending no more than thirty minutes on the whole shebang, that would fit perfectly with the rest of his timetable. It would give him plenty of time for a haircut before the Church and Society Council meeting at 4 p.m. at 121 George Street.

The phone rang, and with one eye still on his diary, he picked up the receiver.

'Hello. Reverend Duncan McPhee speaking.'

'Good morning, Reverend, it's Donald Cartwright. It's just to let you know that my wife's out of hospital, she came out yesterday. It may not be for very long, but it was to tell you that she's home now, out of hospital for the moment at least.'

'Splendid news, Donald,' the minister replied, switching on his computer and cringing at the sudden notes of the Windows theme. Would Donald recognise it? Too old and too much of a fuddy-duddy, with luck.

He opened the first of his emails. It looked dull enough, a communication from Christian Aid Scotland, no doubt seeking further donations. The second, however, caught his eye, and reading it, he almost cried out in his excitement. The subject field read 'Nomination Committee – Membership'. Thrilled at these magical words he longed to open it, and became newly determined to get his caller off the line.

'I was wondering,' Donald Cartwright said, 'while she's here, in bed at home, whether you'd be able to come out and see her? I know how busy you are, I really do, and she does too, but if you had a minute to spare it would make a huge difference to her. She wants to speak to you . . . she wants to talk to you.'

'But of course, Donald. If I can make it, I will. If for any reason I can't, then my assistant, Jim, will come instead. You know him well. So, don't you worry. One way or another we'll see Mary at home. Now, was that everything?'

'You'll see her, Reverend?' The man was not to be fobbed off so easily.

'Me . . . or Jim.' Jim had plenty of time on his hands. He could do it.

'She'd love to see you. It would make her day and, to be honest, I don't think she's got that many more of them. She especially asked to see you.'

'As I say, it'll be me or Jim. I'm sorry, Donald . . .' the minister said, knocking with his knuckles on his desk and watching with delight as the dog ran out of the room, barking wildly, 'but I've got to go. There's someone at the front door. The dog's going bananas. But don't you worry. Jim – or I – will be around in the next day or two.'

Putting down the phone, he clicked on the email. As he scrolled down it, he felt his heart almost burst with joy. It was a three-line message from the Secretary requesting that his name be put forward to the Assembly to be considered for inclusion in the membership of the Select Forty-four. 'Thou hast anointed my head with oil and truly, my cup runneth over,' he murmured into the silence.

For a single second, he contemplated picking up the phone and calling his wife, letting her know that all that he had been predicting for so long was finally coming to pass. Had he, or had he not, told her that the invitation to dinner with the Moderator in Charlotte Square had presaged great things? Oh, the doubting Thomasina would be confounded now!

Granted, it had not been the same as an invitation to Holyrood with the Lord High Commissioner, but it was the next best thing. All those years of drudgery – the school chaplaincies, the convenorship of dull and power-less committees, hours spent in obscure working groups – were finally paying off. He might have started his days in a small Lanarkshire village with no hope for the future but, by his own efforts, he had confounded them all now.

No one had expected a McPhee to become the Dux of the school, or get a scholarship to university. But he had done it, and in his probationary period he had, at last, washed away the traces of coal dust clinging to his name. Even within his charges he had made steady progress, moving from Carstairs to Coalburn, and then eastwards and upwards to Carrick Knowe and Colinton. All the Cs.

No, he would not phone her and have his hopes dampened, could not bear that. Instead, he would leave a printout of the email on the kitchen table. Its significance would not be lost on the daughter of a former Moderator, and even the children's horrid jibe, calling him 'the Reverend I. M. A. Loser', might be forgotten for good when he added 'The Right Reverend' to his name.

The grandmother clock in the corridor outside chimed eleven and, deliberately trying to quell his excitement and concentrate, he turned his attention to the day's post. The first envelope was a small brown one and was, he thought, probably more Ecumenical Relations Committee papers. Sure enough, it contained a report prepared by the minister from Carnbo who had been deputed to attend the conference in Grand Rapids, USA. Topics covered included 'Peace amongst All Peoples', a contribution to the Ecumenical Decade to Overcome Violence. Overall, the correspondent noted, there had been inadequate time for any proper dialogue about joint-ministry, oversight or evangelism due to a terrorist bomb scare, fortunately false, which had resulted in the premature termination of proceedings. The next envelope contained a number of fabric samples sent by Wippells, for him to consider for his new preaching gown. That was Juliet's department, so she could choose for him, he decided, putting it on one side.

Opening the third envelope, he found a crumpled note from the organist, Mrs Tyrell, written as usual on lined paper and in red biro. Someone had, she complained, smeared superglue on one of the organ pedals and she suspected an 'inside job'. Who but a member of the congregation would be aware that she always operated the pedals in her stocking feet? In the privacy of his office, Duncan McPhee rolled his eyes heavenwards and gave an exasperated growl. This was not the woman's first accusation against the culprit whom she named. They were legion. Following her first complaint he had, foolishly, taken it at face value and confronted the child's parents, only to emerge with egg all over his face. The boy had, both his parents assured him, never owned a pet mouse, far less incarcerated one within the organ stool. No. This time Mrs Tyrell could pursue her own vendettas, be her own investigator and judge. He crumpled the note into a ball and tossed it into the wastepaper basket, making a mental note to tell her so himself, face to face, after the first service on Sunday.

His lunch consisted of little more than a chunk of bread with some pickle and grated cheese. The Irish stew that his wife had left for him in the fridge remained untouched, congealing in its bowl. He did not need it. A good meal could be expected from Ellie that evening whatever happened, and allowing, encouraging even, one's waistline to expand beyond thirty-six inches was, according to modern science, no less than a slow form of suicide. His trouser buttons, his early warning system, should not be ignored.

Two hours later the school assembly was well under way. In the chilly central hall, there had been no interruptions or heckles and his homily, equating the dead lion with evil itself, seemed to have held the pupils spellbound, or at least speechless. Only one girl put her hand up to ask a question. She was over six feet tall and seemed to be wearing only a pelmet over her flesh-coloured tights. In an innocent tone she asked: 'But, Sir, what about Aslan? He was a good lion, wasn't he?'

Where do I begin? the minister thought, his mind racing, confounded by the surreal quality of the query. But before he had opened his mouth to reply, the headmistress said in an irritated whisper, 'Ignore her, Reverend. It's the McGonagall girl, a well-known troublemaker.'

This remark was picked up by his radio microphone and broadcast to the assembled children. Prolonged and loud laughter ensued, and the tall girl stood up and took several bows, acknowledging the applause and smiling at the headmistress who looked on, impotently, unwilling to hazard another word.

Driving away from the barber towards 121 George Street and the Church and Society Council Meeting, Duncan McPhee enjoyed himself, contemplating to whom, among the membership, he would impart his good news. Graham would, undoubtedly, take it well and be genuinely pleased for him, but Susan's expression would be worth watching. Horror, masquerading as joy, a difficult one to pull off.

Entering the meeting room a couple of minutes late, he felt all eyes upon him. Nodding to all and sundry he took his place at the long table. His antennae twitched, picking up a definite frisson in the air. So the word must already be out, and dwelling amongst them.

As had become customary, by the time the tray of drinks was brought into the meeting the coffee in the jug was tepid. No one seemed to have remembered about biscuits. A female minister moved to fill up the cups, then, seeing that none of the males present was going to help, withdrew her arm. No one else stirred.

A paper on 'The Ministry: Current Day Celebrity Culture and the Church' was being delivered by a Gaelic-speaking minister from the Outer Isles, and he had already taken up most of the two hours allocated. 'The Church has its own X-factor,' he explained earnestly, 'the cross of Jesus . . .'

Duncan McPhee heard nothing of the talk. His mind was elsewhere, going over the changes in his life that he would have to make now that the Nomination Committee membership was on the horizon. All those loose ends would have to be tied up, otherwise he himself might become tangled up in them. Things must be simplified, whatever the cost.

'Have you any views on this, Duncan?' the Vice-Convenor asked.

'About?' he replied, emerging from his meditation and playing for time. He had no idea what 'this' might be.

'About the "Britney" effect?'

'No,' he said, truthfully, looking round the room and braving the surprised glances that his uncharacteristic brevity had provoked. To make no contribution to the debate was a first for him. Ten minutes later, and bobbing his head cordially to all once more, he gathered up his papers and joined the queue that was forming to leave the building.

Back at home, now standing in front of the mirror, he brushed the hair-trimmings off the shoulders of his black jacket. He straightened his badge and sucked in his belly, admiring his own reflection. Surveying it for a second time, he saw himself in the garb of the Moderator and in those robes he seemed, in his own eyes at least, literally to have grown in stature. Beside him he imagined his mother, alive once more, dressed as for church, accompanying him to some official function, a garden party, perhaps, or an official dinner. But he could not maintain the fiction for long. It became too alarming. What might she say? What might she do? So he readjusted the fantasy, conjuring her up in her front room as she watched him on television, her pride and delight undisguised as he opened the General Assembly.

For the short walk ahead the dog would stay by his side on the pavement, so he did not bother to search for the lead. Had it been a Labrador or a collie, he would not have had even to consider such a precaution, but Juliet had always been drawn to unintelligent breeds. Except me, of course, he mused, I'm the exception to that rule.

As he was going through the hall, he caught sight of a photograph of his wife. It was a head-and-shoulders portrait, showing her in her graduation gown. Looking into her familiar eyes, for a split-second he felt a pang of guilt. Here he was, betraying her again with another woman. How could he do it to her, his spouse of over thirty years?

But that was the answer, of course. Familiarity had long since doused their fires. At some level, she must know about Ellie, he reflected, comforting himself with the thought. How could she not? And, knowing, she could not have minded. Could she? Otherwise she would have said something, done something. It was not part of her fiery nature to keep quiet about something like that. So, in its way, that was all right then, wasn't it? No one had been hurt. And if by some odd fluke, some strange chance, she had never known, then that would be fine too – better, because what she did not know could not hurt her.

In any event, it was all academic now, or it would be soon. Because this, really, would be the last time. Of course, the whole thing had been his fault. He himself had been at fault; he had to accept that, he was entirely to blame. But it had all been so unlikely. Only a saint could have resisted Ellie, and he made no pretence to sainthood. He had never expected, certainly never intended, that their long discussions about agendas, any other business or the minutes should somehow move from the sitting room to the bedroom. How had it happened? Perhaps he had had too much to drink and lowered his guard?

Certainly, her loneliness had been no secret. It shone from her like a lighthouse beam. Or, perhaps, more accurately, like light from a wrecker's lamp, luring ships off their course and onto the jagged reefs! Very soon a proper course would be resumed. Ellie had gone in with her eyes wide open, knew he was married, knew his calling. With membership of the Nomination Committee on the line, the equation had suddenly changed and the reward, certainly, no longer outweighed the risk. For him. Now there was far too much to lose.

Yes, he would tell Ellie tonight as he had resolved earlier, explain the impossibility of their affair continuing and wipe away her tears. He had to think of Juliet. Had to consider Ellie's interests too, because she deserved commitment and undivided love. More than he could ever have offered.

Perhaps he should end the relationship by simply not going? But could things be adequately explained in a letter? Probably not, and it would look decidedly cowardly, unworthy of him. And the Irish stew had looked so unappealing in its Pyrex dish. In any event, she deserved to be told in person. It was the least he could do.

Having so settled matters to his own satisfaction, he closed his front door behind him and inserted his key into the lock.

———

When Alice arrived at Ian's studio at 9 p.m. everyone else had already gone for the night. Crossing the cold concrete floor, listening to the sound of her footsteps echoing in the recesses of the place, she felt suddenly chilled and slightly afraid. The place felt different. The harsh strip-lighting made the shadows deeper and darker, capable of harbouring some malign thing, and the stillness in the air felt dead, like the stillness of the tomb. But the inventory must be done, she had promised his mother it would be ready by the end of the week.

Aware that an irrational fear had begun to stalk her, she told herself off, telling herself that she had been there hundreds of times before and come to no harm. But that proved a mistake, because the calming voice which she had summoned up, ruthlessly reminded her that, when she had come before, it had invariably been in company. With Ian. Not once had she been there on her own.

An unwelcome thought flashed into her brain, almost made her run for the door: had her mystery caller tracked her down? Was he, whoever the hell he was, waiting for her in here? No. She had the key, had unlocked the place herself.

Forcing herself onwards, she pushed her way through the cold, grey dividing sheet into Ian's area, and saw that his easel was still up and had a half-finished canvas resting on it. She looked closely at the picture but at first sight it appeared incomprehensible, an incoherent jumble of colours. The background was made up of greys and blues, merging at the bottom into a solid block of pale yellow. Two-thirds of the way down ran a thin, horizontal strip of silver. She stepped back a few paces from the unfinished work to give it a second look, and as she did so, miraculously the colours and brush-strokes started to cohere and make sense. Of course, it was obvious now. Tyninghame.

How many times had they walked together through those deep, dark beech woods, with the dried leaves crunching under their feet, into the tunnel of buckthorn and sea holly and then out into the light? To see before them a view of the sea, smooth as glass and with that characteristic slash of silver defining a horizon that merged into the vast skies of East Lothian.

His favourite palette knife lay against the picture, as if recently discarded, and without thought she picked it up, trying to feel him through something that his hands had so recently touched. Nothing came. She closed her eyes, limp with despair again, finding herself surrounded by his things but without him. Surely to God, if he was anywhere, he would be here beside her, paint-spattered and alive.

The silence was broken by loud shouting outside in the street, as one man taunted another, sounding vicious, yelping and hooting as if egging someone on. A third voice joined in, screaming at the top of his voice and revving a motorbike. Listening to the sounds, she stood still, petrified, unsure what to do. Should she go and see what was going on or should she radio for assistance instead?

'Christ!' she said out loud, exasperated by her own passivity and aware that she was as nervy as a cat. Once she had been confident, bloody competent, in fact. She would not have dithered and agonised over what to do next. She would just have done it. It would only be a drunken fracas or some such thing, basic police work.

Deciding to take a look outside, she scrambled over two rows of broken kitchen chairs, covered in torn and dusty sheeting, and climbed up onto the windowsill. Perching there, she put her face close to the glass and looked through the dirty pane onto the street outside. As she peered through it she thought she heard a voice saying, 'Alice?'

Less than a second later a brick came hurtling towards her through the pane, shattering it, smashing it into a thousand pieces and sending tiny daggers of glass in every direction.

12

'Foot the ladder for me, Stevie,' the tree surgeon shouted, surveying the scene around him from his elevated viewpoint and glorying in the prospect of the Dean Bridge that his perch gave him. Cars sped along it, and the heads of a few pedestrians, all early birds, were just visible above the parapet as they tramped across its span on their way to work. The sky above the Holy Trinity Church on Queensferry Road was a gelid blue. A wind from the north had driven away most of the clouds but a small drift of grey, lowering cumulonimbus had somehow eluded it and remained directly above him, marring the otherwise pristine perfection of the heavens.

Getting no reply, he looked down towards the base of the beech tree on which his ladder was propped and saw, to his irritation, that no one was there.

'Stevie!' he bellowed but, once more, to no effect.

'Stevie!' he shouted again, unwilling to start on the diseased, lifeless limb on which his chainsaw rested until he was certain that his ladder was secure. The ground below was as hard as iron after last night's frost, slippery in patches too.

Yet again receiving no answer, he raised his visor and began to plod wearily down the rungs of the ladder in his steel-toed work-boots, his chainsaw swinging from side to side with each step.

Taking on his nephew had been a mistake, he decided. He should have stuck with his own instincts and never listened to the rest of the family. His was a business, not some kind of youth rehabilitation scheme, not some kind of bloody charity. Now where had the lad got to? No doubt he'd be hiding somewhere to sniff his miaow-miaow or whatever the latest stuff was called. Months and months of community service had had no more effect on him than a slap on the wrist. Some folk didn't deserve second chances.

For the next ten minutes he busied himself stamping along the frost-whitened gravel paths that crisscrossed the gardens, heading downhill, in his search for his elusive apprentice. Every so often, self-consciously, he yelled the boy's name.

Eventually, enraged by the lack of response, he roared at the top of his voice, 'Stevie, where the fuck are you?'

An elderly woman, little more than her eyes visible between her mauve woollen hat and the striped scarf wound around her nose, mouth and chin appeared around the corner. Her pet, a Maltese terrier, strained on its lead, attempting to sniff the workman's boots.

'Have you lost your dog?' she asked.

'Eh . . . yes,' he said weakly, unwilling to attempt to explain his predicament but incensed at feeling the need to lie.

'What sort of dog is it?' she asked brightly. 'We'll keep our eye out for the renegade, won't we, Digger?'

'Eh . . . a mongrel. Just a soddin' mongrel,' he replied, edging quickly away from her as if she carried the plague, cursing the boy silently in his head once more.

By the lowest path the Water of Leith rushed along, tumbling over itself, in spate. Its cloudy waters were flecked with an ochre-tinted foam, and a single tree-stump blocked half the stream, the city's flotsam and jetsam collecting around it. Beyond the beavers' dam of twigs, litter and traffic cones, he noticed a half-submerged ironing board held upright by the current, white eddies forming on either side of it. Its rigid metal legs were extended skywards as if in surrender.

Raindrops began pattering onto his yellow hard-hat. He swore out loud, hastily retracing his steps, initially to the diseased beech tree and then, on finding nobody there, to his van. Yanking open the door and leaping in he found his apprentice, Stevie, cowering in the passenger seat.

'What the fuck are you doing in here?' he said angrily. 'The rain's only just come on and I spent the last quarter of an hour looking for you.'

'I'm sorry,' the boy moaned, shaking his head, 'but I couldn't stay out there. Not with that man . . . like that.' He, too, was wearing a yellow hard-hat and his green overalls were too large for his slim body, swamping him. Neither hand was visible beneath his overlong sleeves.

'What the hell are you talking about? What man? Like what?'

'The dead one – near the bottom of the tree.'

'You found a dead man?' The tree surgeon was incredulous. No doubt this was the drugs talking. 'You sure about that? It wasn't one of those pink elephants or whatever you see with your weed?'

'Aye. Aye, I'm sure. And he's got no clothes on! He's only about ten yards from our tree.'

'Sure?'

'Sure!'

'Christ's sake! Why didn't you tell me then? Why did you not come and get me?'

'I did. I tried,' Stevie protested ineffectually. 'I shouted at you when you were doing the lower branches, using the chainsaw.'

'So I never heard you! You idiot! I'd have stopped if I'd heard. Are you sure the man's dead?'

'He's lying down – half hid in the undergrowth. He must be dead otherwise he'd have moved. It's freezing out there.'

Leaving the boy trembling in the van, his boss braved the downpour once more to search the dense clump of rhododendrons on either side of the beech trees. With raindrops stinging his cold cheeks and running off his waterproof cape onto his jeans below, he scoured the edges of the bushes until he found what he was looking for. A pair of white feet, their soles wrinkled as if from an overlong bath, heels resting on the frozen ground.

Moving closer to the body he stared at its pallid legs, strands of ginger hair clinging to the skin like strands of seaweed on a rock. Gradually he allowed his eyes to travel upwards. In less than a second, he had confirmed that the man was dead and, disturbingly, as naked as the day he was born.

———

'A wifie rang to report a dead dog, Sir,' DC Elizabeth Cairns said to Eric Manson as he entered the office. Omitting any greeting, she added, 'It's a Dalmatian. Little more than a puppy, the lady says.'

'Why were we called?' the DI asked, taking a sip of coffee from his polystyrene cup. Then, grinning, he walked to his desk and added, 'Was it murdered or something? Raped even? We're supposed to be the Criminal Investigation Department, not the Cur Investigation

Department.' He looked over at her and guffawed, expecting some kind of reaction to his witticism.

'Nope,' the constable responded, deadpan, 'but it didn't die from natural causes either. It was run over on that big stretch of road opposite the Travel Inn on Learmonth Terrace. The lady found it in the gutter. Its name tag says it's called Ailsa and there's a phone number too. But the owners are not answering.'

'Alas, poor Ailsa – but she has nothing to do with us,' the DI said, removing the paper napkin from his bacon-and-egg roll and looking at his breakfast fondly. 'We're busy, Liz, with Crime. C.R.I.M.E. You and I are off to solve the mystery of the naked corpse in the gardens. Sounds like something out of a Sherlock Holmes story, eh?'

'Do we know why he was naked, Sir?'

'I certainly don't, love, but I can make a few guesses. Perhaps he was a midnight naturist who blew his gasket while out on a stroll? Or maybe he was mid-tryst in the gardens with the gardener when his ticker gave out? Or, a long shot, he might have been having a swim in the Water of Leith when his clothes were stolen by somebody . . . then he died of cold.'

'Or, and forgive the speculation,' the Constable chipped in brightly, 'a giant hoover might have descended from the heavens, scared him to death and sucked every natural and man-made fibre off his body.'

'Exactly. At the moment, God alone knows. DC Galloway's there already and he's talked to the poor folk who found the stiff. So to speak. We're short this morning, as DS Rice is to join us later, she's seeing her GP. She got cuts in her face when a vandal threw a brick through a window. By the way, how do you think she's coping?'

'Coping?'

'You know – you've been working with her these last few days – coping with the grief, shock or whatever. I thought she looked a bit pale, stressed and everything. Maybe she came back too early.'

'She seems pretty sharp to me.'

'Good. Good, glad to hear it. We'll be seeing her later, after she's seen the doctor. She's got to talk to the fiscal about Moira Fyfe too, hand over all the papers.'

Looking at the dead man, DC Cairns felt embarrassed on his behalf. For some unknown reason, hearing about him she had conjured up in her imagination the vision of a muscular, youthful corpse with well-defined pectorals and pert buttocks, such as she might have admired on a Grecian vase or an underwear ad. Instead, on display was a flaccid, middle-aged one with a sagging bottom, love-handles and swollen ankles. Someone's granddad was splayed out on the ground in front of her, face down, in the buff, subject to the scrutiny of all and with a strange, greenish, leopard-spotted slug lodged between two of his toes.

Puffing out steam in the cold air as he jogged, DC Galloway arrived at her side and stood looking at the body for a second or two.

'No clothes anywhere,' he sighed. 'We've searched the whole place and there's nothing. Not so much as a pair of Y-fronts or a single sock. But surely to God he can't have walked bollock-naked through the town to get here?'

'It does seem a bit unlikely. Someone else could have taken them, I suppose?'

'The phantom clothes-collector, you mean?' DC Galloway said in tones of disbelief, shaking his head at her suggestion.

'No, not a clothes-collector. A thief, or possibly whoever murdered him, if anybody did. Or, for all we know, he may have been dumped in there like that, starkers, by others. They would have clothes on.'

'Someone just might have noticed that, a . . . '

'Good, because we'll have no clue from footprints or anything like that,' DC Cairns interrupted, thinking aloud, taking no heed of his words. 'The ground's like concrete and has been for days. Nothing will show up there.'

'As I was saying before you interrupted me,' the Constable said, fixing her with his unblinking eyes, 'someone lugging a naked corpse is an odd enough sight to attract most people's attention. We'll soon find out, anyway. The DI says we've to make a start on the door-to-doors. Clarendon Crescent, Eton Terrace, Lennox Street, you're to do them, and I'm on the other side of the road, Buckingham and Belgrave . . .'

—

Lennox Street lay at right angles to the Dean Gardens, separated from the park by elegant railings, which somehow survived the demands of the Second World War. Beyond the railings was a roadway of patched tarmac dividing the two sides of the street. The street itself was short, its buildings low, comprised largely of two bay houses, each crowned with ornate balustrades and constructed of honey-coloured stone. But Edinburgh's smut-laden air had not left the dwellings unmarked: the miasma had penetrated their fabric, leaving stains of black soot on them like the blemishes on a centenarian's skin. Dainty, decorative lamp-posts punctuated the pavements, and some of the residents had softened their frontages by growing ivy or other creepers over their own stretches of filigreed ironwork.

In this street at 11 a.m. on a weekday morning, only the elderly remain at home. Those of working age had long since vacated their reserved parking spaces and were now busy drafting dispositions, diagnosing illnesses or power-ing up and down the lanes of Drumsheugh Baths or those of other elite health clubs. Their offspring, too, passed their time elsewhere, dressed in brightly-coloured blazers, getting to know each other, networking in the nurseries of Heriot's, the Academy, Fettes or Stewart Melville.

When DC Cairns arrived at a doorway halfway along the street, excited yelps and barks greeted her before she had even rapped with her knuckles. The instant the cerise-painted door opened, a trio of long-haired dachs-hunds cascaded out, nose to tail, milling around the young policewoman's ankles and looking up at her with their anxious black eyes. Feeling a damp nose on her calf, she was sorely tempted to give the most insistent of the dogs a quick kick, to push it away as an example to the others. But she managed to restrain herself, and as she waited there was a high, piping sound followed by words of command: 'Toffee! Marmite! Pushkin! Inside, the lot of you!'

It was the voice of the pack leader. Immediately, the three little dogs trooped back indoors, and a large lady with buck teeth and a mass of fair curls watched them return into the hallway. Noticing Cairns's fixed smile and assuming it to be one of admiration for her pets' conduct, she declared, 'Obedience classes!' Met with a look of

177

blank incomprehension, she added, 'Me – I teach them.' She had a whistle around her neck which bounced off her bust as she walked, and as DC Cairns followed her inside, the three dachshunds, all in a line, led the odd procession. When they reached the drawing room, without further instruction, each animal filed into its own bed, all of them looking up expectantly at the two human beings as if for further entertainment.

'I saw or heard nothing, nothing unusual, I'm sorry to say,' Lavinia Travers began, exposing an excessively large area of gum and tooth with her generous smile. 'More's the pity! We could do with a little excitement around here. Nothing has happened since Mr Furnell, across the road, turned himself into Miss Furnell. In Morocco, Tunisia or some other nice hot place like that. I've only been to the Gambia myself. That was not a police matter, of course, and now we have two ladies of the house, Miss Furnell and Mrs Furnell. Although, oddly enough, they're married.' She grinned toothily again, her eyebrows shooting up in an inquiring look as she waited, expectantly, as if for some exciting titbit to be offered in return.

'The description I gave you. No one comes to mind?' DC Cairns ploughed on, determined not to be distracted by the woman's gossip, however diverting it might be.

'No. Could be any old middle-aged man and, frankly, they all look the same to me nowadays . . . unlike you, diddums,' she added in a comforting tone, bending down to stroke Pushkin, the dachshund closest to her hand.

'A man with reddish hair, balding and with hazel eyes? There aren't that many redheads about, are there?'

'True. At a pinch I suppose it could be Duncan McPhee. He's the only ginger hereabouts. A bad-tempered fellow who lives with his poor beleagured wife somewhere or other in Learmonth Terrace. I call him "Ginger Snap", not to his face, obviously, just behind his back . . . because he is. It's only the truth. He's on the Garden Committee, the Tennis Courts Committee, the Amenity Committee, the Committee Committee. He's a "Committee Man" and he makes my life a misery. He's the worst sort of Holy Willie.'

'Holy Willie?'

'He's a Church of Scotland minister for his sins – or, more likely, ours.'

'Do you know his exact address?'

'No. As I said, Learmonth Terrace, I think, but I'm not sure and I may be talking out of turn now. But you're just as likely to find him further up this street. That's where a certain lady lives, another keen committee member. They're tireless, the two of them, often needing to discuss "committee matters" at all sorts of odd hours. I've come across him late at night, going home, when I've been putting the dogs out. They're both extraordinarily conscientious.'

'Did you see him go into Dean Gardens at any time yesterday or . . .'

'No,' Lavinia Travers replied, interrupting the question. 'He always uses the Clarendon Crescent entrance, so I'm none the wiser. I can't see it from here.'

At that moment a well-dressed old man, with a black Homburg hat pushed to the back of his head, shuffled past Miss Travers's window and she exclaimed excitedly, 'Isn't that Lord Spurgeon? If so, it's his second trip this morning. I wonder where he's off to now?'

Without waiting for a response she rushed over to the window and positioned herself slightly to one side, most of her figure being obscured by a thick, lined chintz curtain, and watched the man's progress until he disappeared out of view. DC Cairns was unable to prevent herself from smiling, amused at the woman's unabashed snooping.

'City bound,' Miss Travers muttered to herself, oblivious now of the policewoman, 'but with no briefcase. Mmm. Shopping, most probably, except that the Tesco van called yesterday, so he might be off to the New Club.' She glanced at her watch and added, as if expecting some comment, 'But it's too early for lunch, isn't it?'

Her brow still furrowed in thought, Lavinia Travers returned to her armchair, looked her guest in the face, smiled as if at an accomplice, and then picked up the threads of their conversation.

'I'm not sure what Mrs McPhee makes of it all – the "committee work", I mean. Poor dear. Blinkered like an old mare hauling a milk cart. So, what exactly has Ginger Snap been up to then? Bit of a Jammie Dodger, is he? Up to his old Twix? It must be more than a parking fine, otherwise you wouldn't be interested, now, would you?'

———

No signs of life were visible at the McPhees' house, and ringing the bell at the front door produced no response. Determined to follow up every possible lead, the young constable retraced her steps to Lennox Street. Standing on the doorstep of the house that Lavinia Travers had indicated, with the wind whistling up the street and rattling the joints of the scaffolding at the southern end, she had second thoughts. The information she was acting upon was probably no more than the meddlesome outpourings of a spinster neighbour who didn't have enough to do with her time. Feeling distinctly uneasy, she peered down into the basement window but saw nothing, and while she was wondering whether she still had time to retreat, dignity intact, the main door opened.

Behind it stood an ancient, white-haired woman who was leaning forward at an unnatural angle, supported by a Zimmer frame. Catching the old woman's watery eyes, Cairns felt herself becoming agitated. This woman was obviously not somebody's mistress! It was preposterous! There could be only one explanation. Miss Travers, with her impish sense of humour, must have set her up, and was, in all probability, watching her this very minute, shaking with laughter at her discomfort while safely concealed behind those thick curtains. This 'older woman' had one foot in the grave, and was more likely to be in need of an undertaker than a toy boy.

'I'm sorry to bother you,' she began, any remaining confidence draining away, 'but I wondered whether Duncan McPhee was here by any chance?'

'Who?'

'Duncan McPhee.'

'I'm sorry, dear, you'll have to bellow,' the old lady said, bending even further towards her. 'I'm as deaf as a post nowadays.'

'Is Duncan McPhee here? I understand that he lives nearby on Learmonth Terrace.'

'He's not here, dear. If I were you I'd try Learmonth Terrace. That's where he lives, you see?'

The old lady smiled kindly at the constable, thinking to herself that the girl's youth probably explained her cluelessness. On the other hand, perhaps she had been born terminally dim.

'You're on the committee for the Dean Gardens?' DC Cairns blustered on, aware of the complete non sequitur but determined to establish if there was so much as a smidgen of truth in any of the information given to her by the mischievous spinster.

'Yes, I am. But, really, it's in name alone now. I do little more than adorn the notepaper. Is that what you're after? A key to the gardens? Why didn't you say so? That's all handled by the Reverend McPhee, as I expect you know.'

⁓

The Reverend McPhee's wife enjoyed driving. Her car was inexpensive, a second-hand Fiat Panda, but it was speedy and, more importantly, it had an excellent sound system.

Accelerating past a lorry which was straining slowly up a steep gradient, thick grey smoke coming from its rusted exhaust, Juliet McPhee held her breath. Gasping for air after half a minute, she closed the window before more of the poisonous fumes seeped in.

All the time, in her mind she was accompanying the soprano in 'Soave sia il vento', and the sound she was making in her brain was every bit as pure, as crystalline, as that made by Elisabeth Schwarzkopf. It was blissful, she thought, to be on one's own, surrounded by incomparable music, with the blue Lomond Hills on the left, the shadow of clouds scudding across them and sunlight falling on the Kinross plain.

And, best of all, there was no Duncan beside her barking orders: 'Overtake now!', 'Indicate now!', 'Park there!' or trying to 'rationalise' her route. He would never learn. It was easier to obey his commands than resist them, but obedience, too, took its toll.

If she timed it right, she thought, squinting at the clock on the dashboard over her glasses, she could ensure that she arrived home in his absence, and luxuriate in a few more hours of solitude, with Ailsa alone as company. Thinking about her husband, she reminded herself that she must be fair to him. After all, once upon a time, long, long ago, his dominant traits, his natural authority and his orderliness had attracted her. That had to be admitted. In their early days, she had found them almost reassuring, believing that his strong character kept the forces of chaos at bay, protected her.

But those charms, his charms, had dimmed once she had realised what lay at the true core of his being. Fear. An unspoken, unending dread that he would lose control and be discovered, be found out. That people would see through him and he would be found wanting, shrink, and become wee Dunkie McPhee again, the miner's boy. Nowadays, the pliant and those he had overtaken socially were ordered about, lorded over. Those he considered above him had their egos massaged until they, too, were overtaken. Then he showed his teeth.

And at all times, offerings were made to his real deity, the great God of Respectability. Doubtless it was not his fault, this weakness, but, surely to goodness, by the age of fifty-five he should have got over it, have exorcised those ghosts from his past? Had I known then, she said to herself, growing angrier by the second, that I had been chosen to function as some sort of pass or membership card to help him to join the middle classes I would have declined his moonlight proposal. Refused his kisses.

But remembering that night, she softened towards him He had trusted her, allowed himself to relax with her as with no one else, regaled her with funny stories of unexpected, idiosyncratic snobberies within the pit community. He had chosen to expose his vulnerability completely to her, confident that she would never betray him, privately or in public. No greater compliment could be paid by anyone to anyone.

Of course, his judgement had been sound because she had never parted with his secret, knowing that to do so would destroy him. Even the children remained ignorant about large parts of his childhood: the sugar or ketchup sandwiches, fifth-hand shoes and the endless darning. And, in his way, he had been a good father, even if he had lied to them about their own grandparents, their anteced-ents, air-brushing them beyond recognition.

However, she could, she decided, have done a lot worse. Well, worse, anyway, and so could he! Once, she had been a catch with her abundant blonde hair and trim figure. Time would likely weld them more tightly together, and, perhaps in old age, he would finally relax, grow to accept himself and stop pretending to be what he was not. Finally, he would grow up.

'Thou shalt not worship false gods,' she muttered to herself, removing the *Cosi fan tutte* disc and inserting Mozart's *Requiem* in its place.

Seeing the towers of the Forth Road Bridge ahead of her and with 'Qui Tollis' belting out, she began searching in the ashtray for spare coins, deliberately slowing down to give herself time to collect a pound's worth. While she was picking up speed, amusing herself by racing a goods train rattling over the Rail Bridge, it suddenly came to her that there were no toll booths any more and she laughed out loud at her own inability to register change. It showed how often she crossed the water.

As she drew into Learmonth Terrace, the bright win-ter sunshine that she had been enjoying was immediately blotted out by the screen of large sycamore trees parallel to the road. Halfway up the street she saw an empty space almost opposite her own front door, and blessing her good luck, she manoeuvred into it. Her suitcase was heavy and now she would have no distance to carry it. As she walked up the front steps of her house, Yale key at the ready, a uniformed constable approached her, inquiring if she was Mrs McPhee.

13

Once the mortuary assistant had removed the cloth, Juliet McPhee allowed her eyes to rest on her husband's face and body. An overwhelming urge to keen to the heavens like an Arab woman rose in her breast, but she controlled herself and remained silent. She was shocked by her own impulse. But he looked so slight, so childlike and vulnerable. She longed to kiss his cheek, cradle his head in her arms, comfort him. Unthinkingly, she reached out to touch him, drawing back her hand just before she was asked not to.

Suddenly, there seemed too little air in the place, and she became conscious of each breath as she drew it, none being deep enough to give her the oxygen for which her lungs were crying out. Realising belatedly that the strange panting sound she could hear came from herself, she deliberately slowed her breathing as she had been taught at school. She had not fainted in chapel all those years ago and she would not do so here either. He would not like it, would have thought it unseemly, showy, quite possibly Latin and hysterical. She must concentrate. Primed by the policewoman, she reminded herself that she had a job to do.

'Are you OK, Mrs McPhee?' Alice said. Unable for the moment to talk, she nodded her head. Then, in a nearly expressionless voice, she identified her husband's body and calmly remarked on the absence of his signet ring.

'Have you taken it?' she asked the sergeant.

'No. He is as we found him. Can you describe it?'

It had been, she told them, a gift from her in the early days of their marriage, and he always wore it on his little finger. Looking at him again, she noticed the slightly pale band on his bare wrist, and remarked that his watch, too, was missing. It had been an expensive one, she said, a present from the children on his last birthday. Hugh had done well at KPMG and it was a Rolex. He had contributed the lion's share and Flora had simply chipped in to the extent that she was able. Duncan had always had a weakness for good watches.

After a few more minutes, spent in silence, Alice suggested that they should be on their way, but Mrs McPhee shook her head.

'I can't leave him here all alone,' she said. 'He never liked confined spaces, you know. He's claustrophobic.'

'It's not him, though. He's not . . .' Alice said.

'No? Not him? Who is *he* then?' Juliet McPhee cut in, frowning. 'I've just identified him for you. Please don't give me any platitudes about the hereafter. He believed in all of that, the fairy tales, he had to, but I never have. This –' she said bitterly, pointing at the corpse, 'is my husband. There is, and was, nothing else of him.'

Catching Alice's eye, the mortuary assistant nodded his head in the direction of the clock on the wall.

'Where are his clothes? Perhaps I should take them home with me and wash them?' Juliet McPhee then said, in a slightly dazed tone.

'They didn't tell you?' Alice said, holding the heavy mortuary door open. To her relief, the woman moved towards it, apparently now ready to go.

'Tell me what?'

'That when he was found, he was naked. None of his clothes were found with him in the garden.'

'How do you mean? I assumed that you, the police, the mortuary people or whoever, removed his clothes – for this' the woman said, unable to take in the meaning of the policewoman's words.

'No. He was found naked in Dean Gardens. No clothes were found on him or with him.'

'What . . .' she said, in a slow, hoarse voice. 'Naked in the gardens? No one told me. Do you know, officer, I think he'd rather have been found dead in there than naked. If he had been offered a choice. I really do.'

'I'm sorry, Mrs McPhee. I thought you'd been informed.'

'There'll be a scandal, bound to be in those circumstances,' the widow mused. 'Anyone who knew him, really knew him, would tell you that he would rather have died than play any part in a scandal. I hope it can be kept out of the papers – do you think you could do that?'

⁓

They drove back to Learmonth Terrace in silence, Alice's attempts at conversation having fizzled out. Both women were deep in thought. Juliet McPhee was still puzzling over the news of her husband's nudity. What on earth had he been doing? Why would he undress outside in a public place on a cold night in January? To have sex, perhaps? No, surely not! But that would be the natural conclusion, wouldn't it? But, if so, why outside in sub-zero temperatures, for heaven's sake, and with whom? She had been away, and the house empty. There were three bedrooms he could have used, excluding their own. Maybe he had been robbed or mugged, but then why would anyone bother taking his clothes? They were nothing to write home about. What *had* he been playing at?

'What was he doing in the gardens?' she asked quietly, afraid of the answer.

Alice, lost in her own thoughts, mulling over the widow's bleak conclusion about the finality of death, did not hear her.

'I said, what was he doing in the gardens?' Juliet McPhee repeated, fleetingly annoyed at being ignored, at having to steel herself to ask again.

'We don't know. We were hoping you might have some idea.'

'I've drawn a blank. I can't understand it at all. It makes no sense.'

'Have you any idea what your husband was wearing yesterday?' Alice inquired.

'No, I wouldn't know, officer,' said the woman, letting out a deep sigh and looking out of the car window as they travelled over the Dean Bridge. 'You see, I was away. As I told the uniformed constable, I spent the last two nights with my friends in Bridge of Earn. So I haven't a clue what he was wearing yesterday or the day before.'

'I understand that, Mrs McPhee,' Alice replied, 'but maybe we'll be able to get an idea from what's missing in his wardrobe and not in the wash?'

'I see,' the woman said, gathering up her bag and getting ready to step out of the car.

After about half an hour sitting alone in the McPhees' drawing room, Alice heard the sound of the widow's heavy footsteps on the stairs as she returned to attend to her visitor. Leaning against the doorway and sweeping back a strand of hair from her forehead, she said, 'Well,

I've done what you told me. As far as I can see, he must have been wearing pants. I've no idea how many pairs he had but it would be unheard of for him not to wear them. And a vest, he always wore one, summer or winter. I'm pretty sure he was wearing his black undershirt with his black waistcoat on top, his favourite black jacket too. There are only three pairs of black trousers in his drawer and there should be four. None have been put out for the cleaner. So I imagine he'll have been wearing them too. On his feet he'll have had his black brogues, he always wore them and they're missing as well. A symphony in black as usual, it seems.'

'Can you tell me a little about your husband?' Alice asked. Seeing a look of concern flit across the woman's face, she added, 'For the purposes of our inquiry, Mrs McPhee. You see, until the post mortem's complete we won't know whether his death was suspicious or not, but, as you'll appreciate, at the moment the circumstances of his death do tend to suggest that some investigation may require to be carried out.'

'What do you want to know?' the woman said, sitting down on the edge of the sofa and folding her hands in her lap. A thought suddenly crossed her mind. 'Do Hugh and Flora know? Have you told them yet?'

'No, not so far. We had to be sure it was your husband.'

'What happened to your face?' Mrs McPhee asked, in sudden surprise. She was looking hard at Alice, as if the small area of cuts had just appeared.

'Someone threw a brick through a window – I was too close.' Alice put her fingers to her cheek, now self-conscious about her appearance.

'I'm sorry to hear it. So, what do you want to know?' the widow said, wearily.

'Did he like his job? What was his normal routine? Anything about any other members of the family or friends which might be relevant? Anyone, I suppose, who might have wished him ill?'

'He was a minister of the Church of Scotland, the minister of St Moluach's. He did well – he was well respected, spent a fair amount of his time at 121 George Street on committees and so on. He was . . . a good man. A good husband. I can't think of anyone . . .'

She stopped, gazing at nothing, and muttered as if to herself, 'Golden lads and girls all must . . .'

'His routine?' Alice prodded, rousing the woman from her momentary trance.

'His days were varied. Some of his time was spent here, in his study, attending to his sermons, doing office work – preparing for meetings, that kind of thing. You can imagine the sort of dry stuff, I'm sure. Over and above that he had parish work, but he had an assistant to help with that.'

'What is his name?'

'Jim Kenny. He's young. Twenty-five or so.'

'Do you and he have much family?'

'Us, just us. His parents are dead. They both died in the eighties. He's got a brother in Australia and a half-sister somewhere or other. They had the same mother, different fathers. We lost touch with her many moons ago. So, there are the two children, Flora and Hugh, and me. That's about it, I suppose.'

'Ill-wishers?'

'What an antiquated expression! I can't think of any-one much . . .' Juliet McPhee hesitated, before continuing, 'He's annoyed plenty of people in his time – but not to the extent that they'd wish him any real harm, I think. He was a clergyman, not a mafia boss.'

'Who would these people be?' Alice persisted.

'I don't know.'

'He had no enemies?'

'Oh, for heaven's sake,' the woman said impatiently, her irritation breaking through. 'Who doesn't? Really! He annoyed me, he annoyed the children, he annoyed Jim, he annoyed our neighbours – to some extent he annoyed anyone he ever dealt with. But it's all rather trivial, isn't it? He wasn't the easiest of men, officer. He was complex. Jim or Timothy Dawson would certainly tell you that . . . if you need a testimonial to that effect.'

'Who is Timothy Dawson?'

'Someone who knew my husband well. In fact, for a long time, his best friend.'

'I'd like to talk to him, if possible.'

'I'm sure he'd be only too happy to speak to you about Duncan, he usually is. He'll talk to anyone who will listen to him nowadays. And some who won't.'

Then, distracted, the woman started to look around the room as if searching for something. Looking anxious, she rose and disappeared through the door. In seconds she returned.

'Where's Ailsa?' she asked, adding immediately, and as if to reassure herself, 'I suppose you took her, when you came to the house earlier? Where is she? I'd like to pick her up.'

Remembering the report announced by DC Cairns, Alice said, 'Your dog? Is she a Dalmatian?'

'Yes, that's right,' the woman replied, smiling, clearly relieved. 'Ailsa. Can I go and collect her?'

Feeling a vague dread and conscious that she would, once again, be the bearer of bad news, Alice said, 'I'm sorry, I'm afraid not. She's dead. She was found this morning on the road opposite here. A car must have hit her.'

'Ailsa's dead? Oh God, I don't believe it!' Mrs McPhee said piteously, bowing her head and covering her face with her hands, rocking to and fro on the edge of the sofa, oblivious to the fact that she was not alone.

—

A couple of days later, when Alice was sitting at her desk looking at her statement and thinking about the forthcoming FAI, the phone rang.

'Hello, doll.'

'Is that you, Donny?' she said, unsure of the voice. It sounded like her pal from the SART office.

'And I thought you were a quick learner, Sybil. Have your forgotten me so quickly?' Donny replied, his tone letting her know that he was affronted by her inability to recognise him.

'No, not at all. Are you short-handed – needing someone to make the tea for you again?'

'We've a new woman. Aileen from Lost Property has learned to do that now. She's introduced us to Earl Grey and Lapsang Souchong. None of your builders' tea for us these days, Alice.'

'So you just rang up to boast?'

'Yes. Why not? Also, I thought you'd like to know that someone tried to sell a signet ring matching the description you gave us at the Cash 4 U shop up near Lauriston Place. We've tried to follow it up, but whoever it was gave a false name and didn't have the right papers. So the shop wouldn't take it. But, the good news is that we've got the bastard on film. I've arranged for you to see the clip at their premises at two o'clock. That suit you?'

The manager of the shop, Sarah Owen, was dressed in a dark-blue trouser suit and stilettos. With unconcealed haste, she bundled Alice through the security door and into her office, concerned in case any potential customer got wind of the police presence.

'I'll leave you to see it yourself, eh?' she said, pointing to a television monitor among a wall of four, and then sliding out of the room without waiting for an answer.

The first thing that Alice saw on the screen was an image of a bearded man approaching the counter. He was bent over, seemed to be coughing, and was holding a handkerchief close to his lips. After less than a second the camera moved, filming the top of his balding head. Next, his face was panned, his most distinctive feature being a large, hooked nose with a scar running horizontally across the bridge. His handkerchief now obscured the whole of his mouth. After that the doorway was shown as another customer, an Asian woman, walked through it. The last image showed the man leaving the premises, apparently still coughing. The time and date flashed continuously on the film. At that moment Ms Owen reappeared, clutching a single sheet of paper in her tanned hand.

'There's the paperwork, such as it is. He hadn't got any utility bills or other ID with him. So that's all we've got,' she said apologetically, hovering beside Alice as if to read the piece of paper with her. Looking at the form, Alice saw that only one part of it had been completed. Under the heading 'Name' it read: 'Lloyd George'.

'Seems unlikely,' Alice grinned.

'Oh, I don't know,' the woman replied airily. 'We get all sorts in here.'

194

14

The first witness called by the Procurator Fiscal at the Fatal Accident Inquiry into the death of Moira Fyfe was Brian Imrie, the manager of the Bread Street Hostel. He looked incongruous in his ill-fitting charcoal suit, and the gold stud in his nostril only added to the discordant effect. With sweat glistening on his forehead, he said in his soft voice that he had known the deceased, Moira Fyfe, on and off for about six years or so, initially in his capacity as the manager of the Ferry Road Hostel and later when he became the manager of the Bread Street one. Her main problem, he explained, was that she was a chronic alcoholic, and however hard she tried to give up drinking she invariably failed.

'She just couldn't do it. I don't think she could face life without it,' he said, crossing his legs nervously as if needing the toilet. Responding to a further question, he attributed her addiction to her 'underlying issues', and when asked to expand on them, he said, 'loneliness . . . depression, lack of self-esteem. I'm no doctor, but with her you didn't need to be. She felt alone – unloved. Unlovable, I suspect.'

'You'll need to speak up, Mr Imrie, I can hardly hear you,' the Sheriff said, looking down at him from the bench. She was a petite woman, swamped in her oversized gown. Her wig touching her eyebrows, she resembled an aged child who had recently raided the dressing-up box.

'Right. RIGHT. She felt unloved, unlovable,' he said, obediently increasing the volume. He was determined to get this ordeal over with as soon as possible and get out of the place.

'Unlovable?' the Procurator Fiscal, James Brand, queried, inviting the witness to expand his answer.

'She used to say that she'd killed a wee girl. It was an accident, a medical accident, an overdose when she was nursing. We all knew that, but to her way of thinking she had killed that child. And, of course, she had no one. No family. Her own child died, so did her husband. She had nobody else.'

'When you got to know her, was that when she was staying in Bread Street or Ferry Road?' the Procurator Fiscal asked, shifting his weight from one hip to the other. Awaiting the man's reply, he stood stock-still and pressed his upraised biro vertically against his pursed lips.

'Yes, in both of them when I used to work for the Army,' Imrie answered, 'but also after that. Twice we helped her to get housing, once in one of our own settlement flats and on the second occasion we managed to find her a local authority house in Niddrie.'

'What happened to those arrangements?'

'They broke down,' the man replied ruefully, looking quickly up at the Sheriff and then back at his interrogator before saying, in a slightly defensive tone, 'most of them do, you know . . . unless you can fix their underlying issues.'

'In Moira Fyfe's case, why did they break down?'

'Because . . . well, with the resettlement flat, after she'd been in it for less than five weeks she sold every stick of furniture in the place, all of which we'd got for her. She used the proceeds to buy alcohol. She was lonely there, without her friends. A few days after she'd sold everything she abandoned the place.'

'Your voice tailed away at the end again, Mr Imrie,' the Sheriff said, in a tone of warning.

'She ABANDONED the place, Ma'am,' he repeated quickly, fidgeting with his tie.

'She had returned to her old habits?' the Sheriff asked, looking momentarily pleased, finally, to have caught his answer.

'Yes.'

'What help exactly, directly or indirectly, do you offer your residents to overcome their problems – drink, drugs or whatever?' the Sheriff inquired, still smiling at the hostel manager.

'We offer a range of assistance,' he replied, swivelling round in the witness box to face her. 'There are detoxification programmes available which we try to facilitate. We can suggest referral to the alcohol problem clinic at the Royal Edinburgh, and we have regular visits from the Community Psychiatric Nurses. Obviously, AA are always available to help with their twelve steps and so on. We do what we can.'

'Are your residents allowed to drink on your premises?' the Sheriff continued, and the manager noticed, for the first time, her pen hovering over her notebook, ready to jot down his reply.

'No. That's a part of the contract that we insist upon,' he replied, speaking with a new self-consciousness, unable to take his eyes off the moving pen, his words suddenly difficult to find. 'They have to agree not to bring any drink, drugs or whatever onto our premises. Their rooms are checked periodically to see that they're sticking to their side of the bargain.'

'And do they?' she asked, not looking up from her notebook.

'No, not always.'

'On you go, Mr Brand,' the Sheriff said, still noting down the witness's answer but waving a hand at the Procurator Fiscal to signal that he could now resume his examination-in-chief.

'For the sake of completeness,' James Brand began, folding his arms beneath his black gown, 'can you tell us what happened to the accommodation that you arranged in Niddrie for Miss Fyfe?'

'Yes. Something that quite often happens in that sort of situation with our service-users. Something that, in many ways, goes to the heart of the problem. We got her moved in, the place redecorated. I helped her with that myself, and we found her furniture again. But in less than two months things started going pear-shaped. It's very difficult for them, you see. They're often isolated or whatever. Sometimes they're near-suicidal, they're so lonely. At a hostel they've had company, whether they like it or not, but in the flat they're on their own again, with their own thoughts. Some of their pals from the hostel turn up and beg to stay for a couple of nights. Before you know it, they've got four or five, or more, of their friends dossing down on the living-room floor. So, there's noise, mess, complaints – you can imagine. Next thing the police are involved . . .'

'So what exactly happened in Moira Fyfe's case?' the Procurator Fiscal said. Standing with his legs wide apart, he had moved squarely in front of the witness as if about to challenge him to a gunfight.

'Just that. Her pals, Taff and the rest, came to visit her and she allowed them to stay. Of course, they'd drink on them and shared it with her, so all the months and months of good work we'd done with her went down the plughole. There were fights, the neighbours complained and the police had to warn her about her behaviour and the disturbance and noise at all hours. The next thing I heard was that she was on her way back from London. Apparently, she'd left her flat, got herself south somehow and been living rough around King's Cross. After her money and her phone had been stolen while she was dossing in a bus shelter she managed to persuade St Martin's to give her a ticket on the next bus back to Edinburgh. From then onwards she was either with us or in one of the Bethany Trust places, Salvation Army, Streetwise or the Cyrenians. She took whatever was on offer. She had to.'

After lunch the Procurator Fiscal attempted to question Linda Gates about the events at the hostel on the night of 13 January. With the end of her nose scarcely visible above the top of the witness box, she stared defiantly at her questioner. She was, as before, prepared to co-operate only to the extent of providing her name, which she uttered in a high, childish voice. When, after repeated denials, she was finally told off by the Sheriff she appeared to relent slightly, adopting a new tactic.

'So, you were present in the TV lounge of the hostel at about 8 p.m. on the Sunday evening?' the Procurator Fiscal asked wearily, repeating yet again the same question.

'Sorry, pal, I cannae mind,' she replied, grinning broadly as if pleased with her new gambit and allowing her eyes to roam freely around the courtroom as if for applause.

'Can you recall if you were in the TV lounge at all that evening?'

Loud, liquid-sounding coughing from the back of the courtroom made her answer inaudible. A group of four people, all seated in the back row of benches, were watching her, and one of their number was bent double, shoulders heaving, as he tried desperately to stifle the hacking coughs with his hands.

'Nah,' she repeated, unasked, once silence had returned.

'Can you recall if you were in the hostel at all that evening?'

'Nah. I've lost my memory, see? Substance abuse can dae that tae ye, ken.'

'Perhaps,' James Brand said crossly, fixing the woman with narrowed eyes, 'I should remind you, as the Sheriff did earlier, that you are on oath.'

The witness, now panicking, looked first at her interrogator and then up at the bench. Seeing the judge's implacable expression, the remains of her smile vanished and she nodded her head as if, finally, she had understood. This was not a game, or, if it was, it was not one she could win. Thinking things over again, she managed to recall that she had, indeed, been in the TV lounge with Moira Fyfe.

'At any time whilst you were both there, did you accuse Moira Fyfe of having stolen money from you?'

'Aye, answer that one, Linda,' a man's hoarse voice rasped from the public benches. His words were followed by a ripple of applause from his companions, and a tall, thin woman with dark, greasy hair stood up and let out a muted whoop. Looking up from her note-taking, startled by the commotion, the Sheriff threw down her pen and bellowed, 'Silence at the back of the court! This witness is trying to give her evidence and I am trying to hear it, so there will be no interruptions, NO interruptions from the public benches.'

In the ensuing stunned silence, the tall woman resumed her seat. The Sheriff returned her attention to the witness. Catching her eye, she said, in a measured tone, 'Could you now answer, please, Miss Gates?' The order was thinly disguised as a question, but this time the witness recognised its imperative quality.

'Aye,' she replied, 'I did. Because she had. I'd left thirty pounds in my room that afternoon and I'd telt her I'd got the money from the social, like. She was skint and begged a couple of pounds off me. I even gave them her. When I went back to my room after tea it had all gone. A couple of hours later Moira comes back all tanked up and she'd bought a whole load of stuff with her. Bacardi in her cardie, voddy in her body. Where did she get the money for all that from, I wonder, eh? From my bloody room! Where else?'

The girl shook her head in disgust, reliving the anger again she had felt on discovering the theft, and looked hard at the line of people seated at the back of the room. None of them said a word. Having, to her own satisfaction, stared them all out, she sniffed, wiped the side of her nose with her hand and turned her hostile gaze once more to the Procurator Fiscal.

'How did Moira Fyfe react to your accusation?' the man said calmly, ignoring her aggressive stare and looking down at his notes instead.

'She went radge. She tried to attack me, but I was too quick for her. I moved to the side and she fell over, never laid a finger on me.'

'When she fell over, did she hit anything before she landed on the floor?'

Tired of having to cajole, pressurise and threaten the witness to get anything useful out of her, the Procurator Fiscal had already resigned himself to a denial, further evasion or another sudden loss of memory. Linda Gates, however, surprised him. Shaking her head again, she giggled, putting up her hand to cover her mouth like a naughty schoolgirl, and said, 'Aye. The daft old bitch split her heid on a wing chair on the way down. Served her right for taking ma wad.'

—

The group at the back of the courtroom took little notice as the Macer led a plump lady towards the witness box. They did not, initially, recognise her. Only when she gave her name in a soft Irish brogue did they exchange glances, sit up, and start to whisper to each other.

Because, for her court appearance, Maureen McKee had transformed herself. Her normally scrubbed face was now heavily made up, lips a dark red, and her distinctive bushy eyebrows had been trimmed and plucked into perfect arches. Abandoning her habitual T-shirt and jeans, she now sported a figure-hugging black polo neck, a tight maroon skirt and black knee-length boots.

In contrast to Linda Gates, she appeared entirely at ease and seemed to view the giving of evidence as some form of theatrical performance. Speaking slowly, she willingly filled in some of the missing details, providing a fuller, more colourful account of the night's events. Only when asked what Moira Fyfe had said before and after the fall did she hesitate for a second. Then, taking a deep breath, she repeated the litany of swear words that Moira

Fyfe had unleashed, enunciating each one as if it came from a lexicon entirely foreign to her.

Getting into her stride, she told the Procurator Fiscal about the journey to the hospital and her charge's truculent manner in the casualty department.

'She kept saying, "I'm fine, I don't need to see nobody." But I was having none of it. It would have been more than my job was worth not to follow the proper procedures . . .'

When James Brand asked her if she knew what treatment Moira Fyfe had received, she appeared to be taken aback by the question. Then, in a mildly offended tone, she told him that she had no idea what treatment she had received, adding acidly that their service-users had a right to privacy just like anyone else.

Aware that his witness was on the verge of losing confidence in him, he asked half-heartedly, 'But given Miss Fyfe's condition, which you've already outlined to us, how could you be sure what she would tell the doctors or nurses? If they were to treat her properly they'd need an accurate account of the accident, wouldn't they?'

As Maureen McKee grasped the full implications of the question, including the sly suggestion that she might have failed in her duty, her indignation rose. Leaning over the edge of the witness box as if to get at her antagonist, she put her hands on her hips and proclaimed: 'If you, Sir, think that it is proper to go behind the curtain with someone then that is your business. But I do not. What goes on behind the curtain is private, private between the doctor and the person. Anyway, if I could tell that she was drunk, then, for pity's sake, so could they, couldn't they?'

'I'll ask the questions, thank you, Ms McKee,' Mr Brand said curtly, shifting his weight uneasily from one foot to the other and then back again as he tried to reassert himself.

'Well, all that I'm saying is true, isn't it?' she replied.

Turning to face the Sheriff, she added plaintively, 'I took her to the doctors, Your Honour, so they could see the condition that she was in. There was nothing to stop any of them asking me about anything, anything at all, if they felt the need to, but none of them did. Were you expecting me to go behind the curtain with Moira, as if she was a child or something? It's against human rights, and besides, Moira would have had something to say about that, let me assure you!'

———

The last hour of the day was devoted to evidence relating to the finding of the deceased's body in the Hermitage. By then the courtroom was hot, the air dry and an occasional snore could be heard from the benches at the back. Everyone was tired. The Macer sat slumped in his seat, staring vacantly into space, and James Brand's voice sounded hoarse. The Sheriff seemed to have shrunk into herself, looking from afar like little more than a wig perched on an empty gown.

The scene was set by Simon McVicar, the first person to find the body, and he, too, presented a very different picture from the traumatised, scantily-clad jogger interviewed by the police on that cold Tuesday morning. In his sharp suit, he was crackling with nervous energy, nodding incessantly as if his head was on a spring, licking his lips and answering questions before Mr Brand had finished asking them. Only when called upon to describe the dead woman's appearance did he show any emotion, faltering for a second and putting his hand to his mouth as if he was gagging and might vomit. As he spoke about the flesh missing around the corpse's mouth and earlobe, an audible gasp came from the back of the court.

'Should I go on?' he asked the Sheriff.

'Yes, of course,' she replied blithely, seemingly baffled by his query, as if he had been talking about a recipe for rice pudding instead of describing chewed human tissue.

After he had left the stand, the Sheriff closed her notebook and hooked the clip of her fountain pen over its cover. 'We'll start again tomorrow. Can you tell me who you intend to lead first, Mr Brand?'

'I can, my Lady,' the Procurator Fiscal replied, looking down at his open blue notebook, then leafing feverishly through its pages before adding, in a relieved tone, 'we'll start with Doctor Alton. It's the only time he can come. He was the one who saw Ms Fyfe at the Accident and Emergency Department.'

'Very good,' the Sheriff replied, and as she adjusted her wig, getting ready to stand up, the Macer suddenly got unsteadily to his feet and boomed out, 'Court rise.'

—

The next morning, the young doctor raised his right hand as he had been requested by the Sheriff to do. Then, sounding like an impatient echo, he repeated the words of the oath after her. Looking down at the medical records from the Royal Infirmary as instructed, he said to the Procurator Fiscal, 'Yes, I've found page 42. I saw Ms Fyfe. I don't remember seeing her, but these are my notes, initialled by me.'

'Can you explain your note to us, please, doctor – explain what it says?' Mr Brand said, looking at the photocopies in his own ring binder.

'Yes,' the doctor began confidently, '"Attendance following a fall in the hostel" . . . that's largely self-explanatory, I suppose. That's the history that she must have given me at the time. "Alcohol plus, plus, plus", that's an observation. "C/O of a head injury" . . .'

'Sorry, sorry,' the Procurator Fiscal said, raising his hand like a policeman, 'if I could just stop you there. We need to unpack this a little. The observation about the alcohol – what was that based on? For example, did she tell you that she had been drinking, or was she obviously drunk or did she simply smell of alcohol, or what?'

'I'm afraid at this distance in time I can't be sure,' the doctor said apologetically, adding, 'I suspect that it means the smell, maybe her manner too. Whatever it was, by noting "plus, plus, plus" it means that I thought she'd drunk to excess. Taken a lot of drink. Probably that she was obviously drunk at the time.'

'Very well,' Mr Brand said, nodding reassuringly, 'would you continue?'

'Right. "C/O" . . . that's "complaining of ", a head injury on the left temple. Again that must have been what she told me, the area she pointed to, in all probability. O/E . . . ah, "on examination", yellowish, external bruising on the right temple. So, apart from anything else, that means I saw nothing on the left temple. "Fairly bright" . . .'

'Sorry, I need to stop you again. You say that you saw no bruising on the left temple but some on the right. What conclusion did you reach about the bruising on the right temple?'

'That it was old. It had nothing to do with her fall.'

'If there had been bruising, or any signs of injury, apparent elsewhere on her head, would you have made a note of that?'

'Yes. Given her state and the history, I would have examined the whole of her head, I expect.'

'You don't know whether you did or not?'

'As I said, I can't remember the patient at all in amongst the thousands I have seen, but that would be my normal practice if I'd been given the history of a fall and a head injury by a person clearly under the influence of alcohol.'

The sound of coughing echoed around the courtroom, and after it had continued for over a minute, building to a crescendo, a bent figure stumbled his way to the end of the bench at the back and scurried towards the exit. Once silence had returned, the Procurator Fiscal, who had been momentarily distracted, turned his attention back to the witness.

'If you could continue?' he said, returning his gaze to the photocopied pages before him and trying to find his place.

'"Feeling bright and alert" – well, I suppose I'd be looking at her demeanour, her state of mind, her memory, checking that she wasn't confused, disorientated, sleepy, vomiting and so on – those sorts of things. In short, checking that there were no signs consistent with a serious head injury, concussion.'

When there was no immediate follow-up question, the young physician looked across at his interrogator expectantly. The lawyer said nothing, his eyes still scanning the page for an elusive entry. After a few seconds, Mr Brand resumed his questioning. 'Very good, very good. Next, you have written "PERLA" – could you tell us what that means?'

'With head injuries, you check the patient's pupils,' Dr Alton replied. 'You look to see if they are equal, react equally to light and accommodation. It's an acronym. You shine a torch into each eye to check both of the pupils' reactions, and then make them focus on a close object to see if each one constricts and constricts equally.'

'Did you X-ray her skull, give her a CT scan or an MRI scan?'

'No.'

'Why on earth not? She might surely have had a hidden injury, a skull fracture or a bleed?' The tone the lawyer adopted was one of mild incredulity but, being a bit of a ham, he overdid it.

'There wasn't time. I don't remember her but I do now remember that night. We were inundated. There'd been a pile-up on the bypass and we were run off our feet. A bus had been involved and it was all hands on deck.'

'When did you first recall this rather important detail – about the crash, I mean?' Mr Brand asked, looking genuinely stunned by the news.

'Last night. I was looking at my diary and I'd recorded it in there.'

'And you're sure that the pile-up was on the same night that you saw Ms Fyfe? You've never mentioned it before.'

'Positive. It'll have been in all the papers. You could check it there.'

'In any event, going back to that particular night, you didn't even assess her on the GCS, did you?'

'Yes, I did!' the doctor said hotly.

'Before you go on,' the Sheriff cut in, shaking her head to make her exasperation with the Procurator plain but addressing her remarks to the witness, 'perhaps you had better tell us what the GCS is, exactly?'

'The GCS is the Glasgow Coma Scale. It's a neurological scale devised to produce an objective way of recording the conscious state of an individual. They're tests – can the patient respond verbally? Do the eyes open responsively? There are scores for each exercise, and the total, in a healthy individual, is 15.'

'Fine. On you go, Mr Brand,' the Sheriff said, pointing at him.

'Doctor Alton, there is no reference to the GCS in the notes, is there?' the Procurator Fiscal said. He looked paler than before, and was scanning his file closely, his eyes darting all over the page as he tried to make sure he hadn't missed anything.

'Not in the copy notes you showed me a month or so ago, no, but in the principal records that I've now got in front of me there is. I can show you. It's in my writing. I've given her a score of 15. That means she was normal, drunk or not drunk.'

The doctor held out the principal records, pointing at the relevant page as if to display the entry to the court.

The Procurator Fiscal looked hard at his photocopied notes and then in an agitated tone asked the Macer to take the principal records from the witness and pass them to him. After an interval of about a minute, during which the remaining colour drained from his cheeks, he found the entry and said slowly, 'Right enough, I see that.'

Once the witness had the records in front of him again, the Procurator Fiscal continued his examination-in-chief, but he sounded less fluent, less confident than before. It was as if he was now feeling his way, aware that the ground beneath his feet was no longer solid.

'What about advice – did you advise her to return if she experienced any of the classic head injury symptoms? There seems to be no reference to that in your notes . . .'

'I'm afraid there is,' the doctor said, looking almost disappointed for the lawyer. 'It just didn't appear in the photocopies. I think someone must have cut it off in some way in your notes. In the principal records it says, "Usual advice, to return tomorrow".'

'You asked her to return the next day?' the Procurator Fiscal said, his tone one of undisguised dismay and amazement. He glanced quickly across at the Sheriff. In return, she flashed him a slightly annoyed, quizzical look and said, 'You'll appreciate, Mr Brand, that none of these entries are in my copies either. It looks as if whoever copied them did not do a very thorough job.'

'I'm sorry, M'lady. I'll ensure that full copies are supplied to you for tomorrow.'

Swallowing hard, the Procurator Fiscal turned his attention back to the witness.

'You were saying, Dr Alton?'

'I did tell her to return. I told you, because of the pile-up the place was in pandemonium, and I wanted to be one hundred per cent sure of the woman. After all, I hadn't been able to have her X-rayed, scanned or whatever, and she was drunk. I couldn't rely on her reading the head injury advice card I gave her.'

'Where do we see that?'

'The notes say "HIAG" . . . see, near the bottom of the page. "Head Injury Advice Given".'

'Go on,' the Procurator Fiscal said.

'That's it, really. The examination at that time showed nothing to suggest any kind of focal or diffuse head injury, but I wanted to be sure. There could have been, for example, a slow bleed, and if so the clinical signs would only appear later. That's why I will have wanted to see her the next day.'

'Would you like to sit down?' the Sheriff asked Professor McConnachie. She had noticed the elderly witness starting to tilt forwards slightly as he gave his evidence, a hand resting on the base of his spine. He had declined her earlier invitation to take a seat, but she risked asking him once more. It was obvious that an hour of non-stop standing had taken its toll on the old pathologist.

'Thank you, M'lady,' he replied, grateful for the Sheriff's keen eye and no longer too proud to accept. Resting his bony buttocks on the chair, he tried not to grimace as another twinge of sciatic pain shot down his left leg.

'To continue. In your view, did the fall that Moira Fyfe suffered on the thirteenth of January 2010 cause the subdural bleed?' Mr Brand asked.

'Yes, I think that was the most likely cause. It appears that when she fell she struck her left temple on the edge of the wing chair, the padded chair, and the left temple was the location of the bleed.'

'The bleed – the collection of blood between the dura mater and the arachnoid mater that you mentioned – could that have been responsible for Ms Fyfe's death?' the Procurator Fiscal continued.

'There was sufficient blood, certainly. However, I can't say for sure, because, as I explained earlier, I have little doubt that Moira Fyfe also suffered from hypothermia. At post mortem I found multiple erosions of the gastric mucosa, Wischnewsky ulcers, plus lipid accumulations in the epithelial cells of the proximal renal tubules in her kidneys, and frostbite lesions.'

'Professor, there is one thing I am having difficulty with,' the Sheriff interrupted. 'If the woman was cold, was suffering from frostbite, then what were her clothes doing all over the place? Why on earth would she take them off? You'd think it would be the last thing she'd do!'

The Professor nodded his head before answering her. 'It's a well-known phenomenon, M'lady, known as "Paradoxical Undressing". In the moderate to severe stages of hypothermia, the victim usually becomes disorientated, confused. Sometimes they become fearful; they can even suffer from hallucinations or become combative. In her case, the alcohol she had already consumed will have, obviously, accelerated the effects of the hypothermia, including the confusion. In such circumstances, the victim discards their own clothing – usually that covering their lower body first, as in this case . . .'

'But why,' the Sheriff asked, brow furrowed in puzzlement, 'if they are feeling the cold, do they undress? Surely they'd be desperate to keep their clothes on?'

'Indeed. It does seem rather contradictory – or paradoxical – doesn't it?' the Professor agreed politely. 'But the probable explanation is that, initially, in order to conserve heat the patient's peripheral blood vessels contract, so as to ensure that his vital organs remain warm, but the muscles contracting the peripheral blood vessels eventually become exhausted. Once that happens they relax, and that leads to a sudden surge of blood, and therefore heat, into the patient's extremities, which fools the person into thinking that they are now overheating. They feel too hot. Consequently, they try to cool themselves, they remove their clothing . . .'

'One other thing, Professor,' the Sheriff said, glancing at the Procurator Fiscal to let him know that she was not hijacking his witness, 'you described, earlier, the scratches, abrasions or whatever you found on the deceased's hands, and, to a lesser extent, on her feet, and the mud under her nails. From the photos we've been shown, it looks as if she'd been scrabbling in the undergrowth, the earth even, as if trying to escape from something or someone. What's your explanation for that?'

Moving surreptitiously on his seat to try and prevent another lightning bolt of sciatic pain, the Professor said, 'It's another recognised, though odd, phenomenon. The Americans call it 'Hide or Die' syndrome. We tend to call it 'Terminal Burrowing'. It seems to be the result of an autonomous process of the brain stem which is triggered in the final stages of hypothermia, and produces a primitive burrowing-like behaviour for protection. Something similar is found in hibernating animals. In deaths from hypothermia indoors, the deceased is sometimes discovered in a small enclosed space, for example, a wardrobe. Outdoors, the victim is often found in a crevice or culvert. Here, it looks as if Moira Fyfe was trying to burrow her way into that thicket of trees. Also, with the hypothermia, she had, or may have had, hallucinations, seen and heard things. Someone chasing her, for example.'

⁓

Her own curiosity finally satisfied, Alice Rice left the courtroom and walked towards the central hall. As she passed an empty witness room, she noticed a man sitting inside, choking, tears in his eyes as he fought between bouts of coughing to take a breath. For a second she caught his eye and glanced at his face. Snaking across his hooked nose was a white scar. As she moved on the realisation slowly dawned upon her that it was a face she had seen before. But she could not remember quite where or when.

'Well, that was a sodding fiasco!' Sean Lyle said. He was the Assistant Fiscal and had, while she had been deep in thought, silently fallen into step beside her. Sweat had made his brow shiny and dark stains were visible under the arms of his light grey jacket.

'I don't disagree,' she replied, sounding unconcerned, still puzzling over the identity of the coughing man.

'You lot should have made proper photocopies! It was just bloody slack, missing bits like that. If they'd been complete there never would have been any inquiry. No public money wasted. Heads will roll for this!' He wagged his finger at her as a teacher might at a small child.

'Yours, I hope,' Alice replied, turning to look him in the face, angered by his crass remarks. Seeing his wagging forefinger, she added, 'You lot should have checked the principal records. None of us even saw them, including the Professor. You decided an inquiry was necessary. Before doing so *you* should have checked them, instead of relying on photocopies of photocopies. Don't try and shift the blame onto us for your own incompetence.'

'I beg your pardon, for what?' he blustered, daring her to repeat her accusation.

'I said FOR YOUR OWN INCOMPETENCE.'

Still incensed, she turned back to take another look at the man in the witness room, but he had slipped out while she was arguing with Lyle. In her mind's eye she saw his face again, but this time the image conjured up was in black and white, as if on film. And she heard him coughing as he had been in court, but this time she saw him somewhere else, bargaining at the counter in a shop, trying to flog the minister's signet ring.

15

Alice pushed the courtroom door open, and as she did so its hinges creaked loudly, producing a sound like the braying of an ass, distracting the Sheriff and making her look up and glare in Alice's direction. Apart from a lone, reedy voice, the room was silent, and the silence became complete when, realising that the Sheriff's attention had moved elsewhere, the witness stopped speaking. Everyone looked towards the door.

'On you go, Doctor Smith,' the Sheriff said testily, returning her attention to the forensic scientist. Noticing that the witness looked like a frightened rabbit, she made an effort to replace her own intimidating expression with a more encouraging one.

Embarrassed by the disturbance she had caused, Alice slid into a seat at the back and, after a moment, began surveying the room. A little further along the row sat the three figures she had noticed earlier. One of them had his chin resting on his chest, a baseball cap pulled low over his eyes, and appeared to be sleeping. The cap, which had once been white, had decorative gold braid along its edges which had begun to fray and unravel. The two women with him were sitting bolt upright, gazing intently at the witness. When their neighbour suddenly snored loudly, one of them elbowed him in the ribs, causing him to start and release an involuntary, childlike whimper.

Fifteen minutes later, and with no other interruptions, the witness's ordeal came to an end.

'Thank you for your help, Doctor Smith. You may go,' the Sheriff said to the relieved scientist. Stepping as gingerly as if she was on ice, the woman got down from the witness box, her high heels clacking on the varnished wood. The Sheriff waited patiently until she had left the court before starting to address the Procurator Fiscal.

'Well, Mr Brand, have you another witness?'

'I have, M'lady. Next is . . .'

His sentence was left hanging as he rifled through a blue notebook searching for his list of witnesses, inwardly cursing himself for not being more methodical. After over a minute's delay and no apparent progress, the Sheriff decided to spare his blushes.

'I think we'll start his, or her, evidence, whoever they may be, after lunch. It's seven minutes to one now, so we'll adjourn and restart proceedings at exactly seven minutes to two. 1.53.'

As the judge disappeared through her private exit, the three figures seated along from Alice began to rouse themselves, murmuring to each other in low voices and shuffling in a line towards the door.

'Could I speak to you for a minute?' said Alice, trying to catch up with the whole trio and halt their progress. The nearest one was the tall woman who had harangued Linda Gates earlier in the proceedings. She turned round, her surprise at being waylaid palpable, and said, 'Me? You want to talk to me?'

'Yes.'

'Why? Who are you?' she asked, looking annoyed.

'I'm from Lothian and Borders Police and I'd like to talk to you – all of you, if possible.' Alice spoke loudly, catching the eyes of the other two as they hesitated at the end of the row, looking back at her. 'I'm trying to find your friend,' she added, 'the one who was coughing, the one who left earlier, half an hour or so ago.'

'She mean Taff?' the man asked, directing his remarks to the woman next to him and ignoring Alice. He sounded puzzled.

'Yeah, Taff. You mean Taff?' the woman demanded. She was walking on the spot, her head going from side to side like a clockwork toy.

'If that's what his name is. The guy with the bad cough.'

'Why do you want to speak to him?' the man asked, twirling one of the loose strands of gold braid on his cap between his fingers.

'It's in relation to an investigation we're carrying out. Do any of you know where he's living at present?'

'Aye,' the marching woman replied, 'I do. He's back oot and aboot. Oan the streets again, like.'

'No, he's no'. He's back in Ferry Road, is he no'?' the man said. As he spoke he pushed up the peak of his cap. He seemed genuinely taken aback by her answer.

'No. He's had enough of all of them. Vinnie's back. Enough said, eh?'

'Do any of you know where I'd find him now?' Alice asked.

'Nae idea,' the tall woman said, turning her back on Alice, 'and I'm needing my lunch. We've not got long for it. And Stew and Frances here'll have nae idea either.'

Alice looked at both of them and was met, as had been predicted, with a blank expression on each of their faces.

'Sorry not to be able to help you, pet,' the man in the baseball cap said, holding the door open for Alice and gesturing with his hand for her to go through before him.

Listening to Alice, and having carefully picked all the cress out of her egg sandwich, DCI Bell was just about to take a bite from it when she found that her appetite had quite disappeared.

'Are you telling me that you never even looked at the principal records?' she asked, putting her half-full teacup on her desk, intending to use her saucer as a plate for the sandwich. The question, although asked in a neutral tone, was filled with menace.

'Yes,' Alice replied, standing her ground, waiting for the storm that she had foreseen would break all around her. On her walk back to the station she had calculated that it would be better to be the breaker of the bad news rather than the one to receive it from her superior. Neither role was, of course, desirable but given her involvement in the Fatal Accident Inquiry, and the fact that it had now collapsed like an unsuccessful soufflé, the DCI's reaction would have to be faced.

As the messenger she would, at least, be in a position to explain or justify things, if things could be explained or justified. And she would have the advantage of preparation. All of her responses would be rehearsed, fully considered, and any rash comments rejected. Whereas the verbal assault about to be unleashed on her would be quite different. It would be instant, explosive and, hopefully, incoherent.

'Why not?' the DCI demanded, colour rising to her face.

'We got the original photocopies through Fyfe's GP practice. I passed them on to the Professor. None of us then had any reason to believe they would be incomplete.

When we needed further copies we simply photocopied them.'

'But you didn't think, at any stage, to check the copies against the originals?'

'No. Why would I have done? It's all very well with the benefit of hindsight to see why now, but at that time I had no reason to believe the copies weren't accurate. The Crown Office must have recovered the principals. They lodged them for the hearing after all. They decided that an FAI was required. Surely, if anyone should have checked them before the hearing, in fact before any decision was made, then they should have been the ones to do so . . .'

To her ears, at least, it sounded suitably plausible. Persuasive even, please God.

'Let me get this straight. You didn't think to check, yourself?' the DCI repeated.

'No,' Alice said. 'I've already said as much, haven't I, Ma'am? Obviously, it would, in the light of what happened, be better to have done so, but I didn't. I never even saw the principals. In contrast, the Crown Office will have had them in their possession and, as I say, if anyone should have checked them then they surely should have done so. They're the decision-makers, not us.'

'Their failure doesn't absolve you. You took your eye off the ball, this time, Alice. This will go further,' replied the DCI, looking past her subordinate and out of the window at Arthur's Seat, almost speaking to herself.

'I know,' Alice responded. 'Sean Lyle said as much. And I quote him – "Heads will roll".'

'That fat little runt!' DCI Bell said dismissively, picturing the tight-suited, roly-poly figure in her mind and adding, as an afterthought, 'his, I hope.'

'That's just what I said, Ma'am!' Alice retorted, delighted, trying not to smile.

'Is it? Well, here's hoping that all our wishes come true,' replied DCI Bell, before adding, in a slightly anxious tone, 'Alice, I know life . . . well, things . . . are more difficult for you just now, what with . . . well, everything that's happened.'

'That had nothing to do with it, honestly.'

'You would tell me – if things are getting on top of you?'

'Yes. I am fine, and "things" had nothing to do with it.'

'OK. OK. Now, from what you've told me, it sounds as if that doctor, Alton, is definitely off the hook. So what's the likely verdict?' The DCI picked up her discarded sandwich, noticing that part of it had gone soggy due to tea spilt in the saucer.

'Probably no fault anywhere. Just a mishap like you thought. An aged drunk falling and hurting herself, dying in the cold. No one will be found responsible now. The Professor gave a long, involved explanation about paradoxical undressing and terminal burrowing, and judging by all the scribbling the Sheriff was doing as she was listening, I reckon she was persuaded by it. After all, all the forensic evidence, or lack of it, pointed in the same direction, didn't it?'

'Do you think that the Reverend McPhee succumbed to the same paradoxical urges?' said DCI Bell.

'Maybe, but it'd be a bit of a coincidence. I don't know . . .' Alice hesitated for a second, thinking. 'Moira Fyfe's clothes were found round about her, near her body, weren't they? All of them. Yet despite all the searches we carried out there were no signs of his anywhere.'

'True,' Elaine Bell mused, breaking her sandwich in two and preparing to take a bite out of the dry bit, 'but somebody could have taken them, after he had removed them himself. Perhaps they checked the pockets for valuables and then threw them into the nearest bins. I know we found nothing in them but they'd been emptied earlier that same morning. Eric confirmed that with the Council yesterday.'

'Somebody could have taken them, granted, but surely they'd go through the pockets there, in the gardens, and leave them there. And, don't forget, Dean Gardens are private, you need a key to get into them.' She paused again to think about it. 'Vandals could get over the railings, I suppose. They've done it before. But would they bother checking out the old man's clothes? I don't think so. They'd be far too busy smoking grass in the Pavilion or burning trees. Only this morning . . .'

'What about the dog?' the DCI interrupted her, finally taking a bite out of her sandwich.

'That's another mystery, if you ask me. If it was in the garden with the man, and that's where he usually walked it, how did it get out?'

'You said "Only this morning . . ."' DCI Bell prompted, her cheeks bulging with the bread she was chewing.

'Yes, this morning, at the FAI, something happened. There were a number of people at the back of the court – they'd been there since the inquiry began and on odd occasions they got quite rowdy. All of them were down-and-outs, I think. One of them, I'm fairly certain, is the man who tried to sell McPhee's signet ring up near Lauriston Place.'

'Have you brought him in, then?' the DCI said excitedly.

'No. He left before I'd managed to place him, but I think I know who he is.'

'Who is he?'

'Taff.'

'Taff who?'

'Just Taff. No-one seems to know his surname. He was a friend of Moira's.'

The phone rang and DCI Bell picked it up. After a short pause, she fixed Alice in the eye and said, 'Yes, Sir. I've heard all about it from Sergeant Rice. A very unfortunate mistake for the Crown Office to have made, I must say. They'll surely have to review their procedures. I understand that Sean Lyle may be involved. Up to his neck.'

Still holding the receiver to her ear, she mouthed to Alice, 'Find Taff', and then, pointedly, returned her attention to the Superintendent.

❧

Ringing round the drop-in centres in the city produced no sightings. From a hurried conversation with the manager of the Bread Street Hostel, and a more leisurely one with the manager at Ferry Road, she learned that Taff occasionally spent the night in Greyfriars churchyard. Alice decided to wait until after dark and then try to find him there. If all else failed she could check out the care shelter for the night at St Cuthbert's Church.

Sitting at her desk, staring blankly at her computer, it gradually occurred to her that she had no real picture of McPhee's character, no feel for him as a living, breathing individual. But he had been found stark-naked, as well as dead. If there was some strange sexual element involved in his death, it would be useful to have some understanding of him and of his foibles. His wife might be aware of any kinkiness, of any exotic predilections; on the other hand she might well be entirely in the dark about them. Even if she knew, she might be reluctant to speak. She could take offence, possibly. He had been a Church of Scotland minister, after all, and she a minister's wife. Both of them, superficially at least, were pillars of respectability.

However, an old and trusted male friend might prove more forthcoming. Hurriedly collecting her coat from the back of her chair, she rose, determined to go and speak to Timothy Dawson, Duncan McPhee's old pal, in the remaining hours of daylight.

With little traffic on the road, the drive from St Leonard's to the man's address on the edge of the city took less than twenty minutes. Every traffic light, even the final, unending series at Barnton, turned to green at her approach as if to speed her passage towards him. Shortly before the Cramond Brig turn-off, the wind rose, rippling through the trees on the edge of the gorge and tearing off any remaining leaves, sending them spiralling high in the air like motes of dust in sunlight.

On Dawson's Crescent, parking was easy. The force of the gale had ripped a branch off a nearby fir. Jinking onto the road to avoid it, she ran towards his house. 'The Larches', like the rest of the houses in the street, was a white-harled bungalow, topped with red tiles and enclosed within a high holly hedge.

Dressed in dark-brown corduroys and a green turtle-necked jersey with frayed sleeves, the man himself showed her into his small hallway. It smelt strongly of burnt toast. As he led the way he apologised profusely for the mess everywhere. Oily car parts rested against the chipped skirting boards in the hallway, and old newspapers occupied the three hard chairs in his study. Moving one pile onto the floor to free a seat for her, he said, in a deep, patrician voice, 'Take a pew, officer.'

He was a tall man, well over six foot, but it was not his height that caught Alice's eye. It was his perfect hairlessness. Neither eyebrows nor eyelashes shadowed his bright eyes, and all available light seemed to be reflected off his glistening, bald pate. As he bent over to clear more papers so he could sit opposite her on a stool, she noticed that he was wearing odd socks, one black and one green. Once he was seated, a sinuous Siamese cat appeared from nowhere and leapt onto his lap, arching its back and rubbing itself against him. His large hands stroked it and he beamed at her as she began to purr. Alice noticed, looking at the pair of them together, that their eyes were an identical shade of blue.

'Despite what you said on the phone, I'm not sure I'm the right person to help you,' the man said, looking anxiously at Alice and pulling the cat closer as if it was a shield.

'But you're a friend of Duncan McPhee, the Reverend McPhee?'

'I was. A very close friend.'

'Then can you tell me a little about him? What sort of a man he was?'

'You don't know, do you?' Dawson said, sighing deeply and shifting uneasily on his seat, but keeping the cat cradled on his lap.

'Don't know what?'

'Anything. Anything important, at least. Juliet didn't tell you, did she?'

'Tell me what exactly?'

'I'll tell you and then you can decide whether you still want to hear from me about Duncan, OK?' The man's naked brow was furrowed, two neat perpendicular grooves forming at his nose where the ends of his eyebrows should have been.

'OK.'

'He and I go back a long way. We first came across each other in our early twenties when we were both reading theology at Glasgow University. We come from very different backgrounds. I went to Harrow, you see. But we found we got on. I don't know exactly why we did . . . but we just did. You know how it is?'

Alice said nothing but nodded.

'We both married at about the same time. Had our children at about the same time, too. Flora and Imogen are the best of pals to this day. But, gradually, as the years passed our careers diverged. You see, as a minister I was content, happy even, simply attending to my parish work, but he had set his sights on other things.'

'Other things?'

'"Higher" things, "better" things, he would have thought, if not actually said. He wanted to advance up the hierarchy of the Church, whereas I was quite happy with my parish, with my lot.' He hesitated again, his fingers caressing the cat's fur and making it close its eyes in ecstasy.

'So, what happened?'

Alice shivered in the unheated, spartan room, desperately prodding him to answer the questions so that the interview would come to an end as soon as possible. The window was wide open, letting in a howling draught, but he seemed oblivious to the cold, to any discomfort.

'So, he became increasingly involved in committee work, getting to know the right people, people in high places.' He stopped speaking, his expression mournful.

'Do you really want me to go on? Is this really the sort of thing you want to know?'

'Yes. Why did you fall out – because your careers diverged?'

'No,' he replied, fixing her with his round, candid, cornflower-blue eyes, 'that wasn't it, dear. It was much more basic, much simpler than that. That's just the backdrop, the background to everything.'

He hesitated briefly, looking at her as if trying to catch a glimpse of her soul, took an audible breath and then began to speak more quickly.

'What happened was that I had an affair with a parishioner of mine. That was the real catalyst for everything. It did not last – as, perhaps, you can divine . . .' He allowed his eyes to rove around the room, stopping briefly on a long-dead pot plant and the stained carpet, witnesses to the lack of a female touch in his life.

'There was a complaint, it was upheld and I was suspended from my parish for three years. I appealed it, and at the hearing at the General Assembly – that was how it used to be done – I expected Duncan, if nobody else, to support me. He knew me, after all. He knew it was a temporary, uncharacteristic lapse, a silly, trivial . . . infatuation. But he chose not to do so because, and I hesitate to say this about anyone, I think he put his career before me, before our friendship. Fortunately, enough of my brethren took a different, more compassionate view, and after debate my sentence was reduced from three years to one year. And, for a bit, a short while, I managed to keep my parish.'

'So you no longer consider the Reverend McPhee as your friend?'

'Correct. He dropped me like a stone,' the man replied, looking fixedly down at the cat on his knee.

'Are you his enemy, then?'

'Oh, no,' he said, lifting his head up quickly with a shocked expression on his face, 'not that. What a black-and-white view of life you must have! Of course not. I'm not his friend, but I'm not his enemy either. However, I lost my wife, my faith . . . and my hair . . . and he had a part to play in all of that.'

'I'm sorry.'

'Despite my alopecia, Fu Manchu didn't desert me,' he said, playing with the cat's chocolate-coloured ears.

'What sort of man was Duncan McPhee?' she asked.

'In a way I think I've given you a clue already, haven't I? A man who put his own preferment above everything else. Ruthless, in his way. A man who has climbed and climbed – I expect I helped him on his way in the early days – but not for the view from the top. He climbed as if driven by some strange fear, some strange compulsion to escape from the "bottom", as he would have described it. I should feel sorry for him . . . but I don't any longer.'

'Was he a happily married man?'

'To the best of my knowledge. Why?'

Alice hesitated, reluctant to reveal too much. But something would have to be said to nudge him in the right direction.

'When his body was found in Dean Gardens, he was completely naked.'

'Gracious! What are you suggesting?'

'Nothing. I'm simply reporting a fact. I'm just trying to find out anything I can about the man.'

'I know nothing whatsoever about that side of his life. He wasn't some sort of Tom Jones type, a "swinger" or anything like that. In fact, he was rather prudish as a young man.'

'Can you think of anyone who'd wish him ill?'

'Mild ill, slight ill? Too many to count. You don't climb as high as he's done without alienating people along the way. By blocking someone's preferment, "stealing" a position someone has earmarked for himself or herself, slighting people by picking them up and putting them down to suit yourself and your needs. It happens in every area of life, doesn't it? And the Church is no different from the rest in that respect.'

'But no one in particular springs to mind?'

'I can think of no one who wanted him dead, if that's what you are hinting at. There are a fair few, I suspect, who would have gloried in his fall. I hope I wouldn't be amongst them, but that's a different thing, isn't it? Many might have paid to see him humbled – but not injured, let alone killed.'

———

Crossing from the end of Chambers Street, Alice saw the heavy iron gates of Greyfriars Churchyard before her. Little illumination from the streetlights penetrated the gateway. As she glanced up, the moon's light seemed to be fading before her eyes. An endless stream of clouds scudded across its face, driven by the same wind that was now lashing her cheeks and trying to pull her coat off her back. Unsure which path to take, she started off to the left to avoid having to head into the icy gusts.

By the light of her torch, she peered into a succession of low-walled grave enclosures. Those with roofs had padlocked gratings to prevent the living from camping inside them, but the few which remained open to the heavens were ungated and provided shelter of a sort. There was a terrace of them, stretching into the distance southwards like a street constructed for a race of midgets or children.

As she approached one particularly ornate memorial, something moved inside its four walls. The thing rustled a few dead leaves before squeezing through the railings and scampering over her feet. Involuntarily, she gasped, frantically dancing from one foot the other to shake it off.

Shuddering with revulsion, she scanned the walls of the mausoleum with her torch, revealing the relief of a skull with a fat cherub lounging below on a pile of fleshless bones. As she shone the torch downwards, a hunchbacked rat on a recumbent effigy came into view, its eyes reflecting the light back to her. For a moment they stared at one another, the rat immobilised in the beam.

'Boo!' a loud voice said behind her. She whirled round, suddenly terrified, finding herself inches away from an unshaven face peering out of a hoodie. In the obscurity he appeared ghostly, like a medieval monk in a cowl. As if aware of the impression he was making, he raised his hands and released a long, low howl.

Brandishing her torch as a weapon, she raised it above her head ready to strike. Immediately, he stopped and backed away.

'OK – OK, calm doon. It wis just a joke! Nae harm meant!'

'Well, it wasn't bloody funny,' she replied, aware that her whole body was now trembling. Slowly lowering the torch she kept its beam shining in the man's eyes, until he said plaintively, 'Could ye no' move it just a wee bit, hen. You're blindin' me.'

Trying to sound calm and in control, she said, 'Police. I'm looking for Taff. Is he here tonight?' Her voice sounded unnaturally high, like a choirboy's treble.

'I dae ken. But if he is, he'll be under yon scaffolding – through the Flodden Wall. Everyin's there. Sleepin' below the wooden boards.' He pointed in a vaguely downhill direction, then, looking her in the eyes and smiling winningly, he added, 'Can you spare some change, hen? It's awfy chilly, an' I'm needin' a cup o' tea.'

Alice handed him a pound coin. As he palmed it he said, as if he had had a change of mind, 'Tell ye whit, dearie. I'll save ye the bother. It's a wild night. Taff's no there, right? I seen him earlier and he was complaining aboot the cauld. He's chicken-hearted. He's away fer the free grub at the night shelter.'

'Sure about that?'

'Scout's honour. Would I lie tae you?'

Distrusting his reliability, she checked out the scaffolding and found a couple of homeless men bedded down underneath it, both cocooned in blankets and polythene sheeting. The ends of the polythene flapped noisily in the gale, adding to the sounds made by the creaking metal and producing a constant cacophony which was loud enough to wake the dead. One of the men was lying on a mattress of planks and the other was huddled close to the boundary wall, a lining of old newspaper insulating him from the cold, wet stone.

Shining her torch on their faces, apologising as she did so, she examined them. Neither of them was Taff. One, his hand protecting his eyes from the glare, let out a stream of foreign-sounding invective at her but his companion told him off, calling her 'Petal' and apologising to her in a melodic Geordie accent.

Hurrying back towards the gate with her torch in her hand, now desperate to leave the dark, windswept place, she wove in and out of the tombstones, trying to avoid any that had fallen. Through the moans of the wind, she heard the ringtone of her phone. Putting it to her ear, she heard a breathless, male voice.

'Is that you?' The inquiry sounded urgent.

'I don't know. Who do you want to speak to?' She racked her brain, trying desperately to put a name or face to the voice, but nothing came.

'You, Alice.'

'Who are you?'

'Are you scared?'

'No, I'm not,' she lied instinctively, a shiver passing through her body as she pleaded again for an answer, 'but who are you?'

She looked round, trying to catch a glimpse of him, overwhelmed by the conviction that he was close by and could see her as he spoke. Her fear made her nauseous.

'You should be. You really should be. I'm waiting for you.'

'Who are you?'

Then she heard a click and the line went dead.

16

Slamming the car door shut she sat motionless, feeling safe at last. She held her head in her hands and tried to force her brain to make sense of everything. As before, the caller had withheld his number. One fact could be denied no longer. Someone, in a twisted and unpredicta-ble fashion, was pursuing her, intent on terrorising her. In isolation each incident could, almost, be explained away, but together they formed a sinister pattern: the music played down the phone, the brick through the studio window, the chilling calls and the person following her. Put them together and the threat felt real enough. It was real enough, only a fool would pretend otherwise. This was no prank, no silly joke to be shrugged off. Someone was stalking her, playing with her, intent on terrifying her or making her lose her mind.

Dropping her head, she felt overwhelmed, impotent in the face of such a nameless, shapeless force. And as she cast around for a way of escape, a voice in her head reminded her that there was no one to turn to for help. She was alone. Ian was gone, beyond all her pleas for assistance. Her parents had been frightened from the first day she joined the police, convinced she would be beaten up or murdered in the course of duty. She inhabited a world entirely alien to them, one sometimes violent and sordid, and they were too old, innocent and powerless to provide comfort, never mind any kind of defence. Simply confiding in them would make the remaining hair on their heads stand on end. Everything about her current predicament was so far outside the scope of any of her friends' experience, it would probably sound like self-dramatising nonsense or a cry for help. They had their own lives to live.

No one at work must know, of that she was certain. A few of the episodes could be explained away as wrong numbers, the acts of vandals or, possibly, and far worse, as signs of neurosis. Had she really heard her own name, or dreamt it? Word might spread in the station that she was 'fragile' following her lover's death, and before she knew it she would be steered gently towards the occupational health people, with a diagnosis of 'stress'. A big, black mark would ruin her career.

She was teetering on the edge. And that bloody fiscal, Sean Lloyd, had almost made her fall off. Only his shocked face when she shouted the word 'Incompetence' at him had stopped her from really letting rip. Because he had somehow released a surge of anger from somewhere deep and hidden within her, such that she herself had been taken aback by its ferocity. But worse than that, his complaint had contained an inescapable truth; she had forgotten to check those bloody photocopies. Something she had never failed to do before.

Maybe she was losing her grip. How could she not, when half her mind was occupied, day after day, with Ian.

But, if forced to take leave, without the daily grind of work, all her thoughts would return unbidden to dwell obsessively and exclusively on that one dismal, unchangeable fact. That Ian was dead, and she would never see him again. Never touch, or be touched by, him again. And now this.

She closed her eyes and breathed in deeply, trying to quieten her pounding heart and to think straight. Who the hell could it be? There had been so many people she had arrested, imprisoned, whose lives she had derailed. Police work did not lead to popularity among those who committed crimes. If she was looking for someone who wished her ill, she was spoilt for choice.

She must keep calm. She looked out onto the steps of the museum and watched idly as a sheet of newspaper was tumbled along by the wind. Seeing it tossed to and fro, it dawned on her that her search for a solution was going nowhere. It was like trying to catch a ghost in a net, or smoke in a sieve. All that she could do was to try to be extra alert, and hope that at some stage the person or persons who were menacing her would overplay their hand and make themselves, in some way, visible. That they would emerge into the light.

Apart from the small cuts on her face, she had come to no harm so far. She would not let fear paralyse her. She would use it as a spur to keep going. Telling herself out loud to get a grip, she turned the key in the ignition.

———

The twin baroque towers flanking the domed apse of St Cuthbert's were both brightly lit. Beyond lay a sea of darkness stretching towards Princes Street, and the church itself seemed like a beacon in the night.

One of the red double doors on the east side was propped open and a band of smokers clustered round it. A young woman with piercings in her nose, forehead and lower lip was dodging hither and thither between them, laughing loudly, playing tig with another teenage girl. The smell of food mixed with the cigarette smoke got stronger as Alice moved from the grand outer hall, with its symmetrical stone staircases, to the inner hall beyond.

As she walked by a trestle table covered in empty serving dishes, an elderly woman bearing a large flask asked whether she would like tea or coffee.

'Neither, thanks. I'm looking for someone called Taff.'

'I don't know anyone called Taff. Is he Polish? If so you'd best ask Stephen,' she replied, pointing towards a large man who was sitting at one of the tables set up on the right side of the hall. The room had been arranged to look like a café. He was talking excitedly to a small audience of bystanders, waving a heavily-tattooed arm in the air.

'No, he's not Polish.'

'Then probably best to ask around or try one of the Bethany people. I'm from St Cuth's so I don't know the men, I'm afraid. We're just providing the venue for the night.'

Walking between the bed mats, Alice saw a smartly-dressed man folding up a couple of blankets and directing someone else to the mat closest to him. Approaching him, Alice said, 'I'm looking for Taff.'

The man turned to face her and then let fly an unintelligible rant, gesticulating excitedly and ending his tirade by throwing his blankets on the matting.

'He's Polish, and he doesn't like this place. He wants to go home,' a voice from the floor said. It was an elderly man, his balaclava-encased head peeping out from the top of his sleeping bag. 'Aren't you, Karol? Polski, eh? You're a Polski, aren't you?'

Karol, who seemed familiar with his neighbour, nodded vigorously. Then, almost barging Alice out of the way, he began to make up his bed on the mat.

Kneeling down beside the old man who had spoken, taking care to avoid his bottle of water, Alice asked him, 'Is Taff here?'

'I've no idea, dear. Best ask Janice, she's in charge tonight. She went out earlier. There was a wee bit of bother, someone brought some smack in. Nothin' she couldn't deal with, she's a big lady, luckily. But she should be back by now. She'll likely be checking on the bedding.'

'Turn out they fuckin' lights!' someone shouted. 'I'm trying to get some sleep here!'

As if in response to his words, the dormitory was plunged in darkness, the only remaining light coming through the doorways leading to the outer hall. Immediately the atmosphere in the place became calmer as people snuggled down in their sleeping bags, making themselves comfortable and settling down for the night.

Standing by the light switch was a vast woman, her hair tied back into a couple of bunches like a little girl in a nursery. She was casting her eye over the sleepers, her mouth moving silently as she counted them.

'Janice?' Alice asked.

'Forty-one, forty-two . . . Aye. Do you need something, pet?' Her eyes remained on the figures on the floor, her lips still moving as she continued the count.

'I'm from the police. I need to speak to someone called Taff, if he's here.'

'He's here. I served him his dinner myself. Three times and that was without a sweet. See those chairs stacked in the far corner? He's the one at the end over there.'

Trying not to disturb the sleepers, Alice made her way towards him. He had a torch in his hand and was reading a book. Some of the light was reflected back onto his pale face, and she could make out one of the features she remembered from the CCTV footage, the large hooked nose with the scar running diagonally across it.

'Excuse me, are you Taff?' she whispered, conscious that most of the noise in the place had died down.

'Maybe. I might be or I might not b –' The last part of his reply was lost as he doubled up, coughing uncontrollably, spluttering, unable to breathe.

'Want another sweetie for your cough, Taff?' a female voice in the darkness piped up.

'No thanks, Effie.'

A crooked smile spread across Taff's pale face as, now panting slightly, his coughing having subsided, he looked up at Alice.

'So, love, what are you wanting?' he asked, inhaling deeply as if it might be his last breath. He looked tired and had rings as dark as bruises below his bloodshot eyes. Every so often, a crackling, wheezy sound accompanied the movement of his chest.

'You're a hard man to find!'

'You think so?'

'I do. I'm from the police. I've been trying to track you down for weeks. You were a friend of Moira Fyfe. I saw you at the FAI. You were her best pal . . .'

'And? She's dead and buried now. History, apparently.'

'But you knew her. How come you know the Reverend McPhee?'

'Who?'

'The Reverend Duncan James McPhee.'

'I don't know any McPhees, dear. You must be thinking of someone else.'

'You had his signet ring. You recently tried to dispose of it at the Cash 4 U near Lauriston Place. If you didn't know him, can you tell me how you came by it?'

'No problem, pal. I didn't know who it belonged to. A friend of mine gave it me. Alex. He gave it me. Well, strictly speaking it was more of a swap really. I had something he wanted rather badly and he had the ring.'

'Alex?'

'Alex . . . Higgins. Well, that's what he calls himself. Alex must have known the McPhee man, I suppose.'

'Where,' she began, now feeling tired, her limbs suddenly heavy and stiff at the thought of this seemingly never-ending trail, 'where exactly would I find Alex Higgins?'

'You'll find him at the Ferry Road Hostel, at least that's where he lives just now. He's happy there, been there for months and months. That's where I came across him. They were hoping to get a house for him but nothing's come up yet.'

'Did he give you anything else?'

'Since you ask, love, that's all I got from him. Why d'you ask?'

'Sure about that?'

'Aye. I'm sure about that. I said why d'you ask?'

'Can you give me your full name?'

'Do I have to?'

'What do you think?'

'Edward Alexander Welsh.'

'Taff?' It was the same voice which had offered him a sweet earlier.

'Aye?'

'Shut the fuck up, pal, will you?'

◆

'Alice?'

To her relief, the unfamiliar voice at the other end of

the receiver sounded female, light and musical, quite unlike that of her anonymous caller.

'Yes.'

'Hi, it's me. Celia.'

Celia Bloody Naismith. Other than the stalker, no caller could be less welcome.

'Celia. Hello,' she said, aware as she spoke that her tone sounded both guarded and leaden. With luck, this would be attributed to grief.

'How *are* you?' Sincere Concern, as enunciated by a failed am-dram enthusiast, dripped down the line, and when Alice failed to respond at once the question was repeated with a new note, one of anxiety. Somehow the woman's attentions would have to be fended off.

'Fine, thank you. How are you?'

The response was immediate.

'Don't do this to me, Alice, please. Not to me. Really, how *are* you?'

All the worse for hearing from you, Alice thought, but she managed to prevent herself from saying so, replying instead, 'I'm fine, thank you, Celia.'

'Of course!' Celia shot back as if she had just had a revelation, and could not contain herself. After a suitably dramatic pause, she elucidated: 'You're in that blasted office of yours, aren't you? So you won't be able to speak to me. Freely, I mean. How silly of me! How could you talk there? There of all places. Forgive me, Alice, for my stupidity. But we'll speak properly sometime soon. I'll make sure of it. You must come over to my house or something. I don't think you've ever been here, have you?'

'No.'

'We'll soon put that right. Now, I'll tell you why I'm giving you a bell, apart from just to see how you're coping,

239

and I hope you'll understand . . .' Her voice tailed off, rising in pitch for dramatic effect.

'Try me, Celia.'

'What I would like, what I want, and I do hope you don't mind me asking, is to have one of Ian's works. I really don't like asking you. I didn't mention it before, you know, when we spoke about . . . things. I've been putting it off and putting it off . . . but you're the gatekeeper to his oeuvre now, so to speak, aren't you? I'm certain, quite certain, that Ian would want me to have something of his because . . . because . . . well, we were, purely artistically, of course, soulmates. Naturally, you shared a certain amount with him, I know that, but on the creative side . . . well, that was where we bonded. He and I, I mean.'

'You'd like one of his paintings?'

'Not necessarily in that medium, Alice, because he did other things too, didn't he? It could be a drawing, an etching, a lithograph, a collage. He used so many different techniques in his art. But, yes, I would like something created by him.'

'Have you anything in mind?' Alice asked, managing to keep her tone colourless. It took effort, because with every word the woman said, she could feel the embers of her antipathy being fanned. If this conversation continued much longer, they would spring to life and produce a fierce blaze.

'Sort of. What I'd like to do – what would be the sensible thing in this situation to do – would be to go to his studio and look through his stuff? Then I could put aside one or two pieces. He gave me one before as well and I could pick that up at the same time, couldn't I? I don't know if he told you about it. They would be just for me, you understand, Alice, not to sell or anything like that. They would be, purely, mementos of him. And it's so important that his stuff is kept safe, and appreciated. It would help me to remember him at his best, happy in his studio, instead of . . . well, at the end. You know, broken, after that final, horrible row . . .'

'I'm sorry, Celia, but what are you talking about?'

'Oh, you know. The big row and everything.'

'You had a row with him? You didn't tell me that before.' Alice was startled, though not displeased, by the news.

'No, of course not. Don't be silly. Not him and me. The row you and he had.'

'What do you know about that?' Alice said sharply, the words escaping her lips before her brain had a chance to censor them.

'Well . . .' the woman hesitated, as if savouring the moment, 'as you may know, he did tend to confide in me. As I said, we were soulmates after all. But, truly, Alice you had no cause . . .'

'No cause?'

'To be jealous. Of me, of my relationship with him. It was completely different from yours with him, obviously. I met him on a spiritual, cerebral level, as you might say. Not on a more elevated plane, I'd never claim that, but on a . . . different plane. On the night he died he was – and I don't really need to tell you, do I? He was *so* upset. I've rarely seen a man drown his sorrows like that. I told you that, didn't I?'

'No, you didn't, you didn't tell me that. You said he was getting argumentative, that was all.'

'Well . . . perhaps I underplayed it a bit because – well, you were so raw. Actually, it was as if he wanted to blot everything out, but I was . . . how can I put this . . .

a confidante, a rock in his time of trouble. I calmed him down. That's what friends, real friends, are for, I always think.'

Alice closed her eyes, feeling that she would not be able to take much more of this conversation. Resolved to terminate it as quickly as possible, she said, 'You'd like to meet at the studio? Did you have a particular day in mind?'

'As a wage slave, with your police work and everything, it would have to be in the evening for you, wouldn't it?'

'That would probably be easier, yes.'

'Well . . .' Celia thought out loud, 'let me see. I'm going to Benjamin Ross's opening at The Gallery tomorrow, and the next day I'm supposed to see that splendid mime artiste that everyone's been talking about. She got rave reviews. How about the next night? Friday? Shall we say Friday? What about seven, unless you have a late "shift" or whatever it's called. You don't work nine to five, do you? How about 7 p.m. at his studio?'

'Fine,' Alice replied, prepared to agree to almost anything simply to get the woman off the phone.

Listening to her, the revulsion she felt was almost visceral, and a picture flashed into her mind of some kind of scaly, venomous reptile lumbering from side to side on heavy legs in pursuit of her. A creature with hooded eyes and a ribbon of a tongue that flickered in the air, probing, as it tried to pick up the scent of its prey.

Putting down the receiver, relieved to break off the connection, she quickly switched on her computer. She was hoping to see something which would distract her, put all thoughts of Ian, 'broken' by their row, out of her mind.

But it was no use. The damage had been done, and as her eyes scanned the text of the witness statement, they took nothing in. Her attention had been wrested away, her brain busily going over old and unproductive ground as if it was fresh and fertile. Part of her seemed to have learnt nothing from the useless hours spent churning over the same old stuff, was oblivious to the futility of it all. That endless sapping round was beginning again.

Had she, in all her foolish jealousy, brought about Ian's death? The path of logic leading to such a conclusion was well worn. Her dislike of Celia had led to a row. If they had not had that row then he would not have drunk so much. Had he not drunk so much he would not have stepped out in front of the car. QED.

Had it not been for her and her stupid, small-minded dislike of Celia, he would still have been alive. It was inescapable, but also too painful to bear. And now she knew that he had spoken to Celia about their row, confided in her, confided in that bloody reptile.

Alice stood up, determined to do something, anything, any activity which would disrupt this agonising train of thought. Work would keep her sane. Alex Higgins must be found. She would go now, this very minute.

Walking out of the door, she almost collided with DC Cairns who was dawdling in the doorway, glancing at her newspaper while eating a sugar-covered doughnut.

'So, does our friend Taff have a record?'

'No. I checked him out last night. The shelter are going to let me know when he leaves, and where he's going.'

'What about Higgins? Has he a record?'

'I need his real name.'

'Are you off to see him now?'

'Higgins, you mean?'

'Yes. If so, I'm to come with you. The DCI phoned when I was on my way up the stairs. Where does he live?'

'According to Taff, in the hostel on Ferry Road.'
'"The Lifehouse", you mean.'

———

For over ten minutes they waited in the secretary's office, the dreary hum and click of the photocopier breaking the silence which reigned in the stuffy room. Occasionally, a phone would ring but, from an eavesdropper's perspective, such calls were dull listening; one concerned a consignment of bed-linen and the other was answered by a single, offended 'No!'

After reading everything on the noticeboard, DC Cairns passed the remaining time staring out of the window. There was an extensive gravel-covered turning area and a grove of trees screening the building from the traffic on the road, the only excitement being the emergence from the undergrowth of a couple of illicit smokers. Concluding that the place must be worth millions, she turned her attention back to its interior, noting again the elegant plasterwork on the ceiling and the wooden panelling on its walls. Without its clutter of filing cabinets, desks and computer screens, the room could hold its own against many put on show by the National Trust.

As she was examining the large marble fireplace, its hearth filled with boxes of paper, an unexpected scent tickled her nose.

'What do you think they're having for lunch?' she whispered to her companion.

'Mmm.' Alice sniffed the air. 'I don't know. Maybe French onion soup or, if it's a good day, steak and onions?'

'Lucky buggers! I think I'll declare myself homeless and come and live here.'

Alice, preoccupied, mulling over Celia's words again, did not reply.

'Think about it, Sarge. In lots of ways it would be a good life. No bills or hassle of that kind. Three meals a day, all cooked for you. A lovely Victorian house like this to stay in. No horrible flat in Portobello with a cracked basin. And nothing to do here all day except play ping-pong or snooker or, if you're bored, watch the TV.'

'No alcohol, though, Liz? Do you think you could manage without that?' Alice asked.

Before her companion had time to answer, the manager strode in. Tucked under one arm was a thick, brown file and in her right hand she held a long-spouted watering can. The woman had the air of a small sergeant-major, commanding obedience from her troops wherever she went.

'You take that, Nettie. Snow White's needing a drink,' she ordered the nearest secretary, holding out the can and gesturing at a white cyclamen plant on her desk.

'I'll give Red Riding Hood a wee pickle after that,' the typist replied. She left her keyboard and pulled a dead leaf off the poinsettia by her computer.

'DS Rice? I understand you'd like to speak to me,' the manager said, looking up at the police sergeant.

'We'd like to talk to one of your service-users, Alex Higgins,' Alice said, automatically stepping forward slightly as if on parade.

'Alex Higgins?' The woman sounded alarmed.

'Yes.'

'I don't know who you spoke to on the phone, but I'm surprised they didn't tell you. I'm afraid you can't speak to him. He's no longer with us.' She looked accusingly at her colleagues. Nettie appeared to be busy watering the pot-plant and the other woman was feeding paper into the printer. Neither of them glanced up to catch their boss's eye.

'Not here! Where the hell has he gone?' DC Cairns exclaimed.

'He hasn't gone anywhere, dear. Well, nowhere you'll be able to visit. He's dead, I'm sorry to say. He'd been inhaling lighter gas up near the old Royal Infirmary, and under the influence, as you might put it, he wandered into the middle of the road. He was hit by a council lorry. It was fairly instantaneous, thank the Lord.'

'Christ!' DC Cairns said, instantly provoking hostile glances from the staff plus a single shocked intake of breath from the manager.

'When did it happen?' Alice asked, conscious as she spoke that the temperature in the room had gone down several degrees. The mild distrust that the caring professions felt for the police had now bubbled to the surface.

'Two days ago.'

'Was Taff still living here then?'

'On the day Alex died? Yes. He left the next evening, after another of our service-users, Vinnie, had joined us. They don't get on, you see. There's a long history between them, and they fight like cat and dog. We tried to persuade Taff to stay, but he was having none of it, so he packed up his stuff and went.'

'What was Alex Higgins's real name?'

'Alex Higgins *was* his real name.'

The two policewomen followed the manager as she huffed and puffed her way up to the second floor and into the room that the man had occupied. Although it had been tidied up, it still contained his possessions, but now it had an unoccupied air, like student accommodation before term has begun. A cleaner was busy inside, hoovering the blue carpet.

'It's a good size,' DC Cairns said admiringly, gliding over to the window and looking out. 'Nice outlook over the garden, too.'

She caught sight of a small pile of clothes and a pair of trainers on a nearby table. Beside them was what appeared to be a bundle of dark-red feathers. DC Cairns picked it up and asked the manager, in a puzzled tone, 'What's this? A wee feather-duster or something?'

'What d'you say?' the manager replied, unable to make out a word above the racket made by the vacuum cleaner.

'I said . . . is this a fairy feather-duster or something?'

'No, dear,' the woman answered, no longer concealing her distate for the visitors, 'it's not. It's a red hackle, if you must know.'

'What's a hackle?'

'The feathers that the Black Watch boys wear in their bonnets. Alex was one of them, a corporal, up until two years ago. He'd been in Helmand and places like that. Came back as damaged goods. You know, PTSD and everything. So, no, it's not a fairy feather-duster.'

—

'That sodding man!' Alice said angrily, once they were back in the squad car.

'How do you mean? I don't suppose he wanted to die. Certainly not by being hit by a council lorry,' DC Cairns said, pulling the passenger door shut.

'Not Alex Higgins. Taff.'

'Why are you angry with him?'

'Because when he told me where to find Higgins, he knew the man was already dead. But he didn't mention it. We'd be more likely to find Higgins in the fridge in the mortuary than in that hostel.'

'Well, that's where I'm to go next, the mortuary,' DC Cairns said, unconcernedly. 'So if you could just drop me either there or at the station I'd be most grateful, Sarge.'

'What's on?'

'Duncan McPhee's post mortem, and I'm looking forward to it. Are you going to go and see Taff now?'

'I certainly am. All roads nowadays seem to lead straight back to him. Let me know how you get on.'

17

Taff, when Alice caught up with him, was eating his lunch in the Grassmarket Project on the corner of Candlemaker Row. The dining-room was full, almost exclusively of men, and the sound of their muted chatter was like the low rumble of thunder. She walked up and down between the tables looking for him, dodging the diners as they pulled out their chairs. A few of them looked up as she passed by, but most continued eating, eyes fixed on their plates like hungry dogs. Spotting Taff, she sat down opposite him, meeting his eye just as he raised his final spoonful of jam roly-poly and custard to his lips.

'Sergeant Rice?' he said, putting down his spoon and looking at her expectantly.

'Taff – you sent me on a fool's errand.'

'How d'you mean?'

'When we spoke last time, you knew perfectly well that Alex Higgins was already dead.'

'So?'

'You told me I'd find him at the hostel on Ferry Road.'

'No, I told you that was where he lived. And that is where he lived. The rest is up to you.'

As they looked at each other in silence, the sounds he made as he struggled for breath became audible and she noticed the exaggerated rise and fall of his chest. After taking a few deep gulps of air he lit a cigarette, his hand shaking as he did so.

'That signet ring you got from Alex. Where did he get it from?'

'Look,' he said, exhaling a short puff of smoke, 'I don't know, love. Why would I? I gave him the bottle that I had and he gave me the ring. A swap. It was as simple as that.'

'Taff, are you going to eat your bread?' a Polish voice asked. A man was hovering close by, pointing with his fork at the roll left on Taff's side plate.

'No. You take it, Marek.'

Nodding, and winking at Alice, the man removed the roll and returned to his place further down the long table.

As Alice's attention was momentarily distracted, a woman pushed her way towards them, gesturing at a piece of paper tacked to the wall. Written on it in large black capital letters were the words 'NO DRINKS. NO DRUGS. NO CIGARETTES.'

'Put that out now, Taff,' she said crossly, wagging her finger at him. 'You know you're not allowed. You'll get us all into trouble.'

'Oh, with who?' he replied. Then, grinning at her annoyance, he took another drag.

'With the law . . . public health, I don't know.' She stood beside him with an irritated expression, her arms crossed tightly over her apron as if to stop herself from snatching the cigarette.

Finally, sensing that she would not budge until he had extinguished it, Taff relented. 'No problem,' he said, dunking it in his cup and adding sweetly, 'Rules is rules, eh. No sheep and goats here. I know that.'

'Well, if you know it, why don't you take any notice of my rules, eh?' the woman demanded, not so easily mollified.

Alice's phone went. She recognised the SART number but, unable to hear the voice at the other end of the line, she moved away from the arguing pair towards an unoccupied table and leant against it. Pressing the mobile to her ear, she tried to make out what Donny was saying.

'She's up there now,' he continued. 'She's waiting at the Cash 4 U in Lauriston Place.'

'Who is? I couldn't make out what you said earlier.'

'The woman, the one who was trying to flog the minister's watch.'

'You've got his watch? How do you know it's his?'

'Alice, how can you ask? I'm disappointed in you. We're the experts, remember? It's got his initials, DJM, engraved on the back of it, together with his birthdate and the children's initials. A Rolex. I don't think it's likely there'll be more than one of those doing the rounds, do you?'

'No, of course. Sorry. Does the woman know I'm coming?'

'Not exactly. The owner, a Mr Khan, has persuaded her to wait. He told her he had a particular customer in mind, a local, who would like to come and see it. The clever so-and-so said that this customer was a collector and would pay over the odds if the watch took her fancy. Little Miss Light-Fingers, or Dorothy Drummond as she's calling herself, fell for it, so she's waiting for you up there now.'

Out of the corner of her eye, she saw Taff edging his way between the diners towards the door.

'I'll head there now. Sorry, Donny, I've got to dash.'

Catching up with Taff as he was pulling his greasy woollen bonnet onto his head prior to stepping out onto the street, she exclaimed, 'Where are you off to?'

'Why?' It was clear from his expression that he was not pleased to be asked.

'In case I need to speak to you again.'

'If it's still a free country, I'll be found at the drop-in centre in Cromarty Street . . . unless I change my mind. You've not charged me so I'm not under arrest, am I? Planning to detain me instead?'

'No.' Her bluff had been called.

'Good. I'll be on my way, then, Sergeant.'

—

Mr Khan seemed pleased to see her. He had been waiting outside in the cold, stamping his feet like a guardsman on the icy pavement, and surreptitiously examining each pedestrian as they passed in the hope that it might be the policewoman.

As she entered his office, Alice saw a mousy woman seated in a chair, looking out of the window and with a rolled-up magazine in one hand. The overriding impression that she gave was of someone downtrodden and defeated, someone whose will rarely prevailed in the battle of life. On Alice's approach she rose, stuffed the magazine into her shopping bag and came towards her, asking excitedly, 'You the collector?' Her hand was touching the flap of her green leather satchel, ready to display her wares.

'Not exactly,' Alice replied. 'I'm from the police. I need to speak to you about the watch you're trying to sell.'

Now looking terrified, the woman said, 'There must have been some mistake. I'm not selling anything, and I'll need to be away home now.'

She moved quickly towards the door, her hand stretched towards the handle.

'Not quite yet,' Alice said, remaining where she was and blocking the woman's only exit.

'The man you tried to sell the watch to, Mr Khan, contacted us and, if necessary, I'll bring him in here to repeat his version of events to you. I know you have the watch, so you can either tell the truth and talk to me here about it, or accompany me back to the station at St Leonard's. It's up to you.'

For a moment, the woman remained silent and then, looking even more forlorn, she said, 'OK, you win. What'd you like to know? I've not got much time. I've got to collect my wee boy from school.'

'Could I have it, please?'

Obediently, the woman fished inside her satchel and handed it over.

'Where did you get it?'

'Em . . . I got it at Christmas from my husband.'

'This Christmas present that you're now trying to sell, it's a man's watch isn't it? Do you normally wear men's watches, then?'

'Aha. I like a big face. Easier to see the numbers, eh?' the woman replied, smiling timidly at Alice as if to charm her.

'The initials on the back – whose are they?'

'Mine.'

'Dorothy Drummond? DD?'

'No, sorry, I forgot. It was secondhand, see. My husband said not to worry about them so . . .'

'What are the initials on your watch? No doubt you'll remember that, since you've had it since Christmas.'

'Em . . . I'll need to see,' she replied.

'I'll read them to you,' Alice said, 'DJM.'

'Em . . . em . . . my dad's name. Donald . . . Jane . . .'

Running out of patience with such half-witted lies, Alice cut in. 'Stop wasting my time, please, Mrs Drummond. Up until about six days ago this watch was around the wrist of the Reverend Duncan McPhee. He was found dead on the ninth of February. Do you understand? It was not for sale, in any shop, secondhand or otherwise, prior to that date.'

'It must have been. Alan bought it for me.'

'We are pursuing an investigation into Duncan McPhee's death,' Alice continued, 'because he may have been murdered. Do you understand that? You may be in possession of the watch of a recently murdered man. It is worth thousands of pounds. Bearing that in mind, shall we start again?'

'Right,' the woman said, twisting her hands together and nodding, having finally grasped the implications of the police officer's speech.

'So where did you get it?'

The woman opened her mouth but nothing came out. Trying again, she said in a low voice, 'In one of the rooms, one of the service-users' rooms. In the hostel for the homeless, the one on Ferry Road. I work there as a care worker.'

'Did you take it from there?' Initially the woman said nothing, then she nodded her head and looked into Alice's eyes imploringly. 'You'll not tell my employers, eh? I need that job. I've never done it in my life before and, honest, I'll never do it again. I can't afford to lose my job. I've learnt my lesson, I really have. Please, please don't tell them, eh?'

'You took the watch from someone's room in the hostel. When?'

'Em . . . it'll have been on the morning of the eleventh.'

'Whose room was it? Alex Higgins'?'

'No. If I tell you, will you promise not to tell them?'
she wheedled.

'No, I can't promise that. But I need to know whose
room you took the watch from.'

'OK, but I'm trusting you . . . not to tell them, I mean.
I'm trusting you, mind. I got it from another bloke's
room, the one called Taff. I don't know his surname, truly.
I really don't know it. Nobody does. You speak to the
manager or the Reverend Davis. Nobody knows.'

—

Hatless, and in the absence of his large, padded anorak and the many layers of jerseys worn beneath it, Taff
seemed to have shrunk. Sitting on the hard wooden
bench of the drop-in centre, he was now dressed only in a
collarless white shirt, a black jacket and worn jeans.

Beside him the drum of a washing machine was revolving noisily, but he seemed oblivious to the racket it was
making. The back of his head was propped against the
wall and in repose his face looked as gaunt as a medieval
death mask, eyes closed, his cheeks and temples sunken.
His mouth had fallen open, accentuating the line of his
jawbone.

Fast asleep, he was completely unaware of Alice's scrutiny. For a couple of seconds she was able to gaze at his
face, studying it as objectively as she might an inanimate
object in a museum. In profile, she thought, he had a certain nobility, and his large aquiline nose only added to
that impression.

The second the washing machine clicked into spin cycle
he jerked awake, but he did not look refreshed or restored
by his sleep. Seeing Alice standing above him, he said in
a slightly thick voice, 'Oh, for Christ's sake, what now?'

Because he looked so tired, and fragile as glass, she found that the anger she had felt earlier had dissipated. Taking a seat next to him she said, 'Taff, just tell me the truth this time, will you? Have you ever owned a Rolex watch?'

'What do you think?' he said roguishly, rubbing his eyes. 'Do I look like the sort of man to own one of them?'

'So you've never owned one?'

'That's what I said, wasn't it?' He stretched his arms above his head and yawned, and as he did so an ominous click came from one elbow.

'Sure about that?'

'Yes. I'm sure about that. Is this some kind of game or something, because if it is I don't want to play. I've got better things to do.'

'Fine. About an hour ago I spoke to Dorothy Drummond.'

'Did you now? How do you come to know Dot?'

'Never mind that for now. Dorothy Drummond was in possession of a Rolex watch and she told me that she took it from your room.'

'Oh, right,' he said, not turning a hair, 'I wondered what had happened to it. She'll be the one to have taken Linda's money too, I bet, even though Moira took the blame. She cleans in Bread Street too. Are you following her up?'

'Not at the moment. I thought you said you'd never owned such a watch.'

'Spot on, love. That's what I said. See that watch on my wrist, there, that's a Sekonda. The Rolex was in my room, I admit that, but I didn't own it. I was keeping it safe for someone else. It wasn't my watch.'

'Really?'

'Aye. Really.'

'So who were you keeping it safe for?'

'For Alex.'

He rose, opened the door of the washing machine and began to unload the clothes. The slight effort involved made him gasp for breath, and halfway through the task he stopped and sat down, resting the pile of damp washing on his knee.

'This won't bloody do,' Alice said, looking directly into his tired, heavy-lidded eyes.

'What are you going on about, dear?' His voice sounded faint.

'Alex was already dead when the watch was taken from your room.'

'Not when he gave it me . . . to look after, not then, though.'

'When you told me about the signet ring you got as a result of a swap with Alex, I asked you if you got anything else from him. You said no. Why didn't you mention the watch then?'

'I didn't get anything else from him. I told you, he didn't give me the watch. I was just its custodian, as you might say. The ring became mine.'

'Have it your way. Apart from getting the watch and the signet ring from Alex, did you get anything else at all? What I mean by that, just to be entirely clear, is did he pass anything else on to you, whether as a gift, an exchange, something for you to look after or anything else?'

'No.'

'So you got nothing else whatsoever from Alex?'

'That's what I've just said, isn't it?'

'Sure about that?'

'Yes, I'm bloody certain about that.'

'This won't do,' Alice repeated, her eyes still fixed on his.

To her surprise he smiled broadly as if pleased by something, and said, 'And why not, officer?'

'Because,' she said, pointing at his lapel, 'You're wearing a black jacket with a small badge on it. Do you know what the badge is?'

'No. I never even noticed it. Tell me.' He was still smiling, but he began to pull up his lapel to get a better look at the badge.'

'It's the Burning Bush.'

'Well, I never,' he said. He stood up once more, but once he was on his feet he sat down heavily again, murmuring, 'I'm a wee bit dizzy.'

'That black jacket you are wearing belonged to the Reverend Duncan McPhee. The badge is the one that ministers of the Church of Scotland often wear. The watch and the signet ring both belonged to him too. Odd that.'

'Well done,' he answered, his eyes closed and his breathing laboured. 'At last. You've finally got there. I thought you might, I thought you might be the one to get there. So you deserve the bloody prize.'

18

'The prize?'

'Aye. You deserve it and I'd like someone to know the truth. To bear witness, as they say in church circles. This time the story matters, you see, to me at least. Moira Fyfe was my best friend, my only real friend . . . nowadays.'

'I'd heard that. I know that,' Alice said, 'but could we talk about Duncan McPhee for the minute? He's the one I need to know about. That's who I'm interested in. The file on Moira's been closed.'

'Patience, woman!' replied Taff, breathing in deeply. 'You'll get everything you're after – everything, you've my word on it. But you need to understand. Moira's file is not closed, not by me, anyway. Like I said, she was my friend. She was my mentor, showed me the ropes in the early days. How to keep myself warm, the golden rules of begging, where you'd get a free breakfast . . . where to buy the cheapest drink. All the things, good and bad, that you need to know if you're going to survive on the street.'

'Yes, but Duncan McPhee's the . . .'

'I said, patience!' he spluttered, wiping his mouth with the back of his hand.

At that moment an unshaven man with a yellowish complexion came into the washhouse and, glancing at the two of them, began to unpack the contents of a thin carrier bag onto the top of the washing machine. Once all his clothes were out, he carefully separated them into whites and non-whites.

'Get out, Terry,' Taff said gruffly to the stranger, his voice sounding heavy as if he needed to clear his throat.

'I've my washing to do. You're no' using the machine,' Terry replied, a placatory look on his face.

'I said, "Out".'

'Why? You're only chatting to her, you could go to the drop-in room to chat.'

'Terry, I said, "Out".'

Taff sounded resolute and as he spoke, he stared fixedly at the other man, his eyes burning into his, until Terry dropped his gaze.

Now looking put out, Terry stuffed his clothes back into their carrier bag and left, mumbling, 'I'm seeing the manager.'

Waiting until the sound of footsteps had died away, Taff spoke again.

'She was my pal,' he reiterated, 'and for a couple of months she'd managed to get right off the drink. The doctors had told her to lay off it and she'd been getting help. It seemed to be working too. She was a good woman. Clever as well. She'd been a nurse for years, one of those kiddies' nurses. A paediatric specialist.'

'I know.'

'Aye, I bet you do.' He started to cough, his face reddening and his eyes watering as he fought for breath between each racking bout. After about three minutes, the coughing stopped and he closed his eyes, taking in great gulps of air. He pressed his hand against his chest, massaging it as if the earlier paroxysms had been painful.

'A couple of days before she died, she'd been begging, on her own, up close to Jericho House. She approached a man and asked him for any spare change. She looked at him and she recognised him. Guess who it was?'

'No idea.'

'Go on. Try. I'll give you a clue if you need one.'

'I need one.'

'It was a man of the cloth.'

'Duncan McPhee.'

'Top marks. It was Duncan McPhee. Know who he is?' He stopped again, giving her the chance to answer and himself time to draw more breath.

'Of course. He's . . . a minister, a husband, a "committee man".' She shrugged her shoulders, letting him know that she had not an inkling of what he was driving at.

'Aye, he's all of those things, but he's more too. He's a brother! He was Moira's half-brother, her only brother. Bet you didn't know that, did you?' He exulted in his superior knowledge.

'No.'

'No, you did not. Chalk and cheese, eh? Moira recognised him and she was overjoyed. She'd lost touch with him ages ago, years ago, long before she lost her house and everything, and there he was, standing right in front of her. Large as life. So, naturally, she goes up to him and embraces him – puts her arms right round him, hugs him tight, but he doesn't like it a bit and he stiffens, pulls away. She can feel him freezing up. He doesn't put his arms about her.'

'How do you know all of this?'

'Never mind that now,' he said sharply, 'I'll tell you in good time. Like I said, he's not pleased to see her. He recognises her all right but, oh no, he's not glad to have found her. Not one little bit. Not Moira the beggar, Moira the homeless person. The drunk. He's disgusted by her,

261

and he doesn't think to hide it, either. But, does he invite his wee sister home with him – put the fatted calf on the table for her, as he should?'

She saw no need to answer his rhetorical question, but when she said nothing he became agitated.

'Well, does he?'

'No?'

'Dead right! He does not. He told her he was in a tearing hurry on his way to a meeting, couldn't stay, emptied out his wallet and gave her all the notes from it. Then he buggers off. No address, no telephone number, nothing. He leaves no traces. So Moira knows the score. It's goodbye for ever. He doesn't want to know her or anything about her. When he was going, she said he looked terrified – terrified of her.'

Hearing the sound of approaching footsteps in the corridor outside, he rose quickly and flicked a switch on a nearby socket and then returned to his seat. He still held his bundle of damp washing intact on his knee, staining his jeans.

'Taff!' the project manager exclaimed. She stood before him, her fleshy bulk hiding Terry's small frame from view, until he peered out from behind her shoulder as if playing peek-a-boo.

'Aye,' Taff replied, not moving and fixing her in the eye.

'Terry needs to use the machine. You've finished your washing.'

'That's true, I have. But I'm trying to talk to someone here, Mrs Farrell. In private.'

'Fine. You talk to the lady. No one's stopping you, but let Terry get on with his washing. You could go upstairs to the drop-in room, couldn't you? It's not very full. Let Terry get on with doing his laundry. Right?'

Taff did not answer, turning his head to one side as if the manager no longer existed. But she was not letting him get away with that.

'You'll let Terry get on?'

'Fine,' he replied, his head still to one side.

Hearing his agreement, Terry immediately began to unpack his clothes again, and Mrs Farrell, having got her way, left the scene with a spring in her step. Putting his first load into the machine together with a cup full of washing powder, Terry turned the knob and waited for the sound of water flooding into it. Silence followed. After a further thirty seconds of tranquillity, he kicked the glass in the front panel. But the machine did not churn into life. Infuriated, he aimed another vigorous kick at it.

'That fucker disnae work!' he said crossly, now hopping around the room on one foot.

'Right enough,' Taff said, watching him as he danced about the floor.

'How did you do yours, then?' Terry said, looking at the clothes on Taff's knee.

'By hand,' Taff replied, quick as a flash, pointing at the sink and adding, 'in there, and it took bloody ages.'

'Ah'm no' doin' that,' Terry said, thrusting the washing back into his crumpled bag and storming out of the room.

Once he was certain that Terry was out of earshot, Taff continued speaking. 'I saw Moira that evening. She'd taken the money he gave her and gone out and bought her usual stuff, Tennent's Super Lager, White Strike and a couple of bottles of vodka. She was crying, and pretty far gone, but she'd told me what had happened. It broke her heart, you see. Seeing him, her own brother, then seeing herself in his eyes, seeing his reaction to her . . . she suddenly saw herself. She told me she couldn't take any more, didn't want to live any more. I'd never heard that from her in all the five years we were pals. You know what happened after that, don't you? You were at the hearing too. She fell and hit her head when Linda was having a go at her. The next day she told me she was going to put some flowers on her mum's grave. Seeing that bastard had stirred memories up for her, more's the pity. But somehow she ended up in the Hermitage, and in that lonely, lonely place she died of cold. She froze to death. But no one is to blame, apparently. Well, I don't agree, you see. Someone bloody was!'

'I don't think that's what the FAI will conclude. She had a haemorrhage. The hospital doctor did everything he could . . .'

Before she could finish her sentence, Taff shouted, 'Can't you see? I'm not talking about him. Someone was to blame all right. But he wasn't on trial, was he? The Reverend Duncan McPhee was never called by anyone to explain what he'd done to his sister. Ignoring her, giving her money to buy drink. Like she was no one, less than no one. He just wanted rid of her. In the chain, he was the first link. But I found him . . .' He stopped, his breath now rasping, and bowed his head.

'Go on,' Alice said gently.

'I will when I can, lass. Give me a minute or two.'

She looked at him, noting for the first time the bluish tinge around his cracked lips.

'After she died I found him easily enough, through the phone-book,' he continued. 'I followed him home a few times, and found out all about the Reverend Duncan James McPhee. On the Sunday night, late, I trailed after him into the Dean Gardens. He'd that dog with him, the spotty dog. The poor brute came out with me. It was cold, well below freezing. I just wanted to talk to the man, really. Let him know what he'd done. Tell him about the Hermitage, about her end. Hear him say sorry. But, you see, he didn't care. He didn't care that he'd killed Moira, his own sister. When I broke the news of Moira's death, a flicker of emotion passed across his face. Just a wee flicker. Know what that emotion was?'

'No.'

'Give it a go.'

'Grief? Surprise? Sorrow?'

'Wrong. What flashed across his face, just for a moment, but enough for me to recognise it, was relief. A problem solved. He even dared to lecture me, in his pompous way, explaining in words of one syllable that it had nothing to do with him. "Drink was her downfall," he said, "not me." He rabbited on about personal responsibility, moral choices . . . kept repeating, as if I was a fool, that if she'd died of the cold then no one was to blame. She'd been an alcoholic. He'd certainly played no part in that. And then it came to me. The big idea. I'd show him something he'd never forget.'

He paused again, his throat sounding dry. Seeing a plastic cup by the sink, Alice filled it and brought it over for him to drink. He took a sip and choked, spilling half the water down his white shirt and ineffectually tried to wipe it away.

'I told him to take off his clothes. Of course, he looked at me as if I was mad and refused, and I couldn't force him. Once I might have been able to . . . not these days, though. Actually, the old bastard laughed at me, at the very suggestion. So I put my hand in my pocket, moved my comb about in it and told him I had a knife in there. It's no more than he'd expect.'

'So?'

'He believed me, naturally. No doubt I look the type, to the likes of him at least. Then just to back it up I said if he didn't strip I'd tell everyone.' He hesitated again, watching her face keenly to see her reaction.

'Tell everyone what?' Alice asked, taking his bait and watching as a slow smile spread across his face.

'Tell everyone that the bastard has a mistress! He didn't believe me, at first. He was all, "I don't know what you're talking about", that kind of thing. So, I said one word . . .' He stopped speaking once more.

'One word?'

'Her name – Ellie. I told him that I knew where he lived, spelled out his address for him, where she lived, where he worked and his wife's name. He'd just come from there, see? His mistress's place. I said I would tell them all. Mrs Juliet McPhee, the good people of St Moluach's, his congregation, and his smart friends at 121 George Street. I would tell them all. Spill the beans about Eleanor.'

'Eleanor what? Where does she live?'

'Eleanor Mills, residing in Lennox Terrace in a basement flat. Below that doddery old wifey . . . the one with the Zimmer.'

'So, what did he do?'

'He asked me why I was doing this to him. I said, "An eye for an eye", and that shut him up pretty quick. He got that in one. I explained that maybe he should feel the cold just like Moira did. Try it. See how he liked it, a taste of his own medicine. He looked at me as if I was a madman, but he saw I wasn't joking. He still thought I had a knife in my pocket. He asked me if I'd give him his clothes back at the end, and, of course, I said I would.'

'But you didn't, did you?'

'Of course not! But I had to say it, to make him take them off, didn't I? I waited beside him for forty minutes or so . . . by which time he was bloody freezing, chittering like a frightened dog. Then I walked off with his clothes and everything in them. He managed to speak then, shouting after me that I'd said I'd give them back, but I said to him, "Wish you'd treated your wee sister a little bit more kindly now, do you?"'

'And what did he say?'

'Nothing. His teeth were chattering that much, maybe he couldn't speak. But he'd showed no remorse, so neither did I. He was afraid of the comb that he thought was a knife, particularly once he was in his birthday suit. I took his watch and the ring off him too. Why not? I had more use for them than him, and I couldn't see him going to the police about it. As I was throwing the stuff I didn't need into a bin on the corner of Willowbrae Road I laughed myself sick thinking about him racing naked through the streets on his way home, trying to explain himself to people, to anyone he met. Mighty vulnerable, he'd feel. Let him experience what humiliation, real humiliation, feels like – get a bucketful of it. She knew all about that. Me, too. We're experts in that.'

'That's not what happened though – him running naked through the streets, I mean.'

'No?'

'No. He didn't make it. He died right there in the Dean Gardens . . . of cold, as far as I know.'

'Did he now? I never knew that.' He paused for a little while, continuing in his hoarse voice, 'But, so be it. He had a chance. He was alive and kicking when I left him. She had no chance whatsoever. But, supposedly, nobody killed her, did they? Just being alone in that cold place did it. Anyway, thinking about it, his death seems like poetic justice to me.'

'Why are you telling me this?'

'I told you. Because someone should know. And there won't be a trial,' he added, 'even if he did die like that. So it might never come out.'

'How can you be so sure that there won't be a trial?' she asked, surprised by the certainty in his voice.

'Take a good look at me, Sergeant,' he replied, stretching out his bony arms as if to invite a full inspection. He did, indeed, make a pitiful spectacle. His clothes hung on his fleshless body as loosely as a shroud on a corpse, and his eyes were dull, as if the spark of life had long since departed.

'How long have you got?' she asked.

'I don't know. A matter of weeks, probably. A month at most. They want me to go into hospital, but I've refused. What's the point? They can't do anything, after all. I'd rather stay out and about for as long as I can. I won't plead guilty to anything, if you take me in. No one was found guilty of Moira's death. McPhee certainly felt no guilt, so, I can assure you, I feel none either. Even after you telling me that he died. It's happening to us all.'

They both looked up as a man, dressed in blue overalls, came into the room. Mrs Farrell followed behind him and Terry, like a pet dog, pattered along a few paces behind her.

'You still here?' she said cheerily to Taff as she walked by, but then, suddenly, she stopped dead and turned to face him.

The other two, meantime, set to their task, cursing as they battled to move the washing machine away from the wall. When they failed, the little man squeezed himself behind it to act as a human jack and lever it away from the wall with his legs.

'You've done it again, haven't you?' Mrs Farrell said to Taff. Her narrowed eyes drilled into his.

'What?' He sounded quite innocent.

'You've turned off the bloody switch!' she said. Without waiting for him to answer, she turned round and ordered the two men to stop.

Terry and his companion looked up in surprise as the manager strode over to the nearby socket and turned the switch back on.

'Do that again, Taff . . .' she said, threateningly, leaving her sentence unfinished.

'Or you'll . . . ?' he replied, his expression eloquently informing her that he did not care what she did.

'I'll . . .' she hesitated.

'Throw you out, you bastard,' Terry chimed in, standing as before behind her protective bulk.

'And I'll . . . I'll kiss you!' she added, laughing, puckering her lips into a grotesque pout and bending towards Taff as if to carry out her threat.

'On you go, love,' Taff said insouciantly, offering his thin cheek to her and closing his eyes as if in expectation of bliss.

'I will!'

While, to Terry's unconcealed distaste, they continued bantering, Alice's phone went. It was DC Cairns.

'Just to let you know the results of the post mortem on McPhee, Sarge . . .'

'Yes?'

'He died of a heart attack. All his coronary arteries were furred right up. Hypothermia may have played a minor part. There were no signs of any injury and the Prof found those Wenceslas ulcers again. No evidence of anything else – no cuts, bruising or anything that couldn't be explained away innocently. He's told the DCI that he doesn't think it was a suspicious death. So we're to stand down.'

'But what does she think happened? What about his clothes, the watch and so on?'

'The DCI's satisfied that he took them off himself like Moira Fyfe did. Then someone must have come along later, over the railings, and stolen them. Nobody's sure, they can't be, but they can't think of anything else, including the Professor. You tracked down the ring and that led to a dead end, didn't it?'

'Alex Higgins, you mean?'

'Yes, to a dead man. Presumably he's the one who originally found the corpse and the clothes, and took the lot. He was a down-and-out wasn't he? He might well have had use for the clothes, not to mention the man's valuables. The dog might have followed him out, mightn't it?'

'It might.'

'So, the trail's gone cold. We're to treat it as death by natural causes.'

'OK.'

'Where are you just now – still with Taff? Have you learnt anything from him?'

Alice paused, looking across at the man before answering, 'No. Nothing important, so far.'

Watching Taff laughing as Mrs Farrell blew him a kiss, Alice tilted her head back against the wall and thought hard. So far, nothing she had done was irrevocable. She could still bring him in, have him charged, tell everyone exactly what he had told her. Tell them what he had done.

But it seemed utterly pointless, because she believed every word that he had said. Not least, what he said about his pitifully short lifespan.

Duncan McPhee was already dead, and dragging the existence of his mistress into the spotlight would achieve nothing. Well, nothing worthwhile. Instead, his wife and children would learn for the first time of his adultery, shattering their image of him and, in all probability, destroying otherwise precious memories. The tabloids would fall on the story like vultures on a corpse, picking out its entrails and fighting over them. Their front pages would compete with headlines about 'Mucky Ministers' and 'Randy Reverends'. McPhee's mistress would probably be pilloried, and the church become the subject of another scandal. And all for what? Taff would be dead before the matter came to trial, and keeping a dying man in custody until his premature death would benefit nobody.

She rose to her feet, conscious that if she did not act now she might weaken, be tempted to play it safe. Protect herself.

'Taff,' she said, 'I'm off.'

He looked at her, puzzlement in his eyes. 'Am I not to come along with you?' he asked, gathering the washing on his lap and putting it in its bag.

'No.'

'Sure about that? I will come with you, if you want me to.'

'No. There's no point. You stay here. Stay in the warmth.'

19

At 9 p.m., and with all her paperwork finally completed, Alice set off from St Leonard's on foot. It had begun to snow a couple of hours earlier, intermittent showers of small flakes quickly turning into a constant fall of white feathers, and already Edinburgh had been transformed into a new and mysterious city.

Crossing onto the North Bridge, heading in the direction of Princes Street, she looked up the snow-covered expanse of the Royal Mile towards the Castle, and her eyes came to rest on St Giles' Cathedral. The tracery of its crown spire and the crockets on the finials were now highlighted in white, standing out in vivid contrast to the solidity of the rest of the soot-covered structure, lending it an ethereal air. It was a breathtakingly beautiful sight, and she drank it in.

Dragging herself away, she hurried onwards, overtaking several groups of pedestrians shuffling morosely across the North Bridge, all desperate to keep their balance on the slippery pavement. Like cows in a storm they had instinctively clumped together into huddles, as if for mutual shelter. An old fellow in wellingtons trailed behind one of them, his arms going like pistons, but with his small, flat-footed steps, he was still unable to catch up.

As Alice continued down Leith Street a feeling of anxiety washed over her, putting her on edge. Something was not quite right. Some extra sense had come into play, warning her that she was being followed again and, at the thought, a cold shiver ran down her spine.

Who the hell was doing this to her? She had to fight against the urge to break into a run. Finally, trying to allay her fears by proving them groundless, she stopped dead and, like a child, forced herself to turn round, look behind her. She would confront the threat. In the impenetrable white-out she could see almost nothing, but the certainty that someone was tailing her remained undiminished. Now, even more scared, she shielded her eyes and took another hard look. But it was hopeless. Snowflake after snowflake continued to pour from the sky, landing on her cheeks and drifting into her eyes, blinding her. Close by, no one stood out from the crowd or halted on seeing her stop, but only a couple of yards away anything could be happening. A man might be brandishing a knife at her for all she could see.

Walking on at a brisk pace, her heart now thumping in her chest, she told herself she was being silly and childish, near-hysterical. She was overdramatising things. After all, she was in a public place and there were a fair number of pedestrians around. But whatever she told herself, the eerie feeling which had taken possession of her did not dissipate but instead became more fixed with every step she took. The muscles between her shoulderblades began to tense painfully, and a strange prickling feeling rose up her neck until it tickled the base of her skull. Telling herself that it meant nothing and was probably the result of fatigue or anxiety at the decision she had taken about Taff, she scurried onwards. But she could not stop herself from looking back every few minutes to check that no one was creeping up behind her.

With her head bent over against the thickly falling flakes, she crossed the road and entered Broughton Street.

As she passed an alleyway a stranger loomed from its mouth, blocking her path. She tried to bob round him but he grabbed her by the shoulders and pushed her roughly into the dark passage from which he had come.

Trying not to panic but momentarily disabled by surprise, she felt his arm encircle her neck and a hand clamp over her mouth. Instinctively, she tried to cry out, kicking at him as hard as she was able and struggling desperately to free herself from his grip. But he seemed untroubled by the blows, increasing the pressure on her windpipe until she was unable to breathe and began gasping hoarsely for air.

Scrabbling with her hands to break his arm-lock, trying to force him to release his grip, she aimed a final kick at his shin and heard a cracking sound as her heel made contact with the bone. Yelling loudly in agony, for a split second her assailant relaxed his hold, and as he did so she wriggled, trying to break free. Before she could escape, he tightened his grip once more and pulled her over backwards, knocking her feet from under her and crashing her down onto the icy ground.

'Bitch!' he said, bending over to rub his shin. As she lay dazed on the snow-covered cobbles he began aiming kicks at her body. Instinctively she curled into a ball to protect herself, but in the next second she felt a boot thump into her spine and she cried out in pain. At that instant, she heard a loud crack, like the sound of a cricket bat hitting a ball, and her attacker fell, slumping heavily on top of her.

Someone pulled his dead weight off her and then she heard a familiar, wheezy voice saying, 'You all right, pet?'

Looking up, she saw Taff crouched above her, panting loudly, his arms outstretched and ready to help her to her feet. Taking both his cold hands in her own, she allowed him to pull her up until they were both standing opposite one another like dance partners.

'Are you all right?' he repeated, looking anxiously at her bruised face.

'Yes, I think so. What happened? Why are you here?'

'Who's that mad bastard?' Taff said, looking at the figure stretched out on the ground.

'I've no idea. He came from nowhere and attacked me. I don't know why he did it. But what are you doing here? I don't understand . . .'

For an instant, she thought her legs were going to give way, so she leaned against the wall behind her, propping herself up.

'I was following you home. I can explain . . . I couldn't speak to you properly with Mrs Farrell there, and I wanted to thank you for what you did.'

'*You* were the one following me?'

'Yes. I wanted to . . .'

He stopped speaking and bent double, overcome by another coughing fit. Regaining his breath he tried again. 'I wanted to give you this.'

He dipped into the pocket of his bulky anorak and pulled out a brown leather wallet, offering it to her.

'What is it?' she asked, taking it from his hand.

'It's Duncan McPhee's. It's got his cards, credit, debit or whatever, I never touched them, and a lot of photos. Mainly photos of a wee boy and a wee girl, his children, I suppose. I thought his widow might want to keep them. I spent the money that was in it, you'll not be surprised to hear. There was hardly any, anyway. Less than a tenner. But I thought she might want to have them back, the photos and that. I've no quarrel with her.'

A deep, prolonged groan came from the body sprawled face down at their feet, and they both looked at it. The man let out another moaning sound. As if to silence him, Taff aimed a casual kick at his ribs. The noise stopped.

'How did you manage to knock him out?' Alice asked, feeling her bruised neck with the tips of her fingers, wincing under the slight pressure.

'With a vodka bottle,' Taff said proudly, patting the bulge in the pocket of his anorak. 'It's come in useful before, not that particular bottle, obviously, but as something to protect myself with, you understand. Just as well it's all but full. I'm not as good with my fisticuffs as I used to be. Not a good fighting weight.'

'How did you find me after I left you at the drop-in centre? I phoned later and you were still there.'

'Did you now? How did I find you? If you think about it, you'll appreciate that wouldn't be too difficult, Detective Sergeant. Well, not for me. After all, you are a policewoman, so you're likely to be based at a police station and one that has a CID to boot. Also, you mentioned Elaine Bell, so I reckoned it would be St Leonard's. I know a little about those kinds of things. I'm not a complete idiot. And I wasn't always on the street, you know.'

'Yes, but I still don't understand. How do you know Elaine Bell? You found Duncan McPhee too – tracked him down, plotted his movements and pursued him like a professional.'

'In another life,' he cut her short, sounding impatient, 'when I was an entirely different person, I *was* a professional, like you. I was a police officer. Satisfied?'

'You?'

'Yes, me. Don't sound so bloody surprised. It can happen, you know. To anybody. Like I said, I wasn't always like this.'

'What happened to you?'

'Does it matter? This isn't really the time or the place, is it?'

'No. Sorry . . .'

'Easy enough to guess, I'd have thought. Alcohol happened, and before too long everyone gave up on me. I don't blame them. And then I joined them. I gave up on me too.'

'Elaine Bell?'

'At Tulliallan, years and years ago, I trained her. Now, what are you going to do about that?' He tapped the buttock of the prone man with the tip of his boot, before adding, 'I doubt he'll stay under for much longer.'

'I'll phone for help.'

'Are you all right? D'you want me to stay until they come?'

'No. You'd better go now. It will just complicate things. Put the spotlight back on you. It would seem an odd coincidence otherwise, you "saving" me, I mean. It would demand an explanation.'

'True. But you'll be hard put to take credit for the blow to the back of his head since he had his arm around your neck. He's left his mark too. He have even have seen me and tell everyone who asks him. Did you consider that?'

'I can deal with it. I'll say that you, my good Samaritan, ran off. If you scarper now it will very nearly be true. Can you live with that?'

'I left the police . . . a lifetime ago. I can live with anything nowadays. But I was wondering, how will you explain away McPhee's wallet?'

'Easy. The same way I'll explain away the watch. I'll say that you got both from Alex Higgins. I'll tell them that he said nothing useful to you, and the story died with him.'

———

'I told you not to come in today. Have you even had yourself checked out by a doctor?' DCI Bell said. She put down the report that she had been reading and glared at her sergeant. Then, shaking her head with exasperation and muttering, 'Look at the bruises on you,' she added, 'No, of course not, Alice, because you don't obey orders, do you? You do your own bloody thing! Go your own bloody way! Sit down. You shouldn't even be in here. As you didn't come in this morning I thought perhaps you'd listened to me – a first, I might add – but, oh no, as soon as lunchtime arrives, you arrive with it. Obeying my order would be too much to bloody hope for.'

'I'm fine, Ma'am. I just wanted to . . .'

But before she had finished her sentence the DCI said angrily, 'And why didn't you tell me?' Her dark brows were furrowed and her mouth set tight as a trap.

A picture of Taff shot into Alice's mind. Somehow they must have found out about him, become aware of the part he played in McPhee's death. Feeling suddenly tired, aware of every bruise on her body, she replied, 'Tell you what, Ma'am?'

She looked DCI Bell straight in the eye, trying to appear confident and assured, to disguise the panic eating away at her. Everything would be all right, she told herself. She had done the right thing. If she was to fall, lose her job, if the whole edifice was to come crashing down all around her, then so be it. She could do no more. Taff would not be on her conscience.

If others took a different, more legalistic view, then that was up to them. And if they got rid of her for it, then the Force was not the place for her anyway. The man's life was nearly over, measured in weeks rather than months, and he should not spend a minute of the time that remained incarcerated. She had no doubt about that. McPhee and his sister were beyond help and reparation.

'What the hell's being going on! You're not on your own, you know.'

'If it's about Taff . . .' Alice began, instinctively starting to marshall the arguments in her own defence as she was speaking.

'It's not about bloody Taff! Forget bloody Taff! No, it's about you, Alice. You. About the campaign waged against you!'

'You mean the mugger or whatever he was last night?'

'No. Not that.'

'What do you mean, Ma'am?' Alice said, temporarily thrown off balance by thoughts of Taff and his predicament.

Without answering, DCI Bell got up from her desk, turned her back on her sergeant and strode towards the window. After a long, heavy pause she turned round, her hands clasped together.

'The man who attacked you,' she said, 'told us everything. He described the late night phone calls, the funeral music, the gouge on the car's bodywork, the punctures and the brick through the window.'

'Him? But I thought he was just a mugger! He was responsible for all of it? Why? I didn't recognise him. Who the hell is he?'

'He's called Thomas Paige, an ex-con with multiple convictions, largely for assault but with one or two for extortion. But it wasn't him who organised the harassment,

Alice, he's just the cat's paw, I'm sure. He's nothing. He was only too eager to talk to us, tell us who was behind it all. First thing this morning we brought in your old colleague, William Stevenson.'

'Stevenson. Why on earth? Did he find out who the man is?'

'He *is* the man. He was behind it all, including the attack yesterday. He was the one directing operations . . .'

'But why would he do that?'

'As you can imagine, he's admitted to nothing. He knows the ropes. But Paige, and another lowlife whose services he used, name of Hunter, have been positively chatty. So we'll get him all right. Apparently, he blames you for the loss of his career, quite overlooking his own misdemeanours, his own little failings. According to him, your evidence at his hearing sunk him, deprived him of the little hope he had. He seems to have considered that the score would be evened up if your career were to come to an end too, so he's been busy softening you up. Trying to make you crack, so that you couldn't carry on with your work.'

'He was behind it all?'

'That's what Paige told us, and his accomplice said the same. Why didn't you tell me, Alice?'

The DCI resumed her seat behind her desk and looked, for the first time, directly into Alice's eyes.

'In all honesty, Ma'am, it took me a while to put everything together. At first I didn't connect things – it didn't even occur to me that the gouge mark and the puncture were part of it. By the time I did make the connection I didn't want to . . . it was too frightening. I didn't want to believe that someone was after me. Why would they be? Also, it sounded, even to me, a little too like paranoia. I thought you might think I was going off my head, imagining things, fabricating things . . . because of Ian's death. I began to wonder myself.'

'If only you had told . . .'

'Jesus!' Alice interrupted the DCI, struck by a sudden dreadful thought. 'Ian. Was the hit-and-run driver Stevenson? Did Stevenson kill him?'

'No.'

'Are you sure? How can you be sure it wasn't him?'

'No. It wasn't him. That possibility had crossed my mind too, but both Paige and Hunter looked blank when I put it to them, didn't know what I was talking about. But they confessed happily enough to all the rest.'

'Murder's different though.'

'Murder is different, of course. But I'm sure Stevenson was not involved. Eric's away as we speak checking out a lockup in Grove Street. Somebody brought a car there to have the bumper changed, and it seems the old one's still there. It looks as if Ian was run down by an under-age joyrider. I wasn't going to tell you until we were certain, but I'm pretty sure that it was a young lad from Fountainbridge.'

'Thank God,' Alice said, covering her face with her hands.

The DCI's phone rang. Apart from the odd grunted assent, she said almost nothing until the conversation came to an end and she put down the receiver.

'That's good news, too, in its way, Alice. It was the lab. I got them to double-check the toxicology results after what you said to me. It seems they had two "Melville" samples on the system and they mixed the results up. Ian had been drinking on the night he died, but his blood alcohol count was under the legal limit, not over double as they originally suggested. I don't know what that idiotic witness, Celia, was talking about. He will have been sober enough, compos mentis enough. The other witnesses didn't say he launched himself out, by the way. We spoke to them yesterday.'

'What did they say happened, exactly?'

'I'll give you their statements later. Basically, they both describe a row between him and Celia. She was putting you down somehow or other, "slagging you off", is how the woman put it. He got cross, said he wasn't going to listen to her any more, left and the rest of them left too. As he was crossing, a car, which was going well over thirty, hit him. It jumped the lights, tore out of a side street.'

'They had a row about me?'

'You can read it yourself. Looks to me as if Celia's got it in for you, for some reason. Ian argued with her, told her he wanted to be at home with you. Just read it.'

'I will.'

'Now, returning to this Taff person, for a second, what were you going to tell me about him?'

'Nothing, Ma'am, nothing. I misunderstood you.'

20

Wearing a thick coat, scarf and woollen gloves to protect herself against the cold, Alice looked around the studio. Leaning against one wall was a mass of canvasses, some used, some unused, some facing it and others facing into the room.

With cold hands, she began to organise them, putting aside the unused ones, grading the others by size and ensuring that they faced the correct way. A wonderful sketch of an ancient goat, almost geometric in style with the animal's spine and hip joint standing out against its spare flesh, jostled for space with an oil painting of a ship on the high seas. The sail of the ship ballooned out as it fought its way through gigantic waves.

She picked up the goat picture and admired it, remembering the day it was drawn. The goat was a milk-white Alpine nanny named Fizz who lived on a farm near her sister's house. The sketch had taken Ian all of fifteen minutes and the end result, although quirky, almost smelt of goat, so successful had he been in capturing the essence of the creature, its quiddity.

The ship, too, had a story attached to it. Explaining the simplicity of the composition to her he had said, almost shyly, that it was a self-portrait. It was an image of himself butting through life, enjoying it and everything it had to throw at him. Skimming along, with the wind in his sails. Looking at it then, she had been touched by the optimism in the work, the joie de vivre it portrayed. No jagged rocks were to be seen in the clear water.

Picking up a papier-mâché model of a hare from the windowsill she placed it with all the other treasures on the floor, and was just about to lift up another painting when she heard the sound of wood tapping on concrete. Looking up, she saw old Mrs Melville, similarly clad against the cold, approaching with her rosewood stick in one hand and Hamish holding the other.

'I thought I might find you here,' the old lady said, smiling and coming forward to kiss her. The little boy, newly released, rushed over to a picture and lifted it up.

'I'm meeting Celia here. She wanted something of Ian's,' Alice said.

'I know, she told me. She said she was concerned you weren't "authorised to dispose of his effects". I told her we'd spoken about it ages ago, and that as far as I was concerned everything of Ian's was yours. But she seemed to have difficulty in accepting that, and asked if I'd pop by to "keep her right". I had to bring Hamish back anyway so there was no difficulty in coming. I tried to contact you earlier but you must have been out. What are you going to give her?'

'She wants to choose herself.'

'Typical. So typical of her. I don't know what Ian saw in that ghastly, patronising woman!'

Seeing all the pictures spread before her as if at an exhibition the old lady asked, 'Which ones are your favourites, dear? I'd hide them away quickly, if I were you. You don't want her to get them!'

'The goat and the boat. The boat's him, you see. He told me that ages ago. He said it was a sort of self-portrait.

What about you? Which ones do you particularly like? We'd better tuck them away too.'

'I've got so many of his at home. I suppose I have a slight weakness for *The Murderous Crow* and I like that one,' she said, pointing at a half-finished canvas. It showed a winter scene, a cottage with a red pantile roof and a tall chimney stack against a snowy background.

A high voice piped up. 'You've not put my picture there!' So saying, the child picked up another watercolour and placed it in the very centre of the line of works propped against the wall for Celia's inspection.

'Hamish, they're laid out like that for a friend of Daddy's to take away. You wouldn't want to lose it, would you?' Mrs Melville said, going towards it, ready to remove it and Alice's favourites from the line-up.

'I don't care,' Hamish said. 'Daddy liked it, but I've got others. Much, much better ones at home.' He looked at it hard for a moment, shook his head doubtfully and then dashed through the sheet which divided the building into separate studios, intent on exploring someone else's territory.

As the material still rippled with movement, Celia Naismith appeared, dressed immaculately as ever with a fur hat and black leather gloves. She looked like a Russian countess.

'Are you both all right?' she said, an expression of pity on her face.

'Fine, thank you,' they replied simultaneously, as if part of a chorus.

'Oh, I do like that,' she gushed, taking off her gloves and making a beeline towards the goat. Moving other pictures aside to examine it on its own, she murmured in a shocked tone, 'What a loss. What a loss . . .'

Keeping it in one hand, she picked up the ship picture and looked at the two of them together, her eyes flitting between them as if weighing them up against each other.

As she peered closely at the goat again, Alice said, more in hope than expectation, 'Isn't it a bit . . . figurative for your taste, Celia?'

'Maybe,' Celia replied, putting the goat picture down and staring at an abstract which appeared to be composed of nothing more than red and blue circles on a yellow background.

'This,' she said excitedly 'is the one I told you about, the one he gave me before.'

As she put it on an empty easel to get a better view of it, Alice quickly concealed the goat behind the pictures Celia had already looked at.

'Oh, and I must have the hare!' Celia said, picking up the papier-mâché model and popping it into the wicker basket that she had over one arm. 'He did so little modelling,' she added, as if in explanation.

'Now . . . one more,' she said, surveying the remaining pictures in the line-up.

As Alice watched anxiously, she hovered beside the picture of the little boat, her fingers twitching above it as if about to pick it up and take it away forever.

'You don't think,' Mrs Melville chipped in, 'that that abstract is rather splendid, do you, Celia?'

'Which one?' the woman asked.

'That one,' the old lady replied, pointing to Hamish's picture with the end of her stick.

'Mmm, I see what you mean,' Celia said, turning her attention to it and narrowing her eyes. 'It is quite a statement.'

Catching Mrs Melville's eye, Alice objected, 'You don't think it's a little . . . childish, though?'

Before the old lady could reply, Celia cut in, assuming that the remark had been addressed to her. Art was her sphere, the sphere where she reigned supreme, and if Alice did not like the work then it was almost certainly good, probably unusually so.

'Childish? Heavens, no. It has, of course, a charming simplicity about it. Its form is bold, daring almost, but "childish", never! Try and look at it properly, Alice. The choice of colours he's used is sophisticated, artful in the proper sense of the word. Those oranges! Those purples! They're not just any old poster orange or any old poster purple, but two colours *made* by him, *chosen* by him to set each other off, to . . . *electrify* each other. Make each other zing! Think of that wonderful flower border at Great Dixter. The more I look at it the more I can see in it . . . '

She stopped mid-sentence, thinking to herself that, perhaps, it was a tad crude. Surely Ian would not have left so many areas uncovered by paint? But how could he have missed them? Worse, maybe poster colours had been used after all? It looked suspiciously like it.

'I believe, dear,' Mrs Melville said mischievously, now enjoying herself immensely, 'that Ian himself did think it was rather good. Of course, I have no idea why.'

'I do,' Celia said. She had committed herself completely and publicly, and she decided her only credible option was to bluster on. Bullshit on. They would be none the wiser. Cloth eyes, the pair of them. The picture was with the rest of his work, with his paintings, it must therefore be by him, mustn't it? Whose else could it be? But could it really have been done by him? Something so . . . so incomplete, so immature?

'Why?' Alice asked, unable to resist.

'Let's say, for simplicity's sake,' Celia continued, taking a deep breath, 'that bands of colour, whether in a straight line or, as here, in a rainbow formation, have a long and venerable history. In lesser hands, that's all we would see, but here in Ian's hand, a master's hands, the combination of forms and colours lift this otherwise simple piece into an altogether different realm. As you may or may not know, Ian was very interested in the relationship between curves and straight lines, the feminine and the masculine . . . silence, white sound and noise . . . how one shape calls out, relates, to another. If any artist understood the importance of contrast, in shape, tone and colour, that artist was Ian. Those other pictures, the goat, the boat and so on, they all show, obviously, a degree of technical proficiency, a good "eye" as you might term it, but, in many ways, that's a commonplace. A given. His talent, his real talent, to my way of thinking, lay in his use of colour and form. And, studying it as it deserves, this picture shows . . .', she paused, trying to inject conviction into her voice, 'perfection, well, skill, anyway, in both boldness of composition and stroke, and an almost breathtaking disregard for the staid, for the conventional. It, by its very existence, separates out the seeing from the blind, the ingenue from the sophisticate.'

That should end the discussion, she thought, nodding her head to add authority to her pronouncement.

'So,' Mrs Melville said, unable to prevent herself from smiling widely, 'it's the one you should have, Celia. God knows, neither Alice nor I have your eye, your appreciation. We thought it was . . . well, just a childish daub – but to you, and no doubt to others like you, it's . . . well, I can't begin to describe it as well as you've done, but let's just say, what? The acme of artistic accomplishment?'

'Mmm . . . or fairly close to it, anyway,' Celia answered, holding it up nearer to her face, closing one eye and, finally, committing herself beyond recall. 'And you're right, I think I will take it.'

Alice glanced across the room at the old lady and gave her a surreptitious wink, getting in return a fleeting thumbs-up. At that moment, Hamish entered the room. He had a splodge of brown paint on his forehead and his lips were covered in yellow, an oversized paintbrush sticking out of his mouth. In one hand he held a picture and, seeing Celia, he wandered up to her and dropped it at her feet. It was another rainbow, this time composed of thick brown, yellow, black, grey and red stripes.

'For you,' he said. 'Watch out, it's wet. But it'll go with my other one, won't it?'